PENGUIN BOOKS

Lives we Leave Behind

Maxine Alterio is a novelist, short story writer,
lecturer and narrative-based researcher. She was
educated at Otago University and the International
Institute of Modern Letters, Victoria University.
Maxine lives in Dunedin, New Zealand.

www.maxinealterio.co.nz

By the same author

FICTION
Live News and Other Stories
Ribbons of Grace

NON-FICTION
Learning through Storytelling in Higher Education:
Using Reflection and Experience to Improve Learning
(co-authored)

Lives we Leave Behind

MAXINE ALTERIO

PENGUIN BOOKS

Published by the Penguin Group
Penguin Group (NZ), 67 Apollo Drive, Rosedale,
Auckland 0632, New Zealand (a division of Pearson New Zealand Ltd)
Penguin Group (USA) Inc., 375 Hudson Street,
New York, New York 10014, USA
Penguin Group (Canada), 90 Eglinton Avenue East, Suite 700, Toronto,
Ontario, M4P 2Y3, Canada (a division of Pearson Penguin Canada Inc.)
Penguin Books Ltd, 80 Strand, London, WC2R 0RL, England
Penguin Ireland, 25 St Stephen's Green,
Dublin 2, Ireland (a division of Penguin Books Ltd)
Penguin Group (Australia), 250 Camberwell Road, Camberwell,
Victoria 3124, Australia (a division of Pearson Australia Group Pty Ltd)
Penguin Books India Pvt Ltd, 11, Community Centre,
Panchsheel Park, New Delhi – 110 017, India
Penguin Books (South Africa) (Pty) Ltd, Block D, Rosebank Office Park,
181 Jan Smuts Avenue, Parktown North, Gauteng 2193, South Africa

Penguin Books Ltd, Registered Offices: 80 Strand, London, WC2R 0RL, England

First published by Penguin Group (NZ), 2012
1 3 5 7 9 10 8 6 4 2

Copyright © Maxine Alterio, 2012

The right of Maxine Alterio to be identified as the author of this work
in terms of section 96 of the Copyright Act 1994 is hereby asserted.

Designed and typeset by IslandBridge
Front cover image by Susan Fox / Trevillion Images;
photo inset courtesy of Sherayl McNabb, NZANS Researcher
Back cover image from iStockphoto.com
Printed in Australia by McPherson's Printing Group

ISBN 978-0-143-56571-0

A catalogue record for this book is available
from the National Library of New Zealand.

www.penguin.co.nz

The assistance of Creative New Zealand towards the production
of this book is gratefully acknowledged by the Publisher.

MIX
Paper from
responsible sources
FSC
www.fsc.org   FSC® C001695

For Pamela Wood

And for my mother, Lorna Ferns

You could not go through the things
we went through, see the things we
saw, and remain the same. You went
into it young and light-hearted. You
came out older than any span of
years would make you.

Catherine Black

Prologue

EARLY JULY and a brisk southerly races up the South Island, shears fresh snow from the Alps, whips across Cook Strait and swirls into Wellington Harbour. Red and white streamers, torn from quayside buildings, sail through the air. The same wind dumps flurries of sea spray on the shivering women and children gathered to farewell their loved ones. Nearby, three older boys blast away on tin whistles. Cheeks bulging, eyes narrowed, they scramble up a stack of tea chests, stand to attention and salute the nurses, doctors, officers and soldiers leaving for Egypt on the hospital ship, *Maheno*.

On the upper deck, seventy nurses, in grey ankle-length woollen dresses and matching cloaks with scarlet-lined collars and silk bonnets, return the salute. Also on board are fourteen nurses who will return with New Zealand soldiers wounded at Gallipoli. There are no musicians to take up positions on the platform, no tubas or trombones to gleam in the drab afternoon light, no conductor to raise his baton and set off a stirring rendition of 'Rule Britannia'. Instead, the *Maheno* edges away from the wharf to the screech of gulls circling its mighty funnels. Right on time, church bells ring across the city, startling a flock of pigeons on the waterfront. They take to the air, their underbellies a silver glint against the winter sky.

As the stretch of water lengthens between the quay and the ship, a hush engulfs the windblown throng on shore and those heading out to sea.

A reporter sheltering in the doorway of a wharf shed takes a notebook from his jacket pocket and writes, 'Our fine men and women, willing servants of King and Country, have responded to the call of the Motherland in her hour of supreme need. Let them be victorious.'

ABOARD THE NEW ZEALAND
HOSPITAL SHIP *MAHENO*,
1915

One

ON THE UPPER DECK, somewhere between No. 3 hatch and the darkroom, Sister Adelina Harrington walked to the handrail, where she gulped in a mouthful of salty air. Nearby a group of soldiers broke into raucous laughter as the crew of a fishing boat steaming alongside took off their caps and waved. The soldiers surged along the deck, sweeping Adelina and two other nurses along with them, not stopping until they reached open space outside the chief officer's cabin. An overexcited young officer, jostling for a better view, knocked into her. Instead of apologising, he grabbed her arm and twirled her around until the plumes of spray cascading over the bow turned into ghostly sea creatures.

The strengthening breeze reminded her of the gusty conditions at home in Riverton the day she'd packed for this voyage. As she slipped an extra pair of shoes into her suitcase, Father had joked that being a brain-box was no guarantee she'd know when to duck. Then he'd said in a serious tone, 'Always wear a tin hat, Adelina.' He'd already warned her of sights that would never leave her, of shrapnel that would rip flesh and bone apart like paper. Mother had fussed too, insisting she take extra bodices as though, worn en masse, they could deflect stray bullets. Neither of them had wanted her to sign up. Even at the farewell ceremony in the Invercargill town hall, Mother had looked on nervously while Father placed his hand on her shoulder and boomed, 'You should carry on nursing here, Adelina. No need to gallivant around the world.'

But she wanted to nurse her country's soldiers. It was her duty – and her escape.

There'd been a great deal to organise before she left. Fortunately, her knack for paperwork had meant a seamless handover at Southland Hospital where she'd worked since qualifying six years ago. She would have to prove her worth all over again at No. 1 Stationary Hospital.

Judging from the chatter coming from the other nurses, many already knew each other, but she didn't feel brave enough to join them so she took a notebook from her pocket and sketched herself a little map – medical centre and operating theatre in front of her, surgical stores and X-ray rooms portside, dispensary and sterilising rooms to starboard. Fixed and swing cots further back, bathrooms and a dining saloon nearer the stern.

Reassured by the layout, Adelina turned to watch two soldiers untangling streamers from their hats. They looked too young to be bayoneting Turks and Germans. When she went to swallow, she found that her mouth was dry and she could feel her heart beating faster.

Her apprehension heightened as the *Maheno* entered open water. It was only last week that she had caught the train to Lyttelton, where she boarded the night ferry and crossed Cook Strait. She'd never left the South Island before. The narrow Wellington streets had felt claustrophobic after Invercargill's wide thoroughfares, as she marched with her fellow nurses and a regiment of rowdy soldiers down Cuba Street and along Lambton Quay past hundreds of strangers lining the pavements. When a jubilant shopkeeper had thrown her a posy of hellebores, she'd tossed it to another nurse and the soldiers directly behind her had given a rousing cheer. Then an ashen-faced middle-aged woman wearing a navy coat had grabbed her arm and said in a desperate voice, 'If my son comes your way, Sister, please take good care of him.'

Now, while she waited for the order to go below, Adelina noticed a pretty, strawberry-blonde nurse stop a few feet away and pull a mouth organ from under her cloak. When she belted out a few notes of 'Tipperary', a well-turned-out officer winked at her and grinned.

MOUTH ORGAN stashed in her cloak pocket, Sister Meg Dutton yanked open the door of the cabin allocated to her and Sister Harrington. You couldn't call it a prime location: on the main deck, next to the galley where pots and pans would clang day and night, close to two electric lifts juddering up and down, ringed by filthy coal hatches. Her room-mate was hovering in the corridor, chewing her bottom lip. Meg would have preferred a jollier sort, but she supposed they could muddle along.

'A bit cramped for two of us,' she said. 'Just as well you're skinny. Are you coming in today or tomorrow? Duck when you decide. You don't want to do the Turks' job for them.'

She squashed against one of the two bunks to give the other nurse room to edge past, but she remained in the doorway.

'I hear you come from Riverton. I nursed there. I didn't see you at the local dances.'

Harrington wrinkled her nose. Surely, Meg thought, she didn't belong to one of those queer religions that banned fun?

'Take off your bonnet and let me get a decent look at you.'

Hmmm, not bad looking – auburn hair, high cheekbones, a bit thin in the face but nothing an extra pudding wouldn't fix. A sprinkle of freckles on her nose; if they were hers, she'd cover them with face powder. Odd left eye, though. Moving closer,

Meg realised it was half-blue and half-green, split across the centre. 'Right, I'll recognise you anywhere. Aren't our bonnets ghastly?'

A shocked expression flitted across her companion's face.

'Golly,' Meg continued, 'you're at least three inches taller than me' – and probably two or three years older, she thought, which would make Harrington twenty-five or -six. 'So we can't swap clothes but we can gossip. I'm mad about film stars.' She tossed her holdall onto a bunk. 'Come in. I won't bite.'

Harrington didn't budge. Anyone this timid should work in a library. 'How many natty officers have you seen? Come on. Spill the beans. Who's caught your eye?' Harrington hunched her shoulders so Meg changed tack again. 'What's your first name?'

'Adelina – Addie.'

'Addie sounds friendlier.' Meg tapped her temple with her forefinger. 'I'm Meg Dutton, short and sweet.' Framing her face with both hands, she moved her head from side to side. 'Were your parents sorry to see you leave?'

The blush that had risen up Harrington's face subsided. 'Yes, Father urged me to change my mind.'

'Pa couldn't wait to get rid of me.' Whoops, she hadn't meant to say that. 'Which bunk do you want?' She flung out her arms. 'I haven't shared before. Have you?'

'Yes, with my younger sister Erin when we were on holiday. Not at home, though.'

That would make sense. Harrington probably had the perfect family.

Meg fished into her holdall and pulled out a coral evening dress. She'd spotted the design in a catalogue and shown a dressmaker, who'd made it in shot silk, an iridescent fabric that flickered like fire in her hands. Heads were sure to turn when she put it on. She held the dress against her uniform. 'What do you think of this?'

Addie raised her eyebrows.

What rotten luck to end up with Miss Goody-Two-Shoes. Not wanting to let her disappointment show, Meg delved further into her bag and hauled out a tuck-box. 'If we can't find a place to stash my aunt's baking we'll have to scoff her Dundee cake and fudge straight away. Do you have a sweet tooth?'

'More than one,' Addie murmured from the doorway. 'Mother fills the tins every Tuesday and Friday.'

'Golly, I suppose she washes on Monday and irons on Wednesday.'

Addie gave an uncomfortable laugh, as if it could be true.

A sudden clatter of shoes in the corridor interrupted the uncomfortable silence. 'Who's there?' Meg called.

Addie checked behind her. 'Three nurses. They went into a cabin.'

Good, Meg thought. One could swap with her. She'd organise it when they reached Adelaide. Nicely, of course, so Addie didn't get miffed. 'Won't you come in?'

Addie stayed put but glanced into the cabin. 'I can't see a shelf for my books.'

Leaning across a bunk, Meg rapped her knuckles on the porthole. 'But we are watertight.' The foaming sea outside the glass made her feel woozy. She took a hand-mirror from her holdall and pinched her cheeks until they were rosy pink. 'Some day,' she said theatrically, 'I'm going to travel the world on the arm of a famous film star, and he'd better have a moustache like Lionel Barrymore. Otherwise kissing him would seem tame, worse than eating eggs without salt. And speaking of food, the army cooks will have to feed us well – I can't work on an empty stomach.' She glanced at Addie again. 'I'm talking too much, aren't I? Blame the sea. Salt water corrodes my nerves. Get in here!' She seized Addie's arm and tugged.

Addie yelped as her forehead struck the wooden doorframe.

Meg gasped. Now she'd done it. 'Sorry. Here, perch on my bunk. Turn your head to the left.' Blow, the area was already swelling. 'Congratulations, you're about to hatch a lump the size of a pullet's egg. Eat my fudge while I fetch a cold compress. I can't afford to scoff the lot.' She patted her hips. 'Men prefer curves, not rolls.'

Addie flushed again and lowered her eyes. Golly, strait-laced as well. 'Don't move.'

In the bathroom, Meg grabbed a flannel and turned the tap on full bore. She was such a clot. It was high time she checked what was on her mind before she opened her mouth.

HER PARENTS always called her Adelina, but she'd been Addie at school, and she didn't mind it. She just wished Meg had asked which name she preferred. To make matters worse, she hadn't slept well. The narrow bunk was uncomfortable and the sheets rougher than she was used to. There was no privacy, either, when it was time to get dressed.

Over breakfast, Meg introduced her to the other nurses and she found herself envying her room-mate's ability to make people laugh and keep the conversation bubbling along, even if it was only about the weather.

After attending a lecture on camp protocol and a forty-five-minute talk on latrine construction and sanitation, which took place on the shade deck in a sitting room that doubled as library, she was free for the remainder of the afternoon. She could go to the cabin and read more of *Lorna Doone*, though it would be difficult to concentrate with Meg prattling on. Alternatively she could knock on the door of the next-door cabin and invite Netta Smith, a fair-skinned redhead, and pretty Helena Isdell, whom she'd sat beside at dinner the previous evening, to play whist, but Meg was sure to tag along.

Unable to make a decision Addie walked towards the companionway, her arms swinging smartly at her sides, thinking that perhaps she could convince Matron to reassign her to another cabin. Deep in thought, she failed to notice two hands come from behind and encircle her waist. Panic hammered in her chest, her feet refused to budge and she let out a series of small yelps.

'It's only me, you silly chook. Who did you think it was?'

She looked over her shoulder. 'Meg! I thought you were a wicked person!'

'Sorry. Let me make it up to you. Come on.'

'Where are you going?'

'No idea. I keep getting lost. Do you know where the isolation hospital is?'

'I made a map of this level when I came up earlier.' Addie held up her notebook. 'I have diagrams of all three decks.'

Meg barely glanced at the notebook. 'Maps don't work for me. I always ask people.'

'What if they give you the wrong directions?'

'Then I end up somewhere unexpected. You should try it.'

Addie stopped to study her sketch. 'The hospital should be near No. 4 hatch,' she said, pointing towards a door.

Five cots next to the funnel were already made up, as were another six against a wall. Fingering a rough grey woollen blanket, sides firmly tucked under the mattress, she said softly, 'This will soon be covering an injured soldier.'

Meg picked up a pillow and hugged it to her chest. 'Yes, our faces could be the last many of them see.'

Tears pricked at Addie's eyes. She blinked them away.

Meg patted her on the arm. 'Everything will be fine. Don't worry.'

'You're right,' Addie said hesitantly. After a pause, she added, with more certainty, 'We're trained for this.'

'What did you say?' Meg called from down the back. 'Come on, slowcoach.'

A smaller cubicle next to two standard-sized rooms would be for infectious patients. Sheets were stacked on an examination table. No, not sheets, too bulky – shrouds.

'Let's get out of here,' said Meg.

Back on the upper deck, a sailor securing a coil of rope that smelled of tar whistled as they went past. Meg gave him a cheery wave. Addie took the next corner too quickly and almost bumped into three officers huddling in a doorway, their hands cupping cigarettes that fizzled in the light rain. The men greeted her warmly, but she pressed her arms against her sides and edged along the walkway. Behind her, she heard Meg call out, 'Not much of a day.' Addie picked up her pace but Meg soon caught up with her.

'Do you ever worry about drowning?' Meg was pulling at a loose thread on her cape. If she kept tugging, the whole hem would unravel.

'No,' Addie said uneasily, 'do you?'

Meg screwed up her face. 'Every now and then I have this nightmare where I'm on a ledge overlooking the ocean. I reach for something – I don't know what – and my hair falls out, curl by curl, until it all ends up in the sea.' She gave a metallic laugh. 'Clumps drift off. I can't reach them. What do you think it means?'

Addie shook her head. 'My training didn't cover dreams.' She wouldn't mention her own recurring nightmare – fleeing at the sight of her first injured soldier. Meg might think she had no backbone.

By late afternoon, several nurses were leaning over enamel basins, necks outstretched, chests heaving. When Addie offered to take those who could walk up to the shade deck for some fresh air, a staff nurse raised her head too quickly and accidentally vomited on the hem of her cloak. 'Don't worry,' Addie told her. 'I'll duck down to the cabin and fetch my cape.' She favoured the shorter scarlet garment anyway: it made her look more military.

Among the invalids were Netta and Helena, whom they'd met earlier at dinner. Once the poor things had settled into the deckchairs outside the library, Addie handed them mugs of water and arrowroot laced with brandy. 'Drink up. It will settle your tummies.' Netta pinched her nostrils together and swallowed her portion straight down while Helena took dainty sips.

Two officers strolled along the deck towards them, faces tilted to the breeze but nevertheless managing to look their way.

'Enjoying the war, girls?' said the beefier of the pair. 'We can't call you officers, can we?'

'We were promised the same rank as you,' said Netta, glaring at him. 'It wasn't our fault we didn't get it.'

'Anyone can make beds and dole out gripe water.'

Netta's pale skin tightened across her cheeks and her brown eyes sparked with anger. She spoke in a firm tone, 'We deserve the recognition, not to mention the extra pay.'

The men sniggered and moved on.

Once they were out of hearing, Netta said, 'We passed the tests – no false teeth, varicose veins or weakness of the heart – and we're registered nurses. It's not right! We should lodge a formal grievance.'

Netta had grown up on a pig farm near Oamaru, which Addie thought might explain her direct manner. As far as she was concerned, there was no point complaining; the men's commanding officer was most likely cut from the same cloth as the rule-makers. In her view, most chaps were big on opinions and short on civility.

MEG COULDN'T STAY cooped up in the stuffy cabin a minute longer – she simply had to go topside for some fresh air. Terrified a mysterious force would pull her overboard, she gripped handles, pipes, fittings – anything attached to solid walls. 'Never look at the sea,' she repeated in her head, 'never look at the sea.' The wind was picking up, flapping her skirt around her legs and causing metal contraptions above her head to clank and rattle. Desperate for company, she peered through the spray streaming over the rails at a uniformed figure coming towards her. 'Careful!' she yelled when Addie's face came into view. The ship pitched into a trough and Addie fell awkwardly against the railing. Meg grabbed the ties on Addie's cape and pulled hard. Addie coughed and gasped, flapping her hands, and Meg hit her between the shoulder blades. 'I thought you were a goner. I couldn't save you. I can't swim.'

As soon as the last sentence left her mouth, she wanted to haul it back in. 'I'm fine as long as there's a deck beneath me. See.' She balanced on one leg. Addie stared beyond her to the lumpy sea, her face set.

'Give me a bustling street or a music hall any day,' Meg called above the roar of the wind. Addie scrunched her shoulders and lowered her head. Moving closer, Meg said, 'If rough weather slows our arrival, I'll scream – in tune, of course. I have a decent singing voice.' The ship plunged into another trough and she lurched sideways. 'Sorry, my balance has gone to pot.' Linking her arm through Addie's, she said, 'Help me, please.'

Addie gave a half-hearted smile. 'I'm not that steady myself.'

Together they stumbled towards the entrance of the ship's electric lifts where Meg stroked the metal trim on the gate. 'I can feel the thrum of the engine. It won't break down, will it?'

'I shouldn't think so. Every cog will have passed a medical.'

So she does have a sense of humour. Not wanting Addie to think her nervous, Meg sought a change of subject. 'Netta could struggle in the Egyptian heat with her fair skin. And that red hair means a temper.'

Addie pulled a face. 'She certainly gave those officers a piece of her mind.' She turned towards the companionway.

'Where are you going?'

'I'm off to fetch another book from the library.'

'I'll come with you. Stay close. Be my ballast.' As an eerie whine ran along a wire strut she suppressed an urge to scream.

Once they were safely in the library, Meg jerked her head towards a nearby bookcase. 'Read any of them?'

Addie ran her hand over the spines protruding from the top shelf. 'Yes,' she said, 'Dickens, Kipling, Conrad, and Cook's life of Miss Nightingale.'

Golly, had she swallowed an encyclopaedia? Meg gazed around the room, then moved towards a portrait of an older man on the opposite wall. She traced the line of the jaw with her finger. His disgruntled expression made her think of Pa.

'Have you read about Miss Nightingale?' Addie asked.

Meg leant against the back of an armchair. 'During training I used to wander up and down the hallway with a candle, pretending I was serving with her in the Crimea. One night I accidentally set fire to a peacock feather stashed in an umbrella stand.'

Addie blinked twice.

'Just teasing.' Meg twirled around as someone coughed in the doorway.

A sallow-skinned ship nurse bustled in, carrying copies of the *Evening Post*. 'Hello there. We met over dinner last night.'

'I remember,' Meg said. 'You passed me the milk jug.'

'Do our facilities impress you?'

'Definitely,' said Addie.

'Top-notch,' Meg added.

While Addie and the nurse discussed the benefits of electric lighting, Meg checked her reflection in the glass of the portrait. Her nose was damp. She dabbed it dry on the sleeve of her dress. There was never enough air in libraries.

'Read these if you like,' said the nurse, placing the newspapers on a table.

'Your patients must enjoy catching up on news from home,' Addie said.

'Yes, they can make a paper last all day.'

Meg reached for a copy and flicked to the entertainment page. 'If we were in Wellington we could have gone to His Majesty's. I adore a good show.'

'I doubt you'll find a theatre in Egypt,' said the nurse. 'Fancy a cuppa?'

'Yes, please,' Meg said. 'We can put on our own plays, can't we?' She nudged Addie, who frowned. Pretending not to notice, Meg asked, 'Where did you train?'

The nurse placed a kettle on the primus and set out three cups and saucers on a side-table. 'I was at Auckland, under Miss Neilson – a real stickler. She insisted we all take the same number of paces down the corridor, regardless of the length of our legs.'

Meg shrieked. 'You had Neilson too! I heard she came from Auckland. She was matron at Riverton when I started. Caught me smoking once. Kicked up a real fuss, and I wasn't even on duty. I was at the races, minding my own business!'

❧

YEARS AGO, when she was about twelve, Addie's father had returned from the Riverton Cup in a celebratory mood. 'Three wins, two places,' he'd called out, waving a wad of notes at her. She'd helped him out of his coat and put it on a peg near the back door. 'It's colder in here than a morgue,' he'd said as he fastened his waistcoat. 'Help me get a fire going, poppet.' Unable to find any newspaper, he'd lit one of the banknotes and tossed it into the coal range. The kindling had caught straight away. She remembered clamping her hands over her mouth while Father pocketed the rest of the notes and yelled, 'I'd better get this lot to the bank before it all goes up in smoke.'

'What about you, Sister Harrington?' said the nurse. 'Did you train in Riverton with Sister Dutton?'

Addie shook her head. 'No, I went through Southland Hospital.' If she didn't change the subject, the nurse would expect her to gossip about her classmates. 'How many men can the *Maheno* carry?'

'Three hundred and fifty, and we have space for another hundred on the upper deck.' She lifted the lid of the teapot and gave the leaves a stir with a long-handled spoon. 'I hear conditions are ghastly in the East. I don't envy you.'

Addie pictured rows of tents full of hideously injured soldiers all needing attention. Her hands began to shake. She placed them in her lap, one on top of the other, to steady them.

Meg tapped a teaspoon rhythmically against the sugar bowl. 'Hardships won't worry me as long as we have first-rate medical officers to entertain us.'

Addie's mouth fell open. She hadn't expected Meg to say such a thing in company.

My Adelina thinks she can look after herself. But mark my words, she's heading for trouble. I know men. Minds like sewers. Never let an opportunity pass. She's pretty. They'll take advantage. Even the injured ones – if they can. I won't be there to stop them. What's more, nursing is dirty work. She shouldn't have to clean up blood and muck. She was a delicate child, prone to bronchitis. Night after night, I paced the hallway with her gasping on my shoulder. Soft wee thing couldn't even watch me kill a chook for Sunday dinner. It broke my heart to farewell her at the train station, but I couldn't tell her. No good with words. Not enough schooling. The old man kept me home to work on the farm. Hate to think what would have become of me if Thelma hadn't taken me under her wing. We're two sides of the same coin. She's the planner, I'm the doer. We've done well, made a packet. Adelina could have a posh wedding. Same goes for young Erin. No boys – we weren't blessed that way. We'll have to settle for a couple of sons-in-law. A month ago, I rustled up a high country station manager for Adelina to consider, but the stubborn little minx buried her head in a book, leaving her mother to entertain the poor chap, who'd decked himself out in a fancy city suit. My Adelina would be a damn sight better off marrying him and having kiddies than serving overseas. She's my first-born and precious as spring rain.

Two

THE COLONEL had had a chalk line drawn on the upper deck, to separate the soldiers from the nurses, but in Meg's opinion no one with half a pulse would take a jot of notice. She stepped over it to chat with Captain Adams, a frightful dandy but loads of laughs, who'd sat opposite her at dinner last night. They'd barely passed the time of day before Matron stormed up the stairs, ruby-red splotches flaring across her cheeks. Convinced she'd upset her, Meg hastily farewelled Adams and shot behind a bulkhead. Safely concealed, she listened to their conversation.

'Is something wrong, Matron?' asked Adams.

'He thinks we're using too much water so he's closed two of our three bathrooms.'

'Who?'

'Your colonel! He doesn't know the first thing about hygiene. Would you believe he reassigned our orderlies to other duties? As of today we're to clean our own lavatories.'

'Surely not.'

'He has no regard for our training or our positions. When I threatened to cable the Minister of Defence, he ordered me to leave.' Matron lowered her voice. 'Would you consider intervening on our behalf?'

Adams gave a slight cough. 'Sorry, I'm no good at that sort of thing.'

No surprise there, Meg thought. She'd already pegged him as more of a good-time boy than a diplomat. As for the colonel, he deserved a big fat boil on his backside and a nurse with a grudge to lance it. She heard Matron sigh. That attitude wouldn't get back their bathrooms. Matron had to flap her birdlike elbows and put up a fight, defend her territory and that of her nurses. This trip would be no fun with Ramrod Ronnie in charge.

Before she'd signed up, her aunt had suggested she run a private hotel in Queenstown. 'A nice hairdo, a manicure and a rest brightens up most women. Nothing wrong with a stiff gin either.' Meg wished there was a glass of the stuff in her hand right now and that she was admiring Lake Wakatipu instead of lurching empty-fisted across the Tasman Sea. But back then she had pictured wealthy women sitting in wicker chairs, tartan blankets over their laps, turnips for brains. She'd said as much to Aunt Maude, who had adjusted her fox fur until two paws straddled her abundant bust. 'There's no glamour in war, Meg. You could have a well-paid position at Lake View, plus a routine.' 'No thanks,' she'd replied. 'I need adventure and this war is my ticket.'

BY THE FIFTH DAY, most of the seasick nurses had recovered sufficiently to join Addie and Meg in the dining saloon. They were no sooner through the door than five or six chaps lounging against the far wall waved at them. Netta picked up a table napkin and shook it vigorously. 'You'd think we were ripe fruit the way those officers are drooling.'

Addie was imagining herself as a plum falling from a tree into the hands of a licentious officer when two men started arguing over who would accompany Meg to the table. Before long, they were sitting either side of her, like bookends.

'Being cooped up is terribly hard on us,' Meg said, flicking a wayward curl behind her ear. 'Oh, don't get me wrong. We're ready for whatever lies ahead. Aren't we, Addie?'

Unwilling to agree too enthusiastically, Addie tilted her head slightly to the side. Thinking she would tidy up before dinner, she'd gone to the cabin earlier, only to discover Meg's belongings strewn over both bunks and the wretched woman using her hairbrush. 'In case you've forgotten, two of us share this space,' she'd snapped, then snatched her cape off the hook on the back of the door and stormed out, ignoring Meg's excuses. There would have to be rules: she'd broach the subject after lights out. She carried on nibbling at a piece of fish drenched in white sauce while Meg's voice echoed around the room.

'It would make such a difference if we could . . . you know . . . keep active.'

The men laughed as a rail-thin adjutant approached Meg. 'Leave it to me, Sister. I'll see to your requirements.'

Meg inclined her head towards him. 'Persuade your colonel to set up a nurses' canteen too.'

'One that welcomes guests?'

Meg grinned. 'If they're charming and know their place.'

'Would you trust him?' Addie whispered to Margaret Rogers, a former district nurse who hailed from Christchurch.

'Not unless he was bound and gagged.'

Addie stifled a giggle. Margaret had an easy manner and a warm open face. Her lips turned up at the corners, giving the impression that she was always on the verge of smiling. She wore her thick brown hair parted down the middle and piled up in a roll at the back of her head. A good-natured woman, Addie decided, sensible too.

Margaret glanced towards the end of the table where two staff nurses were talking. 'Have you spoken to them yet?'

'No,' said Addie. 'Who are they?'

'The younger slightly plump one with the angelic face is Dora Kennard from Temuka. Her brother joined the army early on and she signed up so she could nurse him if he got hurt. I don't know anything about her companion other than her name's Lois Moore and she comes from Ashburton.'

Addie sighed. Lois had untidy hair and her dress needed a decent iron.

❧

BEFORE MEG could check if there was a better prospect in the vicinity, the skinny adjutant whisked her across the sitting room to the gramophone, where he sorted through a pile of records in the cabinet. She fluttered her palm over her heart and swayed when he put Harry Lauder's 'She's the Girl for Me' on the turntable. Next minute he had his hand pressed against the small of her back.

Thanks to the dance classes she'd taken during the first year of her nursing training, she made all the right moves and she looked the part. She'd only borrowed Addie's brush because she couldn't find her own. Another two minutes and Addie would've been none the wiser. Besides, Miss Perfect read every night and never asked if the light annoyed her. There had to be give and take.

When the tune ended, Meg pretended to swoon and half a dozen men rushed to catch her. Slipping through their hands, she sprinted over to the gramophone to put on 'I've Something in the Bottle for the Morning', hoping it might make Addie laugh rather than slink off with Margaret. As Meg reached out to waylay Addie, she felt a button pop off her uniform, revealing a flash of creamy white skin. For an instant, in the ensuing

26

collective intake of male breath, she felt a surge of power but the feeling quickly died away.

BETWEEN COURSES – barley soup followed by roast beef, mashed potatoes and boiled cabbage, then breadcrumb and marmalade pudding – Addie and Margaret toasted King George and Queen Mary. On the other side of the table Meg repeatedly raised her glass and said 'Cheers', but Addie ignored her. Eventually Meg got up, came round and went down on one knee. 'Addie, will you please do me the honour of clinking glasses?'

With everyone watching and laughing, she had to oblige.

Even Iris Hutchison, an older nurse with a prominent forehead and greying hair scraped into a bun, played along. Addie looked around the room. To her left, Helena and Dora were joking with the first officer, who seemed a decent sort of chap, while further along Iris was picking the brains of a medic whose spotty brown face reminded Addie of a morepork. On her right, Lois, Margaret and Netta were organising a card night. Across the table, Meg shrieked at something the adjutant told her.

While they were waiting for coffee, a portly quartermaster arrived with two sets of quoits and a skipping rope. 'Here you are, Sister Dutton. These will help keep you trim.'

'You're a true gentleman,' Meg said in a honey-coated voice. She immediately grabbed a couple of the quoits and spun them on her wrists while launching into:

Bugle calls! Bugle calls! sounding all the way,
Oh, what fun to ride the seas at 5/6 a day!

To her horror, Addie could hear her mother's voice in her head: 'Good manners reflect the moral state of a nation.' When the catcalls died down, a lanky ginger-haired officer refilled Meg's

27

glass of cordial, and somewhat skilfully, Addie thought, backed her into a corner.

'Sister Dutton,' he said in an admiring tone, 'you could be on stage.'

'Then help get me there,' said Meg, ducking under an arm he'd strategically placed in front of her. From the middle of the room, she sang a few lines from 'Heroes in New Zealand' – 'Carry out the piano boys – put it on the deck' – and next thing Ginger was apologising for his colonel's out-of-date attitude and assuring Meg that he could supply whatever she needed.

When Addie got back to their cabin, Meg had cleared her clothes off the bunks and removed her blonde hairs from the hairbrush. That wasn't the point, though. Meg shouldn't have taken liberties. Addie pulled on her nightgown and got into bed. She had a new library book but she wasn't in the mood to read so she turned off the light and waited.

Shortly afterwards Meg tiptoed in. Addie heard her ease the lid off her pot of cold cream, smooth the gloop on her face, then undress and climb into her bunk as quiet as could be. Surprised by her thoughtfulness, Addie decided to wait until morning to raise the subject of cabin rules.

Just as she was nodding off a whisper made its way to her through the darkness.

'Sorry, Addie, I should never have borrowed your brush or used your bunk as a clothes horse.'

Addie lifted her head off the pillow slightly. 'My little sister Erin was always messing up my room. It really annoyed me. I had to put a lock on the door.'

'You won't have to do that here.' The bunk creaked as Meg changed position. 'It must be wonderful to have a sister.'

'Erin can be a pest but I wouldn't change her. Sometimes you remind me of her. She tells amusing stories too.'

As Adelaide came into view Addie stayed with Iris, whose size made her slow on her feet, and Lois, who seemed overwhelmed, although she waved her handkerchief in the air. Because Father had told her to look out for a six-storey skyscraper that belonged to a physician, Addie stared upwards. She thought he'd been pulling her leg, but there was the Verco Building in front of her, towering above the people on the wharf. There was nothing like it in Invercargill – she really was in a different country.

When the *Maheno* docked, society ladies, dressed to the nines, took up ringside positions on the quayside. Addie was well down the gangplank before she realised the scent wafting towards her came from their outstretched wrists. Behind this fashionable set, children climbed onto their fathers' shoulders while their mothers elbowed their way through the crowd to get a decent view. She looked around for Meg, who'd been up near the bow with Helena. They were both behind her, eyes as bright as carriage lamps. She was about to ask if they knew what was going on when a woman thrust a tuck-box at her and crooned in a cultured voice, 'In appreciation of your sacrifice, Sister.'

Meg roared in Addie's ear. 'Don't you just love the fuss?'

'Surely all these people aren't here to see us?'

'Of course they are, silly.'

THE SHIP was about to take on coal. As far as Meg was concerned, that meant filthy black dust which would ruin her complexion and increase her chances of ending up on the shelf. Luckily, the colonel had ordered all non-essential personnel to catch a train into town.

She snaffled a seat in the middle of the carriage and pulled Addie in beside her as the conductor blew the final whistle. Netta Smith, who'd employed a gang of hairclips to keep her fiery red locks under control and anchor her panama, claimed the opposite seat. Margaret and Helena piled in after her. As the train chugged out of the station, steam and soot smearing the windows, Meg stretched out her legs. One summer, when she was small, Ma had painted stars on her ankles and hugged her when she'd said the brush tickled.

'Before I signed up, I hadn't travelled further than Invercargill,' Addie said.

'Me neither,' said Meg. 'So we're in the same boat.'

'Literally.' Netta waved a hand in the direction of the *Maheno*.

Meg smiled and tapped the window. 'Impressive countryside, and the Australian men aren't bad either.'

Addie coughed. 'Well, at least they speak English,' she said finally. 'I don't suppose Egyptians do. We could struggle to make ourselves understood. Things might not go smoothly at first.'

Heavens, thought Meg. She plastered a smile on her face and said, 'Let's play "Spot the Nattiest Chap" when we reach town.'

'What if he's dangerous?' said Addie. 'Besides, I'm awfully hot.'

Meg waggled the hem of her own dress at her. 'Would you sooner walk through town in your petticoat?' Addie's eyes widened. 'Tease and flatter them,' Meg continued. 'That always works for me. Who's game?'

Netta groaned. 'I've better things to do than chase larrikins. There are plants in this place that I can't identify. I need to track down a botanist.' She had a marvellous garden at home. They'd seen the pictures.

Helena and Margaret glanced at each other before saying in unison, 'We'll come with you, Meg.'

Addie hiccupped and said, 'I suppose I could as well.'

If it weren't for her guarded expression, Meg would have given her a hug.

They were five minutes out of the station when three Australian corporals moseyed up, Woodbines dangling from their mouths, thumbs hanging like pegs from khaki pockets. Even their hats were set at a raffish angle. They could be good for a laugh.

'Nurse, was your photograph in a recent newspaper?' the tallest chap asked.

Meg flashed him a smile. 'It could have been.'

His wiry pal shot over to a street-seller and bought her a bunch of bronze chrysanthemums. When she passed a bloom to Margaret, an earwig crawled out of a petal and up her arm. 'You have an admirer too,' Meg said.

The third fellow had a crooked nose, broken more than once by the look of it. He pulled on the ties of her cape, shimmied up a pole and draped his scarlet prize over the light. 'My lady of the lamp,' he shouted, his face ruddy from exertion.

'What a show-off,' said Addie in a hushed voice.

When Meg wagged a finger at her, Addie blushed like billy-o. Damn. She'd gone too far again. It was time to send the chaps packing. 'Off you go before Matron catches us. Bring my cape down first, though. Otherwise I could get into terrible trouble.'

While the cheeky beggar retrieved it, the taller corporal pulled a crumpled paper bag from his jacket pocket and tossed it to her. She peeked inside. Good, they were her favourite toffees. 'Thanks,' she shouted as he disappeared with his mates into a hotel across the road. Beckoning to her companions, she nodded towards a poster on the door of an ornate Victorian building. 'Come on, let's see what that's all about.'

'Are you sure you know what you're doing, Meg?' asked Margaret, patting her hair.

'Not really,' she said, and tossed the bag to Helena before walking over to Addie, who was running her fingers down the window of a bookshop. 'Come and get a toffee.'

'No thanks.'

'Can't you decide which title to buy?'

Addie put her gloves back on. 'I have enough for now.'

There was still warmth in the late afternoon winter sun as they walked back from the station to the ship. No clouds, just an indigo sky, tinged with pink.

Netta was waiting for them at the top of the gangway. 'What took you so long?'

'A dashing officer on a balcony who was determined to sing me a medley of show tunes,' Meg said. No sense in telling a fib unless you made sure it was a beauty. Stories came alive through the decorations you hung on them. Like Christmas trees.

'Come with us next time, Netta,' Margaret said.

'Meg's the perfect tour guide,' Helena added. 'She introduced us to all sorts of attractions: shops, lamps, the locals.'

Everyone laughed, even Addie, which pleased Meg no end. Perhaps they could carry on bunking together.

❧

AFTER THE SERVICE on Sunday, Addie had morning tea in the sitting room with a group of staff nurses and sisters from nearby cabins. Everyone was talking of home. Helena was from Kumara, on the West Coast.

'It's smaller than your Riverton, Addie, and Meg's Tuatapere,' she said. 'We have the Southern Alps to the east, and to the west dense bush that runs almost down to the sea. Anyone straying off a track risks getting lost. And it can rain for days.'

'If you can put up with rain, come south for a visit when this fuss is over,' Meg said. 'My aunt and uncle will put you up. They have an enormous house.'

Addie passed Helena a plate of oat biscuits. 'Yes, please do. We could take you to Monkey Island in Te Waewae Bay. On a clear day, you can see the Solanders. The Maoris have a great story about their formation. They believe a whale called Kiwa bit into the South Island and the crumbs from her mouth fell into the sea.'

Helena sipped her tea thoughtfully as though straining the information through her small white teeth.

The talk then turned to the deserters on board a ship that had come alongside theirs last night. A steward had told Addie that when he'd taken the crew down a billy of tea, they were slicing bread and opening tins of mutton with a bayonet. 'I wouldn't want them as my jailers.'

'It's a waste to shoot deserters,' said Margaret. 'They could roll bandages for us.'

A strand of hair strayed down the nape of her neck and Addie watched her absentmindedly tuck it back into place. 'They mightn't be right in the head,' she said.

'If they're not, there'll be a good reason.' Meg dropped a slice of lemon into her tea, some of which splashed into her saucer. 'I suspect they lied about their age, then got cold feet when they realised what they were in for, poor little blighters.'

'Liars must repent or burn in hell.' Lois spoke loudly and with an intensity that made Addie squirm in her chair.

Fifteen years ago, while gathering cones with a neighbour's son, Addie had accidentally lost Father's torch. The following day the boy found it and took it home, intending to return it when he saw her next. Unfortunately, his older brother thought he'd stolen it and thrashed him. She couldn't look at either of them for weeks.

Late in July, when they were halfway to Colombo, the weather turned foul. Winds lashed the ship and torrential rain pelted down as the sky darkened to a menacing black. Addie covered her face with the sheet as bolts of lightning flashed through the cabin. She could hear the sea hammering on the wall.

At dawn, something crashed onto the floor and woke her. Meg, who was fully dressed and swinging her legs over the side of her bunk, bootlaces tied in double knots, hopped down to pick it up. 'A jar of my aunt's apple jelly. Just as well it didn't break. I need a spoonful of something sweet.'

Addie's own mouth tasted stale. She would gargle with warm water and salt when she went for her morning wash. The ship was slewing, thumping, creaking. 'I should get dressed too.'

Meg turned her back and tidied her bedding while Addie pulled on her clothes.

While she was fastening her collar, there was a knock at the door and Matron poked her head in. 'Harrington, Dutton, go directly to the workroom after breakfast and hem more towels.' The door had barely shut before Meg was mimicking Matron's habit of stroking her nose while issuing orders. Addie hoped she wouldn't start mocking her.

⁕

THE DAY their canteen opened Meg edged her way through the crowd to the counter, where she praised the steward who was overseeing the event. He took her order straight away.

'A vanilla ice cream sets me up for the whole day,' she said, waving her cone triumphantly in the air.

'Keep buttering up those blokes,' Netta said with a grin. 'Who knows what we'll find in Egypt.'

'Camels,' Meg said, loping about as though she had a hump on her back.

When the laughter died down, Addie asked why the colonel had denied them adequate water then given them a canteen. She had a point, Meg thought. 'It pays to cosy up to military men, even the fruitcakes.'

Helena picked up a dishcloth and started wiping down a bench. Some nurses enjoyed scrubbing and sluicing but Meg wasn't one of them. She leant over and pretended to lick Netta's ice cream.

Netta moved her cone out of reach. 'You're incorrigible. Stop it, Meg.'

'I will when I die. Do any of you think about dying?' That wasn't what she'd meant to say. Her mouth still moved faster than her brain.

Helena coughed as if something unsavoury had lodged in the back of her throat. 'We don't need to worry. Our boys must, though.'

Addie said, 'Do you believe in God, Meg?'

'Not God, other things.'

'Like what?'

Meg took a handkerchief from her pocket and wiped a trace of ice cream from the tip of her nose. Once she had everyone's attention, she said, 'People and pleasure.' She raised her hands in the air like an evangelist. 'They are my delights. What are yours, Addie?'

'I had a Presbyterian upbringing.'

'That explains a lot!' To Meg's relief, even Addie smiled.

'Hypocrites rile me,' said Netta, 'praying on Sundays, sinning for the rest of the week. I can't abide them.'

Addie said, 'My parents believe we can rise above sin.'

A well-heeled couple wafted into Meg's mind and plonked themselves down on a snow-white cloud above Riverton, ready to watch common folk perform various depravities. 'How do they think that happens?'

'By respecting one's elders, praying and remaining pure.'

Meg picked up a woven strip of cane and swatted a fly. 'You really needed to leave home.'

'I'm here for lots of reasons,' said Addie. 'Only some involve my parents.'

Meg waved her ice cream cone over Addie's head. 'Any more talk of parents or religion and I'll turn you into a toad.'

We found Meg alone under a Christmas tree that we'd taken over the week before. Her mother had vanished, which made us think she was unwell again. There were no presents in the house, apart from ours. The child's flannel pyjamas steamed with filth and there were lice crawling through her curls. Maude removed her silk scarf and wrapped it around Meg's little head. I fetched a bag. There wasn't much to pack – just a teddy bear we'd given her the previous year. She'd outgrown the jacket and shoes we'd dropped in six months ago when her father was in Invercargill at the yearling sales. He wouldn't have us on the property after we raised concerns about the child's care. I wanted to report Meg's parents to the authorities but Maude thought we should keep it in the family in case they mended their ways. He drinks and Maude's sister mopes. Some days she never leaves her bed. On others, the fidgets come upon her and she heads for the river. To anoint herself, she says. Maude's sister isn't the full ticket. She talks to things we can't see. Reckons they're after her. She blames Meg for her troubles because they worsened after her birth. He can't see beyond the next bottle. Never will. The wee girl nuzzled me like a horse when I scooped her into my arms.

Three

ADDIE WOKE to a shrill dawn chorus coming from outside the porthole. 'You want cigar, sir, cigarettes?' 'Lady, drop a penny for boy.' 'Missus, buy fresh fruit?' She rolled over and, finding Meg's bunk empty, closed her eyes again and cast her mind back to late yesterday afternoon, when they'd steamed into Colombo. The first thing that had struck her was the sticky oppressive heat, the second was the swarms of dark-skinned men on the quayside, stacking supplies and equipment that had been haphazardly unloaded from transport ships, troop carriers and provision vessels. There'd been no way of telling who was in charge.

In her mind she suddenly saw clearly the trawlers at home working their way under the bridge that divided Riverton from Colac Bay and the Rocks, the air chilly, flax rustling in the brackish breeze. For the second time in twenty-four hours, homesickness rolled through her.

She found Meg and a few other early birds outside the ship's dispensary, panamas sensibly shading their faces. Squeezing in beside Helena and Lois, Addie peeked over the rail. Half a dozen whippet-thin youngsters were manoeuvring boats loaded with fresh fruit and vegetables alongside the *Maheno*.

'They're the colour of Worcestershire sauce,' Lois said. 'I can't see inside them.'

A sailor working on a derrick shouted, 'Darkies outnumber whiteys here. You'll have to get used to them.'

Lois clapped her hands over her ears and darted behind Meg and Helena. While they tried to settle her, Addie counted out sufficient coins to throw to a lad brandishing a small bunch of bananas. She was imagining their sweet taste when a senior officer rushed up to her shouting, 'Buy nothing. Plague and smallpox are rife. Don't send your laundry ashore either and there'll be no sightseeing.'

Startled, she dropped the coins back into her purse.

'No sightseeing!' said Meg, fanning her face with last night's menu. 'What else is there to do?'

'Quoits?' said Helena.

Iris and Dora offered to set up a game. They shared a room and from all accounts got on famously, although it was difficult to tell what they had in common.

'Hurry up, Dora!' said Iris. 'The day will be over before we get started.'

'Give me a few minutes,' Dora answered. 'I'm not a machine.'

When Iris thrust out her chin Addie was sure she was going to grump again, so it was a pleasant surprise when she dropped her voice and said, 'Sorry, Dora. Yelling's a bad habit of mine. When you're the last kid in a family of eleven you have to kick up a din if you want anything done.' Dora smiled sympathetically as Iris picked up the quoit stand and paced out the prescribed distance.

'Right,' she said, 'who wants a game?'

Addie moved aside to let Isabel Clark, a nursing sister from Oamaru, make her way through the crowd. She had striking blue eyes and dark hair – and a good throwing arm, despite her short stature. Her friend, Marion Brown, a big-boned woman with spectacles, acted as umpire. When Isabel won the match, the sailor who had upset Lois clanged a wrench on a metal pipe, simulating a drum roll. Iris called for another game.

An hour before the *Maheno* was due to take on more coal – the threat of plague and smallpox apparently forgotten – the colonel instructed eighty or more officers and nurses to pile into horse-drawn gharries and set off for the Thomas Cook tourist office. Addie was travelling with Helena and the dandyish Captain Adams. As the gharry bumped up and down the deeply rutted road, bootblacks plied for trade, bead-sellers thrust trinkets at them and urchins jangled tins in their faces.

Further along a herd of water buffalo thundered into a crowded junction, forcing the horses to stop abruptly, and causing the back of Addie's head to rebound painfully off the canvas-covered frame of the gharry. She rubbed the spot while the drivers of adjacent army vehicles blasted their horns. When the buffalos bellowed back, she glanced at Helena. Both women tightened their grip on the sidebars of their gharry.

'We'll walk the rest of the way,' shouted Captain Adams. 'Out you get, girls. Now watch where you put your feet. We're not on Lambton Quay.'

No matter which way she turned, Addie couldn't escape the ghastly stench that oozed from roughly hewn stone channels overflowing with waste and crawling with sated blowflies. To make matters worse, Ceylonese men kept spitting red liquid onto the ground beside her.

'Betel juice,' said a medical officer, 'a disgusting concoction that spreads disease.'

'This place needs a good scrub down with Jeyes Fluid,' said Iris.

No amount of Jeyes could clean it up, Addie thought. Dirt and disease were part of the city. So were unveiled girls with oiled hair that glistened in the sunlight. Two were standing directly in her path; one had razor-sharp cheekbones, the other, enormous nut-brown eyes. She had to step onto the road to bypass them.

'Back-door beauties,' Meg whispered.

The queue at Thomas Cook stretched down to the corner. There were no verandahs to diminish the glare of the sun. Addie sought refuge under her umbrella while Meg stood in direct sunlight telling an officer she would *not* go back to the ship until she'd seen everything. When Addie enquired about the cost of the excursion, a second lieutenant told her he thought one pound fifteen shillings would cover a return train fare to Kandy, and meals and lodgings in a reasonable hotel. Armed with this information, Addie stepped into the office.

By the time she emerged, ticket in hand, bootblacks had taken over the street. 'Best shine, best price.' 'I quick, you see.'

A suave-looking medic in the middle of a boot polish waved his cane at her.

'Sister, are you up for some sphinxing when we reach Egypt?'

She shook her head and hurried over to Helena, who was standing at the side of the road. In a futile attempt to create a cool breeze, Addie swished her skirt. 'I never know what to say to his sort.'

'Me neither,' said Helena. 'I prefer sick men, They're much nicer, no trouble at all.'

Addie beamed at her.

FROM HER TRAIN window Meg could see mountainous country-side, patches of jungle and even glimpses of rice terraces in various shades of green.

She stretched her arms above her head and pulled on her knuckles until they cracked. In the opposite seat, Dora peeled an orange. Earlier she'd read aloud part of a letter from her brother, which she'd been carting around in her handbag since leaving home. In a seat further back, Iris was harping on about writing a story on the perils of dirty water for their nursing magazine, *Kai Tiaki*. No one at home would read it. Everyone wanted tales about pyramids.

Matron agreed. 'Record your loftier thoughts in your diary, Sister.'

Each nurse had received a diary before leaving New Zealand. Meg was using hers to rank the attributes of certain officers. So far, Captain Adams had the highest score. Before strapping on his holster, he'd been a reviewer of musicals. If she played her cards right, he might get her a part in a show after the war, or at least send her dress-circle tickets.

When the train finally pulled into Kandy station, she grabbed her holdall and made her way through the carriage. Porters in flowing gowns swooped towards her like a flock of magpies as she stepped onto the platform and undid the top button of her belted cotton dress. The last thing she needed was a dose of prickly heat.

'Will it be as hot outside?' Addie gasped beside her. 'My throat's burning.'

Meg took a handkerchief from her handbag and mopped her face. 'You need something cool to hang around your neck.' She spotted a stall that sold necklaces and, as instructed by Captain Adams, beat the owner down to a fair price. 'For you,' she said, handing Addie a strand of amber beads.

'How lovely, thank you. You shouldn't . . .'

'Wear it to our next concert. It might bring you luck.'

Luck was something Meg believed in. You had to if you had nothing else.

Out on the street, urchins buzzed like insects around the waiting gharries that were pulled along by nimble locals. A small boy shouted, 'You want guide? Cheap? You like cheap?' An older boy shooed him away.

'Pile in, Sisters,' said Captain Adams.

He offered his arm to Netta, who bunched her skirt into a tight knot and climbed into a different gharry. You'd have thought Adams was some kind of monster the way Netta carried on. The man was only trying to help.

Then again, she remembered something Netta had said recently while they were folding linen. 'I doubt anything would silence a blowhard like my father.'

'Is he why you have a poor opinion of men?'

Netta had snapped her end of the sheet. 'They think they're better than us.'

The gharry men kept up a brisk pace until they came upon a religious parade. While waiting for the followers to pass, Meg bought two oranges from a vendor and gave one to a boy covered in desert sores. Left untreated, they would scar.

Finally, they were able to move on and the Queen's Hotel soon came into sight, a bang-up establishment if appearances were anything to go by. She was keen to freshen up. Her hair drooped on these stinking hot days. Once inside she stood under a ceiling fan, making the most of the cool downdraft while Adams banged his cane on the desk in the foyer.

'Poor show,' he shouted. 'We booked ahead. You must have sufficient rooms. These girls need beds.'

Because the owner couldn't increase the number of rooms, Meg and six other nurses had to take a second bone-rattling journey, this time through a better part of town.

'Lucky us,' she said as the gharry stopped outside the flashier Hotel Suisse. Morning glory spilled from pots on the steps and, beneath the borage-blue sky, spiky palms cast eerie shadows on white shell paths.

After thanking the gharry chap, Meg followed the houseboy through a pair of ornately carved wooden doors into a spacious entrance hall where rugs covered the tiled floor and a pretty tapestry hung on a wall. She ran her hand over the textured cloth.

A big-bellied concierge appeared, her tiny feet encased in jewelled slippers. 'Come, I take you to room. Who with you?'

Meg pointed to Addie.

In their twin room three red hibiscus blooms floated in a bowl sitting on a low table. Meg walked onto the balcony, which overlooked a triangular lake. In the garden below, vibrant orange and black butterflies flitted among cinnamon bushes.

'Nice, isn't it?' said Addie over her shoulder.

'Nice? It's downright splendid!'

THE GUIDE who took them next morning to the Temple of the Tooth had speckled brown eyes nesting under puffy eyelids. He insisted they break their journey at regular intervals, but not out of concern for their welfare. In his brother's shop, he pressured Addie into buying a sash she would send to Erin and, from the stall of his cousin, whose face was disfigured by eczema, sweet-scented flowers to place before Buddha. The boy persuaded her to take two, then three, then five blooms, so she divided the extras between Netta, Helena, Margaret and Meg. Her dress was already damp and clung to her skin as she began the long climb up to the stark white temple. There was no breeze, no shade, just relentless heat.

Close to the top step, she found a little girl whimpering like a starved kitten. Addie had heard that some Ceylonese used children to beg, so she made sure there were no adults in sight before bending down and folding back a ragged piece of clothing that was covering an infected stump. Pus was pooled there – the leg had obviously not been amputated by a trained doctor. 'Meg, do you . . . ?' She couldn't finish her thought.

Meg knelt beside the child and gave her a drink of water from her own canteen. Then she peeled the second orange she'd bought and offered her a segment.

'Poor wee mite.' Helena placed a handful of coins in a nearby tin.

The sound made Addie think about the treasures she knew were inside the temple. If the holy men sold off a small portion, the profits could feed and house Colombo's poor for years. 'I can't go in,' she told her companions. 'I'll wait here.'

She'd barely arranged the folds of her dress to shade the girl from the sweltering sun when a man and a woman, covered in putrid sores, emerged from behind a column further up the steps, hands outstretched, voices pleading. Perspiration gathered in the hollows of Addie's neck as she backed away, mopping her face with her handkerchief. 'No money left, please leave. Shoo.' The beggars persisted until she shouted, 'Stop! Go away!'

At breakfast Addie washed down the last mouthful of her Bombay toast with a cup of tea while the tour guide went through the day's arrangements. 'We must go while the air is cool,' he said. 'Please be getting ready.'

As they set off up-country in a convoy of gharries to watch elephants bathe in a river, they passed elderly women with baskets on their backs working in the fields. They must have a hard life compared with her mother's, but then again farmers' wives had little time to themselves. She harboured no regrets about the station manager.

They watched the young elephant keeper leading his herd to the water's edge. He was no more than fourteen, yet he handled his charges with ease.

'I needed an orderly with his skills when I ran the senile ward,' said Netta, standing well clear of the swinging trunks.

Addie scratched an itchy bite on her chin. 'I'm not sure if elephants lose their faculties. Dogs do. Erin's old collie can't find his way home from the beach.'

'You'd think he'd get hungry,' said Margaret. 'Or at least want fresh water.'

Dora joked that even blindfolded she could locate her mother's cake tins.

'Stop it,' Meg said. 'You're making me hungry.' She raised her hand to shade her eyes from the brightness of the early morning sun. 'Look at that, will you.'

The keeper was encouraging a juvenile to step over the lip of the riverbank. Meg, laughing, pulled up a tuft of grass and walked over to the wrinkly little creature.

'Dear wee elephant,' said Addie, taking a step back.

FIVE DAYS out of Colombo a monsoon dished up choppy seas and ferocious cross-winds. The last big gust knocked the *Maheno* onto its side and Meg, her fingers aching from gripping the sides of her bunk, feared that if it didn't pop back up, water might enter the funnels, pour down the companionways, race along the passageways and into her cabin. Black-eyed fish might devour her: she could almost hear the crunch of teeth. Addie, as usual, had her nose in a book. When Meg rolled off her bunk and announced that she was off to pad splints, Addie grunted but didn't look up.

In the workroom, Meg slid into a seat beside Helena, who could stitch straight seams no matter which way the ship rolled. 'Need another pair of hands?'

'You could hold this splint while I fasten a tricky corner.'

Dora was hemming. 'I keep thinking of our boys in the Dardanelles.'

'What happened to them?' asked Lois sharply.

'They were injured in a raid.' Meg grabbed the edge of the bench as the ship thumped into another trough. Outside the wind howled and groaned. 'No need for you to worry. The medics will have taken care of them.'

Lois banged a splint down on the table. 'Why can I hear their bones rattling then?'

'That was your teacup, Lois,' Meg said. She rolled out a length of cotton. It had heaps of flaws. Like me, she thought. 'The Turks will roll over soon.'

'I don't think that's likely,' said Netta. 'They're a stubborn breed.'

Meg wiped her forehead with her apron. 'It's like an oven in here. Who wants lemonade?'

Towards the end of the week, Meg awoke to stillness and a calm, oily sea. She threw off her top sheet and slipped into her clothes. It didn't take her long to find Addie on the shade deck, where the temperature, apparently, had topped ninety-six degrees. No one had energy for quoits. A few camera buffs were taking photos but that didn't interest her. She preferred human distractions, like Ginger, who was walking in her direction. She wet her lips with the tip of her tongue. 'Any idea when we dock at Suez?' she said.

He appraised her candidly, appreciatively. "You'll soon be in the thick of it, Sister Dutton.'

'We should throw a concert. Want to help rustle up some props?'

'Girls are better at that sort of thing. We chaps will see to the punch.'

Over lunch – tinned oysters wrapped in bacon, Pigs in Blankets the cook called them – Meg put her idea to the girls.

Addie pushed a scrap of rind around her plate. 'Well, I could organise the costumes.'

Meg grinned. 'You just want to stay out of the limelight.'

'I only meant . . . No, you're right. I would prefer to work behind the scenes.'

'I'll string up streamers,' Margaret said, 'and choose the music.'

Using scraps of linen salvaged from a discarded laundry bag, Dora and Addie whipped up four sailor suits and the same number of pirate outfits. 'Perfect,' Meg said when they showed them to her. She was making a mermaid costume decorated with shells scrounged off a deckhand. When she was eleven years old, Aunt Maude had helped her get the lead role in a repertory production of *Red Riding Hood*. Everything was fine until she tried to kill the wolf instead of leaving it to the woodsman. When the curtain came down, the boy playing this part had yanked on her plaits until she screamed.

On the *Maheno*, her skits, based on the vaudeville shows she'd seen, drew loud cheers and her impromptu verse about their smallpox vaccine brought the house down: 'Each prick a scratch; each scratch an itch / To add to a sea-sick maiden's woe.'

They dropped anchor the following day, August 16th, a mile from Suez. While the crew secured the ship, she gazed across the azure sea to a golden desert and mountains that changed from iridescent pink to deep purple.

'It looks biblical,' said Helena. 'Terrible things shouldn't happen here.'

Meg wanted to tell her that bad things happened everywhere. Instead, she watched hawkers load melons the size of swedes onto sharp-prowed boats. Pa liked swedes. She must have winced because Addie squeezed her hand and said, 'We'll soon be back on land.'

During the worst of the monsoon, Meg had thought her life was over, which was why she intended to make the most of her time in the East.

At a briefing that evening, Matron told them the South Islanders were heading to Port Said and the majority of the North Islanders to Cairo.

Meg whispered to Addie. 'Bad luck. You're stuck with me.'

Addie smiled, but her expression changed when Matron took Dora aside and handed her a cable. As she read it, Dora's face went white and she bit her bottom lip. Next thing her entire body went limp and, before anyone could reach her, she folded like a pack of cards and fell to the floor. After helping her up and telling Iris to take her to the sitting room and give her a brandy, Matron explained to the others that Dora's beloved brother was missing – which didn't necessarily mean dead. Meg moved closer to Addie, who was blinking madly.

'I hope Dora gets a chance to nurse him,' Margaret said. 'That's why she joined up.'

'Picture him alive then,' said Meg. If you believed in something, it was more likely to come true. 'I'm off to stretch my legs.'

'I could do with a stroll,' Addie said. 'Otherwise I'll never sleep.'

'We'll go up to the shade deck.' Meg wanted to get as far away as possible from Lois, who was predicting a gloomy fate for Dora's brother.

The whoosh of the sea had dropped to a gentle murmur and the milky horizon promised cooler weather. Halfway into their first circuit Meg asked Addie why she'd taken up nursing.

'To avoid the suitors Father and Mother kept inviting to Sunday dinner. They think I'm a lost cause at twenty-five.' She rubbed her ring finger dreamily. 'I don't want to be a farm drudge. There has to be more to life. At least nursing got me to the city.'

'So it wasn't a calling?'

'Well, I wanted to do something worthwhile.'

Meg pulled two clips from her hair and shook her blonde curls free. 'Every day on a ward is different. You never know what will happen.' She loosened the ties on her cape. 'How did you find life in your nurses' home?'

'I didn't do much except read.'

'Even on your free days!'

'Oh, if I had a Sunday off, I caught the train home and spent it with my family. Mother always cooked a leg of lamb.'

'I would have given anything for a day like that.'

'What do you mean? Doesn't everyone have a Sunday roast?'

'My aunt and uncle do. It's a different story at Pa and Ma's place.'

Once when she was little and Ma was unwell, Pa had sent her to bed hungry. She remembered chewing the corner of a grimy sheet until her mouth bled. The following morning she'd run down to the letterbox, taken out his newspaper and shredded it, stuffing bits in a roadside ditch. As she trudged back up the gravel driveway, she'd cracked icy puddles with the heels of her boots. Pa's horses had galloped up to the fence, columns of white breath streaming from their nostrils. Addie was standing beside her, waiting for her to continue. 'Are you ever scared, Addie?'

'Sometimes, but I want a bigger life than the one Mother and Father had planned for me. What about you?'

'If I think too much I panic, yet I can't abide the ordinary. Odd, isn't it?'

'Not really. This war is changing women's lives. On my last visit to Riverton, I met a mother and daughter running a butcher shop. When I commented on the sharpness of their knives, the daughter said, "It won't matter if we lose a finger or two."' Addie bent back two of her own and waggled the rest as though they were worms.

Meg was still cackling when a clerk, clipboard under his arm, overtook them.

'Keep it down, the first officer's inside,' he said as he opened the door to the wireless room.

Meg stuck the clips back in her hair. 'I bet that nit-picker knows everyone's business, including who has a romance on the go.'

'Men make me tongue-tied.' Addie sounded worried. 'I don't know how to behave around them.'

Meg put an arm around Addie's shoulder and gave her a squeeze. 'Chaps aren't that different from us. Take Ginger and Adams. They want to travel and make friends, just like we do. If their crusty old colonel wasn't such a stick-in-the-mud we could have loads more fun.' With a toss of her head, she danced along the deck, not stopping until she drew level with his cabin. The light was on. She wanted to bash on his door and tick him off for being a spoilsport.

The flighty one calls me 'Ramrod Ronnie'. Thinks I don't know. Her lot act as if this war is a stroll in the park. Once we reach Egypt, they can do what they like. Until then, their safety is my responsibility. I tried to toughen them up by removing their privileges. They complained. Then most of them got seasick. If they can't manage a swell what use will they be at the front? They'll scream blue murder when they come across shrapnel wounds. Same palaver if they find lice in the seams of a soldier's breeches. As for mopping up the spit of mad-dog syphilitics . . . I can't abide sickness; think good health and you have it. Eat an apple a day in summer and raw cabbage in winter. If you stick to a routine, you won't go wrong. Ladies upset the applecart. I'll never marry. Doubt if I'll be alive this time next year. When my time's up, I plan to go out with a bang, preferably at the hand of Fritz, rather than the Turks. Those dark-skinned savages deserve whatever we throw at them. It won't be long before we beat them back into their greasy holes. I bet my savings on it. Let Nursey put that in her bandage and roll it up.

EGYPT,
1915–1916

Four

THE GUIDEBOOK had described Port Said as a harbour town separating the Mediterranean Sea from Lake Manzala, leading Addie to expect an attractive place, not a low-lying strip at the northern end of the canal, packed with people and dilapidated buildings. Although there were a few grand homes with balconies on all floors and awnings over the windows, much of the neighbourhood looked misshapen, as if hastily cobbled together from odds and ends. Children holding baskets of fruit ducked past men stacking boxes on the wharf and badgered the soldiers coming off the ships, their voices rising when they struck a deal. Everywhere there were signs of war. French ships guarded the waterway and Indian troops lined the banks. Sandbags and barbed wire surrounded trenches and dugouts that stretched for miles. A railway line waited to bring in the ambulance trains. Everything was poised for action and soon Addie would have to play her part.

From the upper deck, she watched Adams disembark with his regiment. At the bottom of the gangplank, he turned and waved to her and Meg.

Over the clamour of winches and weaponry, Lois yelled, 'Natives wear rags on their heads here too.'

'Turbans,' Addie told her. If Lois wanted ordinary hats, she should have stayed in Ashburton.

'What do they want?' Lois was rubbing her eyes. 'Make them stop staring at me.'

The Egyptian workers were waiting for a convoy of army trucks to back into position so they could begin loading them. The sleeves of their tunics flapped above their turbans as they lifted their arms, calling to the drivers who ignored them and waited for the officer in charge to give the orders. The Egyptians were smaller in build than the Europeans, Addie noticed, and quicker on their feet. Their swarthy complexions made them look tougher too. 'They're just going about their work,' Meg said. 'After all it *is* their country.' She fluttered her handkerchief in the direction of the workers.

Addie thought that was going too far. 'You'll give them the wrong impression.'

Meg tweaked the brim of her panama. 'They're interested in our purses, not our charms. Besides, we'll all darken up in this climate, even you, Lois.'

Worried that Lois might explode, Addie picked up her holdall and took her place in the queue Matron was overseeing.

WHILE MATRON checked their travel arrangements, Meg waited outside the office with her chums. It was marvellous to be on solid ground again; why anyone lived on water was beyond her. A decent gust of wind could surely upend the local sailing boats – feluccas, she'd heard someone call them. There were also larger boats under sail, their inhabitants hidden behind curtained windows.

Lois leant closer to her, shoulders rounded, fists tucked under her chin. 'What if I don't like it here?' she whined.

'You'll be fine once we get to work,' Meg told her.

Poor thing had a bad case of the blues. When Meg's ma became ill, she often curled up on the couch in Aunt Maude's living room, tears streaming down her beautiful face. At other times, she paced up and down, unable to sleep. Occasionally, if Meg sang to her, she would settle. Never for long, though.

A motorcar pulled up, the door swung open and Ramrod Ronnie stepped out, bristling with self-importance.

'Ladies,' he said, stamping his boots, 'your new home. Hardly a picnic ground.'

Meg pulled back her shoulders. Matron did the same.

'We're not here to eat sandwiches,' said Netta.

The colonel's eyes narrowed. 'Ladies do not belong in a war.'

Meg stared back at him. 'We've come to save lives.'

A crimson wave spread across his marbled cheeks. He could grump until he was purple in the face; nothing would change the fact that she was here. She placed her hands on her hips and planted her feet firmly in the sand. As far as she was concerned, he could take a running jump, preferably into very deep water.

There was no wind, only a blistering heat. Sand clung to the hem of Meg's dress, spilled into her shoes, stuck to her stockings. Perspiration was forming at the nape of her neck. She'd soon be dripping like a tap. The sooner she got under cover the better, and there wasn't much to see anyway, only a hotchpotch of marquees on a promenade facing the sea and behind them a three-storey building. She glanced at Addie and caught a flicker on her face of something between disappointment and nervousness.

'What do you think that's used for?' Meg said, pointing to the building.

'According to Miss Maclean's report,' said Iris, 'it's the medical headquarters. 'Did you not read it?'

Blasted Iris Hutchison never missed an opportunity to drop the matron-in-chief's name into conversations. Meg batted her question away. 'So we won't be staying there.'

'I shouldn't think so.'

Someone behind them coughed and Meg spun around. Two army officers were trudging across the sand.

'Welcome, ladies,' said the shorter of the pair. 'I'm Simpson and this is Abbot. He'll escort you to your quarters then give you a tour of the hospital. Things are quiet at present – no medical cases, just convalescents. You have time to settle in.'

Spirals of damp hair protruded from Simpson's collar and cuffs. Hairy men must really suffer in this awful heat, Meg thought. It would be like walking around in a fur coat.

Matron stood to attention. 'Thank you,' she said confidently and stepped forward.

As Abbot held out his hand for Matron to shake, a network of veins was visible through the skin, and birdlike bones.

'Righto, follow me.' Abbot set off at a brisk pace. Netta pulled up the hem of her dress an inch or two. 'I can't hurry. My calves have fallen into my ankles!'

Matron inspected the puffy flesh. 'Surely you know how to disperse fluid, Sister. Raise your legs above your heart for ten minutes every hour.'

'What happened to sympathy?' Netta muttered.

An Egyptian lad dressed in a white tunic and a red turban came over to take their luggage, followed by a broad-shouldered New Zealand orderly pushing a cart. He'd come in handy on the wards. There was always plenty of lifting to do.

'Blue,' said the orderly.

'Yes,' said Matron, glancing up at the cloudless sky.

'No, my name . . .'

'Ah.'

Meg covered her mouth to hide her amusement. It wouldn't pay to get in Matron's bad books or she could end up scrubbing the sluice room instead of caring for good-looking soldiers.

'Good chap,' said Simpson.

Blue tapped the side of his nose. 'I can find whatever you nurses need.'

Simpson waved him away. 'Hurry after Abbot, ladies.'

Abbot halted outside a two-storey whitewashed house with wooden shutters. Bird droppings covered the fronds of the inky-black palms planted either side of the door.

'Golly,' Meg said, 'it's like the house in Mary Pickford's last film.'

'That would have been a façade,' said Netta. 'Nothing's real in Hollywood.'

Meg rolled her eyes. As if she didn't know that. 'Who owns it?'

'A Frenchman hiding out in Switzerland,' said Abbot, pulling on a metal door handle.

A blade of sunlight sliced through the long passageway and rooms ran off both sides. If hers was close to the sitting room, she could brew up whenever she fancied and chat to anyone who popped in.

'Close the shutters during the day and open them at night,' said Blue.

'Plato speaks,' Netta said, picking up her suitcase.

That was foolish, Meg thought. You should stay on the right side of your orderlies. 'We'll do as you suggest, Blue. Thank you.'

'Come to headquarters for tea and biscuits after you've unpacked,' Simpson said.

Tomorrow she'd visit the convalescents. None of them had set eyes on a New Zealand woman for months – she'd be as welcome as iced beer.

❦

ADDIE'S MIND was full of images of maimed soldiers and operating tables bloodied as butchers' blocks. To mask her disquiet, she offered to help Matron arrange the accommodation. No one else had a surname starting with E, F or G, so she ended up back with Meg.

Their high-ceilinged room with its ornate wall panels had neither electric lights nor oil lamps. She'd have to read by candlelight.

Meg threw herself onto a bed under the window. 'Golly, this mattress is hard.'

Addie gave hers a poke. 'Mine's stuffed with cricket balls.'

Her corner needed a homey touch. She placed a photograph – her cheekbones replicated in the faces of her mother and sister – on an upturned box. There was also space for an alarm clock, a volume of poetry and a pretty cut-glass scent container and atomiser her mother had given her. She slipped her nightgown under the pillow. There was no wardrobe, so she draped her dressing gown over the foot of her bed and put her extra clothes into a second box. Everything else stayed in her kit.

When she glanced over to see what Meg had done, she caught her taping a photograph to the wall. 'Should you be . . .?'

'Meet Aunt Maude and Uncle Bert,' Meg said.

Her clipped tone stopped Addie asking if she had one of her parents.

Across the hall, Netta was arguing with Lois, her room-mate. Addie moved closer to the doorway to listen. Netta said, 'Thinner than an eel!'

'It could be poisonous!' yelled Lois.

There was a loud creak as if someone had jumped onto a bed. Addie stepped into the corridor.

'A good reason to keep calm,' Netta said evenly. 'Stop panicking, it's leaving.'

What was leaving? Could it be a snake? Addie looked up and down the floor.

'What if it comes back while I'm asleep?' Lois squealed.

'It's probably harmless. Now Egyptian rats . . .'

Meg joined Addie in the doorway. 'Lois has a full steam up.'

'I think there's a snake in their room. Do you think it will come our way?'

'If he does, I'll drape him around my neck and sing him to sleep.'

'I can't stand it,' Lois screeched. 'I want to go home.'

Netta slapped her hands on her hips and raised her voice. 'A snake can leave. We're stuck with the Turks.'

'They don't believe you're dead unless they chop your head off.'

'Who doesn't?'

'The Turks, they hide swords under their head-cloths.'

Netta grunted, then, recovering her composure, announced brightly, 'Captain Simpson said afternoon tea was waiting for us.'

When Lois shot out into the passageway, bellowing, 'I'd sooner eat my tongue', Meg grabbed the speeding girl by the arm. But as she turned, the skirt of Meg's dress knocked the scent bottle off Addie's makeshift bedside table and chips of glass flew everywhere. Lois shook herself free and ran back to Netta.

Meg's hands flew to her face and every part of her went still. She stared straight ahead for seconds before whispering, 'Oh, Addie, I'm so sorry. I'll buy you another one.'

'You can't replace it,' she said quietly and knelt down to gather up the pieces. Her mother had given it to her at the station, running along the platform beneath the open carriage window, telling her to spray her pillow with the scent to remind her of home.

At headquarters, Bland, an army officer whose mouth barely moved when he spoke, and Kemp, a cheerful orderly, explained the laundry and personal hygiene arrangements. Addie jotted down the main points in her diary. She'd already made a sketch of the camp.

'We're to wash in a bath tent,' Lois said, her voice rising, 'out in the open!'

'Soliman will fetch your water,' said Bland.

Lois pressed her hands to her chest. 'But he's a native!'

'Listen to the officer,' said Iris impatiently. 'He's important. See the pips on his jacket.'

Bland continued. 'The worst medical cases go to Alexandria but that could change. We received instructions this morning to set up a surgical ward in the school. Who knows what's around the corner.'

'Pyramids,' said Netta.

Matron glared at her, then turned back to Bland. 'Do you have a primus to sterilise instruments?'

'Yes, several,' said Bland. 'One recently exploded, so use them with care.'

Lois stifled a scream.

'Settle down, Nurse Moore,' said Matron.

Wrinkles formed on Matron's forehead, making Addie think of crepe bandages. 'Do supplies come through regularly?'

Bland twiddled with a button on his jacket. 'You name it, we have it: instruments, tourniquets, splints, peroxide, Eusol, saline, crepe, calico and gauze bandages.' A shadow fell across his boots. 'Ah, here's Bob Stanhope, one of our medical chaps.'

When Stanhope took off his hat, Addie noticed that the sun backlit his hair to the same pale orange shade the farm willows took on in autumn. She dropped her head in case her eyes misted up.

'Jolly brave of you to join us, Sisters,' Stanhope said.

Matron clicked her tongue. 'It's our duty.'

Stanhope tipped his hat. 'Do you know what hours your nurses will work?'

Matron adjusted her buckle, a forerunner, Addie realised, to plain speaking. 'Three weeks of day duty, same for nights, twelve hours each shift. If a convoy arrives, we'll work as long as we're needed.'

⫸

THE CLIP OF HOOVES woke Meg at dawn. At first, she thought it was Pa, out training his horses, as he did morning, noon and night, regardless of the weather or the amount of Dewar's whisky sloshing around inside him. For the umpteenth time she wondered why he pushed himself so hard. It didn't make him happy. The room was already stinking hot. She flung back the bedcovers and went to the window to watch the troops leading their horses along a dusty road. A fiery ball of sun hung over the turquoise sea. Addie was stirring. 'Quick, get up. It's a glorious morning. We can go for a walk.'

Addie reached for her dressing gown. 'It might be dangerous.'

'We're in the middle of a war. There's danger everywhere.'

'Someone else can go with you.'

'Odds on it won't be Lois.'

Addie threw a pillow at her, which Meg tossed back.

'Visit the convalescents with me then.'

The first marquee was full of Tommies recovering from minor contusions, scalds, lacerations and straightforward fractures, not wounds inflicted by the Turks. Halfway down the ward, a simple fellow told a joke about a bishop and a dancing girl who fashioned herself into a collection plate. When he delivered the punch line, Addie turned away, her face bright pink. To break the mood, Meg asked an Egyptian worker if he had a beater so she could make eggnog for anaemic patients. He caught a live beetle, put it in a glass jar and offered it to her.

'No understandee,' said a corporal, tapping the side of his head.

Meg unscrewed the lid of the jar and set the beetle free. 'Never mind, I'll see to it.'

On her way to the kitchen, she met an Irish nurse who was preparing to take up another posting. 'How do you stand this stifling heat?' Meg asked.

'It's a doddle if you can get someone to fan you day and night.'

Within twenty-four hours making eggnog was a distant prospect. Many of the convalescent Tommies were staggering towards the latrines, clutching their stomachs; a lot didn't make it in time. Before the nurses had time to turn around, two-thirds of the camp were down with dysentery.

'We can't seem to contain it,' Margaret said on the fourth day, clicking her tongue in frustration. She dumped another load of soiled towels into a washing basket.

'I blame the kitchen staff,' said Netta in a decided tone. 'They have filthy fingernails. I dread to think what ends up in our food.'

Lois tugged at her fringe repetitively. 'Do they want to poison us?'

'I eat what they give us,' Meg said. 'And I'm still standing.'

When Netta shot her a quizzical look, she sent one back. Lois wasn't her responsibility.

Everyone had more or less regained their health when Simpson came unannounced to their sitting room where they were darning socks for convalescents. Meg stuck her needle into a ball of wool and set down the wooden mushroom that went under the holes as she stitched.

Simpson wedged his thumbs into the webbing of his belt. 'I have distressing news, ladies. Our side has suffered a bloodbath at Chunuk Bair on the Gallipoli Peninsula.'

Meg could feel her heart pounding faster. She pressed her hands to her mouth. This was it.

He ploughed on. 'The worst of the injured are travelling to us under the care of a British surgeon, Captain Wallace Madison. Set up your trolleys, Sisters. Matron, you're to telephone the Canadians if you need assistance.'

'Each of our twenty-one tents can take up to eighty patients,' said Matron. 'Surely there won't be more cases than we can handle.'

Our own boys, counting on her, Meg Dutton, to nurse them back to health. She'd do everything she could to save them.

The first hospital train brought not soldiers with nice clean bullet wounds but groaning, wide-eyed boys with crushed limbs, shattered jaws and missing flesh. Meg gave the less complicated cases to Dora, her staff nurse, and began to treat the seriously injured. Although she'd seen some bad sights at Riverton Hospital, she'd never faced anything like this horror. Each stretcher contained a boy who deserved her full attention but she had to move from one to another and gauge at a glance what to do and in what order.

On her way to fetch extra basins, she overheard Dora asking a chest case for news of her brother. 'He's in your regiment. You must have seen him.'

'Sorry, I can't help. I fell in the first hour along with our captain.'

'Who took over? Please tell me.' Her voice was desperate.

'I have no idea, Nurse.'

Meg took Dora aside. 'No news is good news. Now help me care for these boys.'

Every two hours more cases rumbled in. One chap's jaw was almost gone. Another, swathed in blood-sodden field dressings, had a tourniquet on his right arm, a collarbone studded with fragments of shrapnel, a fractured jawbone and an injured throat. He squeaked like a mouse. She told Blue to take him straight to theatre.

There were hundreds of uniforms to cut off and labels to attach to tunic buttons: 'GSW' for gunshot wounds and 'SW' for shrapnel. Red signified danger. A man with a red label might haemorrhage, or convulse, or require one of a dozen emergency treatments. To lessen the risk of an overdose, she wrote 'M' for morphine on the foreheads of the patients she jabbed and the time they received the injection. There was no chance to take a break. She had to eat on the run.

At dusk, Matron handed her the surgical list for Captain Madison: four amputations, five fly-blown abdominal cases, a chest, two intestines, one bladder, a fractured lower maxilla and three shattered shoulders. 'It's your turn to assist, Sister Dutton.'

The theatre tent was hotter than a smithy's furnace, and a rotten-fish stench rose from a chap writhing on the table. Blue was on insect swatting duty. Edward Ramsay, a beanpole with greyish-blue eyes and curly brown hair, dropped ether onto a mask he held over the patient's face. Once the soldier was under, Madison cut into the lower stomach area and removed a section of intestine. Highly skilled, agile on his feet, a little bulky around the chest, he talked throughout the surgery. Mostly, Meg realised, for his own benefit.

'Nice work, sir,' she said as Blue and Ramsay wheeled the patient out.

He appraised her thoughtfully. 'You kept up your end, Sister.'

'Your commentary helped.'

'No one has remarked on my verbosity before.'

'I always speak my mind. Are you a betting man?'

He laughed. 'Yes, mainly on surgical odds and the ability of certain theatre sisters.'

She looked into his honey-brown eyes.

He held her gaze. 'Would you bet on me?'

'My father trains racehorses. Betting's in my blood.'

'Here's our next case. Ready?'

The dark-haired shaver died before Madison could make an incision. Another fitted during chest surgery. Five criticals went to the moribund tent for the padre to give them last rites. Stable patients waited in recovery until the orderlies were free to take them to wards.

At last the line of theatre patients ended.

While she cleared up, Ramsay asked if she had brothers. 'Only child,' she said.

'Me too.'

A blessing, they agreed, under the circumstances.

Madison removed his bloodied apron and dumped it in a bucket. His face had a greyish tinge. 'Time to turn in, Sister

Dutton. It's been quite a night.'

'Sleep well, sir.'

On her way back to her quarters, dragging one foot after the other, Meg bumped into a gravedigger whose glum expression made her wonder how many holes the shovel over his shoulder had dug that night. A jagged scar ran down the entire right side of his face. When she asked if he'd eaten he told her his stomach was playing up. Any pain? He shook his head. 'All these casualties,' he muttered as he moved on.

She must do something nice for poor Dora – perhaps Blue could track down some proper chocolate. In the moonlight that shimmered across her path she saw a rat scuttle between two marquees, something dangling from its mouth. A body part, maybe the remnants of a foot. The sappers needed to dig deeper pits.

On impulse, she ducked into the non-surgical ward to check a neuritis case. 'Turn him again and give him an extra pillow,' she told Kemp, the orderly on duty. 'Is everyone else settled?' Kemp cocked his head towards a corner where a dark shape crouched. Meg looked more closely. 'Lois! What are you doing here?' There was no time to find out. Two orderlies stretchered in a patient who'd lost control of his bowels. When he apologised, Meg joked that they should bottle the fumes to drop on the Turks.

A PATIENT with a baby face and a gunshot wound to his upper arm had lent Addie a volume of John Clare's nature poems, which she returned before going over his discharge notes. It seemed ludicrous to nurse him back to health so the authorities could return him to the front. She felt like an accomplice to a shady deal.

'Sister Harrington, do you think our side will win?' the boy asked.

'Well, the newspapers are full of victorious accounts about us gaining ground.'

His chin trembled slightly. 'I want to pull back my bedroom curtains at dawn and watch Mount Egmont rise out of the mist. Do you think I'll make it home in one piece?'

'Of course you will.' But she turned away so he couldn't see her expression.

'They're so young,' she said to Isabel during a break.

'One of mine relives battles in his sleep,' Isabel said, 'and a lad in Marion's ward goes off his head at the slightest noise. He has her on tenterhooks.'

Addie gazed out to sea where foam rose in white clusters. Mercifully, her nightmare of fleeing from the wounded hadn't come true. She'd gone from one boy to the next, washing, treating and caring for them. There'd been no time to think. 'I wonder when it will end,' she said. Isabel looked at her glumly and shook her head.

Dawn was barely beginning to lighten the sky when Lois prodded Addie with a stick. 'Hand me my dressing gown,' Addie hissed. 'Meg needs her sleep. She's been in theatre for hours. We'll have to go outside if you want to talk.'

There wasn't much of a moon and a light wind rustled the palms as they walked outside. Abruptly, Lois sank to her knees and began to draw shapes in the cool sand. Trails to nowhere, Addie thought. 'What's wrong? Tell me.'

Lois ignored her.

When Addie finally persuaded her to come back inside, she suggested they make a pot of tea, but instead of heading towards the sitting area, Lois rushed into the room where Meg was sleeping and banged a shutter, rattling the wooden slats. Meg sat up as though she'd been shot. Lois moved to another shutter and tugged on a knob. It flew off and hit Nancy Wilson, a newly arrived nurse, in the face as she peered around the door in search of the source of the noise. She screamed and covered her face with her hands. 'My eye! My eye!'

Addie was at her side immediately. 'Let me see.'

Lois continued to bang on the shutters.

'Stop it,' yelled Meg as she leapt from her cot, 'or I'll tie you up.'

Addie put her hand on the injured nurse's shoulder. 'Can you open your eye?'

Wilson shook her head. 'Do something, please!' Her voice was high and panicky.

'What's going on?' Iris came running in, closely followed by Margaret.

Lois fled past them both, her face twisted and her hair awry.

'Go after her,' Meg said to Iris. 'She needs watching.' Then she knelt beside Nancy, who was now crouched on the floor, and gently raised her eyelid.

'Nasty,' Addie mouthed as she helped the injured woman to her feet. 'Meg, take her other arm.' She tightened her own around Nancy's waist. 'We're taking you to Matron,' she said firmly. 'Steady, we've got you.'

Matron was sitting at her desk sprinkling grains of sand from a saucer into an envelope. 'So the family of this boy has something from the place where he died,' she explained. Then she saw Nancy's face. 'Goodness. What happened, nurse? Did you collide with a door?'

'Actually it was a knob from a shutter that Lois pulled off,' Addie said.

Matron reached for her bag. 'Harrington, help Wilson to a chair. Water, Sister Dutton.' Matron swabbed the area around the eye and examined it thoroughly. Her mouth tightened as the full extent of the damage became evident. Afterwards, she took the nurse's hand and said, 'You must be brave.' Wilson sobbed harder.

Addie barely heard Matron tell Nancy she could convalesce in Alexandria because she was imagining how she'd feel if her own sight were threatened. Besides not being able to read, she'd have to stop writing in her diary, something she looked forward to each day since it helped her make sense of the mayhem she was caught up in.

'Sister Harrington,' said Matron, 'find Nurse Moore while Sister Dutton fetches ice from the kitchen.'

After checking with Iris, who'd failed to locate Lois, Addie eventually found her hiding under a cot, her eyes wide and staring.

'I'm a ladder,' Lois chanted. 'You're a snake. Throw a six. Or you'll never get home.'

'We could ask Matron to play.' Addie squeezed Lois's hand and felt a slight pressure back.

LOIS WAS TAKEN away in the middle of the night, something Meg learnt only when she quizzed a driver. Netta had been on night duty so she'd been none the wiser either.

At the next opportunity Meg got everyone together. There was no powdered milk to go with the tea but no one made a fuss.

Netta shook her head. 'She was my room-mate. Not the easiest I admit but still . . .'

'You weren't to know they'd send her away without telling us first,' Meg said.

'I expect her condition was beyond them,' said Iris. 'She's better off in a place that deals with her type.' She pushed her cup towards Addie, who was closest to the teapot.

'It could happen to any of us,' Meg said, 'even you, Iris.'

Addie set down her own cup. 'It certainly makes you think.'

Meg nodded. 'We have to look after each other. Make sure we don't go the same way.'

'I'll ask Matron for an address so we can write to Lois,' said Netta.

Iris inched her fingers along the arms of her chair and heaved herself up. 'Come on, Netta, we have instruments to sterilise.'

After they left Meg said, 'If it happens to me, Addie, promise not to ship me home.'

Early in October, orders came through to break camp. Meg and Netta had two hours to transfer the patients from their wards to local hospitals and to No. 2 Stationary at Pont de Koubbeh.

'I hear there's dreadful dysentery in Lemnos,' Netta said as they stripped another cot.

'Let's hope we're not going there then.'

Netta piled the linen into a canvas bag. 'The closer we get to the guns the harder it will be to sleep. Lots of boys tell me they can't stand the noise.'

'Others dread the silence when they leave the front line,' Meg said. 'We'll have to become like sloths. They can sleep anywhere.' She launched herself over the iron bed frame until she was virtually hanging upside down. As the blood rushed to her head, it dawned on her, yet again, that her need for attention had outranked her common sense.

Netta said, 'Watch out. Matron's coming back.'

Meg rearranged her limbs. Supple joints came in handy. They'd once helped her escape a nest of rope fashioned by her mother.

'Simpson will notify me once our travel plans are confirmed,' Matron said. 'In the meantime, take in the sights – in groups, mind, never alone.'

'Apparently there's an Italian dressmaker near the bazaar who makes divine cotton dresses,' Meg said to Netta as they walked back to their quarters. 'We don't have to leave Port Said looking like frumps.' She was hoping for France. Aunt Maude and Uncle Bert had honeymooned in Paris and Maude considered the French terribly stylish.

The dressmaker had cherry-pink lips and a frank manner. She told Dora to eat less, then took a bolt of buttercup-yellow material from Addie, saying the colour was more suited to Meg's skin tones, which would have been fine if she hadn't gone on to say it was a pity she lacked the height to do justice to the latest styles. Margaret, she declared, had uneven hips. Netta's hair ruled out every fashionable colour and Helena needed extra darts to compensate for her small bust. Goodness knows what she would have said about Iris.

Meg emerged from the shop feeling as if the dressmaker had squeezed out her confidence like juice from a lemon. 'We need a pick-me-up. Come on.'

At a bazaar across the street a snake charmer was playing a melodic tune on his reed pipe. Opposite him, a conjuror pulled two birds from his trouser pocket. Addie nudged her. 'Look over there.' Hat under his arm, Wallace Madison was rifling though knick-knacks on a table. When he caught sight of them, he waved and a small brass vase glinted in his hand. Splinters of sunlight bounced off his dark straight hair. He was a tall man, not screen-star handsome, rugged rather than rakish: Roman nose, broad forehead, square chin. 'Hurry up,' Meg said to the others as she walked towards him. 'We can't be rude.'

When they were all in the middle of a conversation about hand-woven rugs, Wallace handed her the vase and said in a low voice, 'A memento from Port Said, Sister Dutton.'

'Thank you.' The others would be green with envy. 'So we're leaving?'

'Bulgaria has gone against us,' said Wallace. 'If Greece follows . . .'

'Do you know where we're headed?'

He put a finger to his lips.

'Somewhere that warrants a new dress?' She spun around as if she was already wearing hers. 'Are we travelling together?' she said, coming to a stop in front of him.

'I expect so.'

'Can we look forward to milder temperatures?' said Helena. 'A change would be welcome.'

'Anything's possible.' Wallace was looking at Meg intently.

As they made their way to camp, Meg hung back to be alone with her thoughts. Had she stymied her chances with Wallace? Surely he hadn't expected her to flirt with him in front of the others? Relationships among army personnel were discouraged but that didn't mean they were out of the question. You just had to be careful.

When she caught up to Addie, who was waiting for her, Meg whispered in her ear, 'He visited my ward three evenings in a row.'

Addie looked puzzled. 'Who do you mean?'

'Wallace Madison, our surgeon, of course.'

'Why did he come that often?'

'Supposedly to check on a potential haemorrhage,' Meg said. 'But he spent most of his time talking to me.'

They were hardly through the gates when Iris and Margaret ran up shouting that Blue had heard Simpson tell Matron that they were bound for Salonika via Alexandria.

'We're leaving on a troopship – the *Marquette*. We'll be with some British soldiers – an ammunition column,' Iris said.

'A troopship? Not a hospital ship?' Addie sounded worried and Meg knew why. The red cross on the side of a vessel offered some kind of protection; a troopship was fair game.

Margaret flicked sand off the hem of her dress. 'Don't worry. A French destroyer's coming as our escort.'

'What about the medical officers?' Meg asked.

'Stanhope is already packing.' Margaret smoothed her hair. 'And apparently Captain Madison turned down a plum post to stay with us.'

Meg felt a tremor travel through her body.

I hadn't counted on meeting Meg Dutton the day I arrived at No. 1, or dreaming about her every night thereafter. Could have visited the native quarters but I'm trying to curb that particular appetite now the pox is endemic. I keep myself busy. Not difficult – there are endless boys to save. Last Saturday's surgery left sixteen poor fellows with seven legs between them. Hit a quiet period yesterday so I went shopping. Just as I was buying a brass vase for my wife Evelyn back in London, Dutton burst into view, her hair a golden halo, eyes like sapphires, and I found myself handing it to her. She rewarded me with a splendid smile. Evelyn's damned attractive too, but she's too busy cultivating an unhealthy interest in politics to consider my needs. Why Englishwomen want the vote is beyond me. Power comes at a cost. Take this war. Battles thought up in government offices unravel in front-line trenches and the results end up on my operating table. Sometimes I can hold death at bay. It's a lot harder to keep myself in check.

Five

THE HARBOUR was full of huge ships and Addie felt insignificant as she gazed up at the colossal funnels belching out steam. Which of these towering vessels was theirs? As usual, officials were yelling at the Egyptians, who carried on working at their own speed and in their own way. The entire area smelled of oil and grease, unwashed skin and frustration. She signalled to a few nurses in the crowd to join her and Dora. To their right an officer herded his regiment into single file and marched them up a gangplank. Their young faces reminded her that in her mad dash to get down to the wharf, she had accidentally left behind her notebook. In it were the addresses of several transferred patients who'd asked her to write to their families and let them know where they were being sent. She could have kicked herself for her carelessness.

Once they were all on board and on their way, she could see that Matron seemed out of sorts as well, criss-crossing the upper deck of the *Marquette*, her mouth drawn. Maybe travelling on a troopship bothered her too.

While Addie waited for a sailor to gather up his mops and buckets so she could make her way to her cabin, two officers came out a side door, deep in conversation. She heard one say, 'Yes, I agree, enemy activity is possible', before they glanced at her and hurried away. She wondered if the two incidents that occurred just after they set off from Alexandria had unsettled them as much as they had her: a rag tied around a piston-rod had rendered the steering gear useless until an engineer spotted the problem and removed it; and not long after this, a crew member detected a smouldering case, which he'd heaved overboard.

However, as their fourth uneventful night approached, her worries began to dissolve. The journey had turned into more of a cruise than a transfer. There'd been time to rest, wash her collars, write letters home and take leisurely walks along the deck, as she was doing now. Unfortunately, a cool breeze had sprung up so she considered going below to fetch her cloak, and perhaps Meg's and Helena's as well. The girls were chatting a few yards away, Meg waving her arms and laughing as usual. Then Addie remembered – any minute now there'd be the second lifeboat drill of the day, and the last for the voyage. As she headed along the deck towards her designated station, she became aware of five or six sailors waving from the stern of the *Tirailleur* as it turned away, its escort duty over. She waved back, grateful for their protection.

'They're leaving,' she said when Meg and Helena joined her and they watched the *Tirailleur* steam off.

'What a shame,' said Meg. 'Frenchmen are tasty.'

Really, Meg must have X-ray eyes or a vivid imagination. 'Nothing will happen now,' Addie said.

'Not unless Matron gives the Germans permission.' Meg saluted as if she was in charge.

Helena laughed. 'I'm turning in. We won't get much sleep once we're ashore. Goodnight, you two.'

Back in the cabin, Meg pulled out her tuck-box, handed Addie an oaty biscuit and took another for herself. 'My aunt would adore these.'

'You seem fond of her.'

'Aunt Maude and Uncle Bert saved me.'

'I'm not sure what you mean, Meg.'

'You wouldn't believe me if I told you. Count yourself lucky to have ordinary parents and a sister. I'd swap places with you in a flash.'

Uncertain of how to reply, Addie took a bite of her biscuit.

After a long silence, Meg said, 'I think I embarrass you sometimes.'

Addie waited for her to expand, maybe talk about her family, but Meg rolled over and faced the wall. 'Sleep well, Addie,' she said from under her blanket.

Addie finished her biscuit. 'You're marvellous fun, Meg. Goodnight.'

Beneath the blackened porthole that prevented enemy ships seeing cabin lights at night, and lulled by the familiar wash of the sea – although Riverton's wild waves crashing over the rocks sounded nothing like the placid whispers of the Aegean – Addie thought about the wonder of friendship.

※

MEG COULDN'T get the line 'All your fears are foolish fancy' from 'My Melancholy Baby' out of her head. Nor could she escape Wallace Madison's hands, which felt like hot coals on her skin, burning her to the bone. She woke in a sweat – no one should have this much power over her. Each time she almost dozed off again, she would jerk awake, her body contorting as a newborn infant does when unwrapped from a shawl. Only Addie's steady breathing coming from the next bunk calmed her.

Her mother thought sinners got insomnia as a punishment for being curious. 'I can rinse your mouth out with soap. Unfortunately, I can't do the same for your brain.' Meg had raised her sleeping problems with her aunt, who'd suggested warm milk, a hot bath and calm thoughts. Although she'd often managed the first two suggestions, she usually failed with the third. Her thoughts refused to assemble in tidy patterns. They collided with each other, faltered at jumps, created new trails to race along.

She knew her behaviour sometimes pushed Addie to the limit, though she rarely complained and the shocked expressions that used to flit across her face had almost vanished. If she knew what pleased Addie, she'd do it more often so she'd call her marvellous again.

But if she kept stewing, she'd addle her brain. She might as well get up.

IT WAS SATURDAY. At nine o'clock, Addie joined Meg and Helena on the upper deck. Today the sea resembled a bolt of charcoal taffeta that she'd once admired in a draper's shop window, though the surface was broken by white-tipped waves. There was a slight chill in the air and the sky had turned a dull grey. She thought it might drizzle soon.

'We're nearly there,' she said to Helena, who'd asked if she knew the name of the strip of land visible in the distance. Before Addie could check her guidebook, a passing officer said, 'Platamona Point.' She rested a foot on a low metal rung and double-knotted her bootlaces, thinking she might need the extra support when she went ashore. Wallace Madison had warned them to expect goat tracks, not roads. She wasn't sure what to make of him. No one could fault his surgical skills or his meticulous theatre practices, and he could be rather amusing, but she felt slightly uneasy when she caught him studying Meg who right now was halfway down the deck, arms thrown around a pole, joking with a sailor. There was no sign of the despondency Addie had detected in her last night.

As she puzzled over this change, a loud swish, a ripping of

metal, then a gargantuan blast tossed her into the air like a bundle of laundry. As the wooden deck beneath her cracked and split, she fell awkwardly. Her elbow ached; bitter smoke stung her eyes, her throat. Flames gobbled a doorframe in front of her and a length of rope ignited. The whole ship quivered. Panic-stricken, she scrambled to her feet. Where had she last seen Meg? A massive explosion knocked her off her feet again as a segment of the deck disappeared into a hold. Clouds of smoke blackened the air. Upright once more, she tripped, picked herself up, ran faster. Ahead she glimpsed Meg crouched down, clutching the remnants of a banister, debris in her hair, her dress filthy, her face rigid with terror. 'Don't move, wait there,' she yelled as she rushed below to alert the others, but they were already dashing up the stairs, white-faced but composed.

A steam whistle went off, a bell rang twice and someone shouted, 'Torpedo! Torpedo! To your posts, to your posts!' As Addie reached Meg and pulled her to her feet, a column of water spurted into the air, drenching them. The companionway to the officers' mess was gone. Four or five men formed a human ladder, which others clambered up, one with a piece of toast clamped in his mouth, raspberry jam dribbling down his chin.

In silence, Addie and Meg fetched their cork lifebelts and, as instructed, gathered at the flight of stairs near the saloon. Eighteen nurses, including Dora, Iris and Netta, lined up portside, eighteen to starboard, where she and Meg waited. Helena and Margaret took each other's hands. 'Remember the drill,' Addie said. 'Follow the steps. Stay calm.'

Meg shook her head. 'I'm done for.' Her voice was flat and she lowered her eyes and swivelled the toe of her right boot back and forth over the decking.

'Not if I can help it.' Addie gave her a hug. 'If we end up in the sea, paddle like a dog until I find you.'

The ship was already listing so much that lowering the starboard lifeboats was impossible. The sailor Meg had been talking to earlier yelled, 'Use those on port.' The first boat went down safely. Addie grasped Meg firmly by the arm and climbed into the second. There was so little room that she was almost sitting on Meg's lap. She couldn't tell who was shaking more as six burly soldiers struggled to free their heavy boat from the davits. One swore as the *Marquette* rose sharply. Addie tried to hold onto Meg but there was an immense jolt and their boat plummeted onto the first. Red capes spun through the air. The icy sea closed over Addie, pulled her down, sucked at her clothes, her skin, her hair; tossed her around like a leaf. Stay calm, she thought. Let out small breaths. Follow the bubbles. Her lungs were burning pans of salt, and hot, white panic frothed inside her as she fought her way to the surface, where she gulped in mouthfuls of air. On her right she saw the lifeboat from which she'd fallen, upright in the water and roped to the *Marquette*. Meg was still on board, screaming and pointing. A plank glanced off Addie's shoulder. She hardly had the strength to move her limbs, but she could hear Meg yelling for her to kick, swim faster, harder. Struggling to get enough air into her lungs in the mounting swell, she changed from breaststroke to overarm.

Someone grabbed her hair, then her shoulders, and she felt her back scrape against solid wood. She tried to speak, but water, not words spilled from her mouth. Meg's face loomed over her. 'Never leave me again, Addie. Never, hear me!'

She attempted to sit up but a hand pressed her down. Slats dug into her back. Much later, someone tapped her hand and she managed to pull herself into a better position. A pinched-faced soldier in the water pointed to a limp figure he was supporting and worked his way towards her.

'Can you take a look at him, please?'

She leant over the side of the lifeboat and instinctively checked for a pulse. There was nothing. 'He's gone. Sorry.' The soldier recited a prayer and let his mate go.

High above her, on the *Marquette*, men tried to free the ropes while flames shot around them and wood and metal twisted into fiery forms. Shrill, almost human cries erupted from the hold. Ammunition wagons, mules and horses burst through gaping holes in the side of the ship, smashing into the men and women in the water clinging desperately to planks, hatches and butter-boxes, anything that floated.

A nurse grabbed the tail of a mule, which towed her towards the ship where another lifeboat, finally freed from its davits, struck an iron door, tipping its occupants, including Wallace Madison, into the sea. Meg screamed as the final rope attached to their lifeboat also gave way and she flew through the air.

Cold water pressed vicelike against Addie's skin, dragging her down, deeper and deeper, until she thought her lungs would rupture. Drawing on every ounce of strength, she struggled to the surface, rolled onto her back and wriggled her right arm, shoulder, leg, then performed the same check down her left side. There were no broken bones. She pushed her hair off her face. Directly ahead, a cresting wave tossed up wide staring eyes and a defiant red slash of a mouth. 'Meg, I'm coming!' 'Sister,' yelled a soldier, 'paddle for your life. There's a shark behind you.'

Her head immediately filled with terrifying images. She moved her legs and arms just enough to stay afloat, and prayed. Something rough, raspy – a fin, it must be a fin – rubbed against her shoulder, and she waited for the clamp of jaws, excruciating pain, shocking blackness. A large mass knocked against her and she could feel legs pounding up and down. Legs! She opened her eyes. A mule, it was only a mule. She moved away from the petrified creature in search of something less volatile to keep her afloat.

A lifebuoy materialised to her left. She swam towards it, aware that each stroke was taking her closer to the *Marquette*'s propeller. Two nurses – she couldn't make out their faces – climbed onto the ship's rail, held hands and jumped. Their white aprons ballooned around them as they disappeared into the sea.

Men leapt too, many from great heights. Some landed in the water. Others thudded against the side of the ship. Two landed on the propeller.

The *Marquette* was almost perpendicular. Several men were clinging to a railing but the angle made it impossible for them to hang on. Two hit the stern post; the rest tumbled into the sea. A tremendous crack rang out and the ship jolted forward, as if the engines had broken free and were hurtling towards the bow. Bubbles, steam, smoke, squealing mules, a sinister rattle, then the mast gave a final shudder and the entire ship slipped silently beneath the water.

Shivering, Addie tightened her grip on the lifebuoy. Soon afterwards, a raft packed with shocked faces lurched past and she shouted, 'Has anyone seen Meg Dutton?' Two soldiers shook their heads. A body drifted between the raft and her buoy. When she grabbed a handful of sleek dark hair, the head flopped back and she saw that it was Kemp, one of the orderlies from Port Said. Another corpse followed. Stanhope! The medical officer's rust-red hair fanned out from his scalp. 'Please help me,' she called to those on the raft.

A sharp-featured fellow called back, 'Sorry, we're loaded to the hilt.'

THE AEGEAN pummelled Meg, pushing her from one wave to another. Panic rushed through her as it had the day Pa had thrown her into heavy surf when she was ten years old, telling her it was the best way to learn to swim. By the time he'd pulled her out, she was full of seawater and frantic with fear. Just like today. Her throat burned, her eyes stung. Addie had disappeared, and there was no sign of Wallace either. Her worst fear was coming true: she was going to drown. No death at the hands of the Turks, as she'd occasionally imagined. 'Not a

Catholic among them,' her uncle had said after she joined up. 'Some have three hundred wives,' added her aunt. 'A different one for each night of the year,' ragged Uncle Bert. He'd swum across the Aparima one summer, a sheep under one arm and a rope slung over his other shoulder.

She clung to this memory of his strength.

Bile scalded her throat and she started convulsing. Water, not air, rushed into her lungs. She didn't want to die. There was too much she hadn't done. Using her hands and feet as paddles, she worked her way to the surface.

Straight away strong hands reached out and closed around her upper arms and when she looked up she saw Wallace's face. She coughed. He tightened his grip, then hauled her into the lifeboat. She attempted to thank him, but he covered her mouth with his hand as if he wanted her to keep a secret. Then he applied pressure to her knee and checked for other injuries. Finally, his lips rested near her ear. 'You're safe with me,' he said.

She tried to catch her breath. 'Where is she?' Her voice was hoarse. 'I have to find Addie.'

Wallace placed his hands on her shoulders. 'Another boat will have picked her up.' He looked at the men collapsing around them. 'We need to care for this lot.'

The nearest chap had a gash to his right shoulder, another was bleeding from his temple and a third held his left arm awkwardly across his chest. Others were slumped against the sides of the lifeboat. Wallace used his trouser belt as a tourniquet, assuring a soldier with a badly mangled leg they'd get him to a theatre soon. 'Won't we, Sister?' She raised her head slowly and croaked, 'Yes, sir.' Wallace arched his eyebrows. Meg sat up straighter and tried to speak with more conviction. 'Let's sing so our rescuers can hear us. Who knows "Are We Down-hearted"?'

ADDIE DIDN'T THINK she could hold onto the lifebuoy much longer. Every part of her was aching, including her teeth. A Tommy slipped off a raft and swam over to her – 'It's all right, Sister. You can have my place.' – but before he could help her up, another soldier dragged himself on. No one stopped him. Perhaps they were worried about capsizing or they were too weary to care. Holding onto the buoy with one hand, the Tommy grasped her more firmly around her waist. 'Don't give up, Sister. Someone will rescue us soon.'

She rallied a little. 'We'll need more than one ship. There are so many of us.'

Nearby a chap thrashed the water with purple fists and shouted, 'The sorrows of death encompassed me, and the floods of ungodly man made me afraid'. She recognised the words from Psalm 18. 'Can we help him?'

'He's off his nappers. Nothing we can do, Sister. Jesus, this water's perishing.'

Her hands turned lavender and her clothes hardened like wax as the cold crept into her bones. The Tommy stopped talking. Sleepiness washed over her and she was back in Riverton, on a family picnic near Monkey Island. After lunch, when the tide was low, she'd waded out to collect rock oysters, and later, back on the beach, swallowed their juicy plump flesh.

I couldn't leave her alone in the water. A sister like her nursed me when I had a piece of shrapnel the size of a pinecone in my right leg. The wound turned septic. She injected a hideous cold solution into it every three hours for weeks. Not pleasant but it did the trick. This one has a nice face too, oval-shaped, same as my Ellen's, high cheekbones. I never wanted anyone else. Asked her to marry me the first time when she was six and I was nine. Popped the question every March on her birthday, until fourteen years later she said yes. I bought a ring that afternoon. Her letters went down with the *Marquette*. Doesn't matter. I know every word. She always starts with 'Dearest Clive'. Her best news came three months after my last leave: 'A new little soul is coming into the world.' If we have a son, I'll call him Billy after a young Geordie who caught a shell at Gallipoli. We were sheltering behind a wall, both separated from our units, still in range of the Turks, clumps of dog roses and poppies everywhere. Shrapnel took his head off, left me unscathed.

Six

DOWN IN the engine-room of the *Tirailleur*, peculiar gadgets released clouds of pungent steam into the murky space. Meg could barely make out the face of the sailor who handed her a pannikin of hot wine. It smelt of cloves.

Someone obviously knew basic first aid because stacks of blankets were warming on the vents. Over the racket of the engine, the ship's padre shouted, 'Enlevez vos vêtements mouillés là derrière' and tugged at his shirt. 'Vite,' he commanded, 'avant d'attraper froid.' He held up a blanket so she could duck behind it to remove her tattered petticoat, then he passed her a warm towel. She rubbed her skin briskly, and gratefully accepted a khaki overcoat that came down to her feet. Her bare toes were ribbed like kelp, and numb. She pushed the blanket aside and scribbled in the air. 'Can I have something to write with, please?'

The padre took a piece of paper and a pencil stub from his jacket pocket. She jotted down Addie's name and made a rough sketch of her face. He shook his head when she showed him. 'Je suis désolé.' She didn't understand. Only brainy girls took languages at school. He switched to English. 'I am sorry.'

In the ship's lounge, she grilled an English-speaking doctor but he was no help either. When two French nurses came in and plied her with hairpins and a toothbrush, she badgered them until they looked at her as if she was dangerous.

Addie still hadn't turned up when Meg heard that evening she was to be transferred to the *Grantully Castle*. She talked Wallace into accompanying her and asked him to hound everyone he knew for news of survivors. He told her not to worry – Addie would turn up, everything would work out.

English and Australian sisters on the *Grantully* raided their wardrobes to supply her with a blouse, a toothbrush and other essentials. After filling her with sugary tea and biscuits, a nurse took her to a two-berth cabin, reassuring her that as soon as anyone called Addie came aboard she would bring her down.

Although she was weary and achy, Meg couldn't rest. She had to do something. If Addie were in her place, she'd make a detailed plan of the ship, then search it inch by inch. She should do the same. In her rush to get out the door, she nearly knocked over two English officers. One kept her talking while the other fetched an official who gave her a brandy that went straight to her head.

⚜

THE MUFFLED SHOUTS in a nearby corridor subsided into scratchy coughs as though fish bones had caught in the throat of a careless diner. Addie stopped abruptly, causing the Australian sister behind her to pull up sharply. 'Shush,' Addie said and held her breath. Weariness blunted the footsteps, the reedy cries, but it sounded like Meg. She ran to the end of the corridor and turned the corner. Two cabins away, swamped in a bulky coat, bruises covering much of her face, Meg was about to knock on another door. Choking back tears, Addie rushed towards her.

'I've been frantic.' Meg was hugging her hard. Finally she

stepped back and inspected Addie from head to toe. 'Golly, who gave you those dreadful pyjamas? Did the French find you too? Does your throat feel like sandpaper? Open wide.'

Addie stuck out her tongue.

Meg conducted a hasty inspection, then stroked her nose. 'Take an aspirin and report for duty.' They broke into gales of laughter. Meg leant closer. 'Smell me. I'm saltier than a sardine.'

'I can't believe it. You can't swim.'

Meg barked, then coughed.

Although Addie tried to laugh again, all she could manage was a raspy croak. She looked behind her to thank the Australian sister but she was gone.

'You won't believe what happened to me,' Meg said. 'We need to get comfy. It could take a while.'

They were barely through the cabin door when a steward brought in a jug of mulled wine. Addie filled two mugs and handed one to Meg. 'You have the chair. I'll take the bunk.'

'Wallace rescued me,' said Meg. 'Who found you, Addie?'

'Some chap off the *Lynx* went fishing and caught a petticoat with a bedraggled nurse inside.' She didn't want to think about him hauling her semi-naked into the rescue boat. 'Two sisters jumped from the ship's rail into the sea. Did you see them?'

Meg placed her mug on a table. 'Yes, Isabel and Marion I think.' She felt light-headed and a little green about the gills.

'They'll have been picked up,' Addie said, not wanting to consider any other possibility. 'We'll see them soon. Heaven knows how I got from the *Lynx* to here. The whole thing's a blur.' She reached for Meg's hand. 'Who else have you seen?'

'Netta and Iris, they're both fine, and Dora, though she has a terrible cough.' Meg stared at the purple bruises on her own arms. 'Golly, these look like sea anemones.'

'So do the ones on your face.'

Meg's hands flew to her cheeks. 'Are they bad?'

'They are rather noticeable.'

'Can't be helped.' Meg wrapped her arms around the upper part of her body. 'I keep getting the shakes.'

'Do you need more wine?'

Meg held out her mug. 'You'd better fill it to the brim.'

Struggling to keep her hand steady, Addie topped Meg's up and her own as well. As she put the jug back on the table, she noticed there were no books on it. A sob caught in the back of her throat. Her entire collection had been lost. Meg was watching her. She was so exhausted and sad, she doubted she could keep talking.

'The hardest thing,' Meg whispered, 'apart from worrying about you, was trying to calm a chap from the cavalry unit. He took a swing at me when a severed horse's head and a haunch drifted by. Wallace had to restrain him.' She touched the bruises on her face.

Addie said softly, 'I had a white knight too. He kept me afloat.' She hadn't seen him in the rescue boat, and without his name she couldn't make enquiries. A drowsy warmth spread through her body and she fought back a yawn. 'A steward on the *Lynx* helped me onto his bunk. He gave me two hot-water bottles, one for my back and another for my feet. I'm desperately tired but I don't want to close my eyes in case you disappear.'

'I'm not going anywhere.'

Meg scrambled off her chair and curled up beside her the way Erin used to do if something scared her in the middle of the night.

※

MEG HAD SLEPT, woken and was asleep again when a loud knock startled her. She leapt up and opened the door. The ship's doctor – bushy moustache, bloodshot eyes, hairy hands, the type women settled for rather than chased – waited in the corridor.

'I've come to examine two nursing sisters,' he said.

'Who do you want first?' she asked.

He referred to his notes. 'Dutton, then Harrington.'

Addie sat up and rubbed her eyes. 'Is something wrong?'

'Everything's fine,' Meg said. 'It's just a check-up.' She sat on a chair and held out her wrist. The doctor pressed two fingers to her salt-withered skin.

'How many from the *Marquette* have you seen?' she asked.

He made a note on his chart before inspecting a nasty scratch on her arm.

'I can't keep count. More came in last night.'

She leant forward. 'Any nurses?'

He reached for his stethoscope. 'Quiet, Sister Dutton.'

'We're worried sick,' Addie said from across the room.

He rubbed his chin. 'I recall a fractured femur, three dislocated shoulders, two chest cases, a pierced lung and four or five concussions.' He tapped Meg's chest. 'Take a deep breath, and another. Good.'

She could have told him she was clear of mucus. 'We need names, not conditions.'

He stuck a thermometer under her tongue, a trick she used on irritating patients. 'I can't help you there,' he said brusquely.

She clamped her lips together for the required time.

He checked the reading and said, more gently, 'A list will go up soon.'

After he'd examined Addie, he hung his stethoscope back around his neck and said, 'You're both in remarkable condition considering what you've been through.'

'Well,' said Addie, 'we're alive. We're also desperate to talk to our friends. Are they together somewhere?'

'Everyone's resting and you must do the same.' He packed his bag and walked to the door where he turned and said, 'A roll call will take place shortly. You'll see your chums then.'

Meg turned her neck from side to side to loosen a kink. She must have slept on an angle or wrenched it when she hit the water. 'Did you see Helena after we went down?'

Addie shook her head. 'I heard that five or six nurses reached a copper tank. She could have been among them.'

'I hope so.' Meg gave a drawn-out sigh. 'I wasn't brave the whole time. Especially when a ship veered towards us, then changed direction and headed back out to sea. I thought we'd had it. In desperation, I ripped a strip from the bottom of my petticoat and waved it in the air, and I screamed my head off, but the ship held its course. It was almost dark. I couldn't understand why they hadn't come for us. A soldier reckoned it was because another submarine was in the area, and that really frightened me.' She glanced at Addie. Her friend's head was falling forward so Meg didn't describe the panic that had rolled through her stomach, up to her chest, into her throat or how, when she bent over to rub her feet, she'd seen water bubbling through a small crack in the hull. 'Wallace was sure we'd be picked up before dark.' Addie was yawning. 'You won't believe how much water I swallowed. I'll be coughing it up when I turn ninety.'

Meg reached for her nursing medal, forgetting it had gone. She missed the weight of it. Wallace liked her, she could tell. She remembered him yelling 'Smoke! Smoke!' and jabbing his finger in the direction of the French destroyer, which she now knew was their former escort, the *Tirailleur*. She rolled the name around her mouth. If they ended up in France, maybe she could learn the lingo. Noticing Addie's bare neck, she remembered the amber beads. 'I suppose you've lost your necklace?'

Addie nodded, her eyelids flickering. She was almost asleep.

'Don't worry. I'll buy you another when we berth, and a new bottle of perfume.'

'There's no need, really.'

'Uncle Bert and Aunt Maude said they would wire me money if I kept receipts.'

Growing cold again, she pulled a blanket from the back of the chair and draped it over her shoulders. 'I used to climb into my aunt's wardrobe and wrap her furs around me. Have you ever worn mink?'

Addie murmured, 'My mother's coat is fox.'

'Tell me what you need, please, Addie.' There was a queer desperation in Meg's voice.

'Just to hear everyone's safe.'

'Yes', whispered Meg. 'I want that too.'

OVER A DOZEN nurses came aboard the *Grantully Castle* on Sunday and, during the next afternoon, another eleven were winched aboard, some in tattered cotton uniforms, others clad in shrunken woollens. One minute, they were joking about their appearance, laughing too loudly, the next, quiet and wistful. Two or three stood back from the main group, staring into space, their faces and posture showing the strain of their ordeal. Eventually, two solemn-looking officers escorted them all to the saloon where Addie and Meg drank more tea and talked in hushed voices to Dora, Netta and Iris. Addie wanted to keep touching her friends to make sure they were real, not images she had dreamt up. No one had seen Helena or Margaret. Whenever the door opened, the room fell silent as heads turned to see who was coming in.

During the silences in Monday's roll call Addie fought back tears. Afterwards Meg took her arm and they walked without speaking back to their cabin.

On Tuesday the CO asked the *Marquette* survivors to gather on the main deck, where Addie noticed most of the men were salt-burnt and many wore the shock of Saturday on their faces. The poor CO looked as if he had been up all night writing reports, or condolences.

'I've organised accommodation,' he said solemnly. 'As of tomorrow nursing sisters will be quartered in hotels, but I'm afraid you chaps will be in a cotton mill. Ladies, Salonika is in a state of political upheaval so please remain indoors. Rescue boats will continue to search for survivors.' He thumped the tip of his cane on the deck, an action Addie interpreted as *they will be found*, but when he raised his eyes to the skyline, she realised he had already placed the responsibility in God's hands.

⋘

MEG HAD barely spoken to Wallace since they transferred to the *Grantully* but they'd managed a few words after the CO's announcement while people milled about discussing the arrangements. He'd commented on her bruises and carried out what others might have thought was a cursory medical inspection but to her felt like a caress. His eyes had never left hers. But that was hours ago. She was now out and about in the hope that she would bump into him. If he asked her to meet him in Salonika, she would. So what if everything about him screamed danger. She wasn't exactly humdrum herself. Besides, she knew life could end in a flash. There was no point waiting for the right time and place: it might never happen. There was still no word on their missing friends. She tried not to think of them during the day but their faces tormented her at night. Neither she nor Addie could sleep soundly.

Up ahead four medics were talking. She recognised Wallace's broad back, the line of his shoulders, his long legs. If he sensed her before she got any closer, it meant he fancied her as much as she did him.

Bang on the button he turned and sent her a wink. She smiled and kept walking. If he came to her hotel and asked her out, she would need something better to wear than a second-hand coat. Maybe she could borrow Dora's uniform, which was in good condition, unlike poor Dora, who was bed-ridden with a terrible cold. Meg had taken her a cup of tea and two biscuits earlier. She shouldn't be thinking about clothes at a time like this. Besides, before she let Wallace slip anything off, she would have a smart new outfit. Hussy, she thought, and swallowed a delicious idea.

Life didn't flash before my eyes as I floundered in the drink: my thoughts turned to Meg and what I might miss if my number was up. She's an itch I can't stop scratching. An itch that keeps me awake at night. Previously when the cravings came upon me, I found a bar girl, handed over the money, dropped my trousers and rammed her. Payback, I told myself, for Evelyn's cold shoulder. I felt buoyant at the time, rotten later. Native girls don't satisfy me. Never will. I need someone who comes up trumps in every department. I think Meg will. She's bright, funny, sweet. We talk. She listens. When the torpedo hit I ran the length of the ship looking for her. A rush of relief went through me when I saw her get into a lifeboat. Only then did I board another earmarked for us medical chaps. Both boats turned turtle. I went into a spin until the Aegean swept her into my arms.

Seven

AT THE SPLENDID PALACE hotel, Addie had time to rest, although whenever she sat in the teal armchair in her second-floor room, a maddening restlessness came upon her, compelling her to rise and touch the furnishings, smell the rose water, stare into the mirror. Her parents would be horrified if they could see her peeling skin or knew she was struggling to recall what had taken place in the past few days. It was as though a tide had rolled in and washed away the details, leaving behind a multitude of questions. Why did she live and others not? Would anyone else be found? Would the officials send her unit home?

A persistent braying drew her to the window. Directly below an elderly man was beating a donkey, his face contorted with rage as he let out a string of what sounded like swear words. Steam rose from fresh dung, obscuring the pleasant fragrances that had previously floated in from the traders' spice baskets. Everything about this place struck her as blasphemous: the maimed children, the loud horns, the drunken soldiers, the annoying beggars.

Either side of the city wall, she could see rows of tents, ambulances and wagons. To the west, on the edge of the Vardar

Plains, troops were marching between rows of wooden barracks. To the east, beyond the cemeteries and the tree-lined boulevards, aerodromes dwarfed the bell-shaped tents of the Anzac camp set among trees on the shoreline beneath the slopes of Mount Hortiatis. She felt unable to climb back into her skin, as if some nameless part of her had vanished – and she mourned its absence as much as she would a limb. Young soldiers had spoken to her of losing their innocence during their first battle. Perhaps something similar had happened to her. She needed someone to listen to her fears, not try to jolly her along, as Meg seemed to want to do. Dora had a similar tendency, which intensified after her brother sent a cable saying he was in a general hospital recovering from a minor wound. She'd shaken off her cough and bounded from her sickbed full of goodwill.

Addie would have preferred to stay in her room, but her companions were waiting in the hotel lounge, so she brushed her hair and headed for the stairs.

As she walked through the door, Netta, who was dividing up a floral-scented semolina syrup cake, swivelled round in her chair. 'I think you'll like it, Addie. Apparently it's called basbousa.'

'Thanks.' Addie draped a napkin over her lap and surveyed the group. 'Where's Meg?'

'She sent her apologies,' Dora said. 'She's gone off to see a dentist.'

More like a surgeon, Addie thought. 'Is there any news of Matron?'

'She has pneumonia,' said Netta, 'and some paralysis.'

Addie said, 'Can we visit her?'

'The doctor wants her kept quiet,' said Netta. 'There's talk of sending her home.'

Dora slipped another slice of cake onto her plate. 'I wouldn't be keen to travel while there's still a threat of U-boats. Would you, Addie?'

95

She thought of Matron, so far from family and home. 'Not unless there were special circumstances.' She drove a teaspoon into the sugar bowl. 'Ten of us are still unaccounted for.'

Netta twisted her napkin into a ball. 'They might still come ashore. Don't give up, Addie.'

She picked up a teacup with a leafy pattern and thought of Helena talking about the rugged West Coast bush. She was among the missing. 'Do you think the Germans would have fired if they'd known nurses were on board?'

No one spoke.

'We're the enemy,' Netta said finally, 'even if we are women.' She picked up the teapot. 'More tea for anyone?'

Addie sighed and held out her cup.

FROM HER HOTEL window, Meg watched Australian and New Zealand soldiers enter Floca, a café famous, according to Wallace, for its varied clientele: Russians, Italians, English, Greeks, Indians and Albanians. He had assured her over dinner last night that these men got along famously unless some faction objected to the politics of another. Even if a brawl broke out, it was unlikely to affect her. Salonika was nowhere near as dangerous as the CO had made out. There were hundreds of Tommies patrolling the streets, and there was nothing to stop Wallace getting an army motorcar and taking her sightseeing. She would slip a note under his door. He'd already left two for her.

Usually she enjoyed sprucing up, but she had no rouge or lipstick so this time she had to make do with a thorough wash, a vigorous clean of her teeth and a hundred brushes of her hair. She checked her appearance in the gilt-edged mirror in her bedroom. The borrowed uniform didn't do her figure justice. Nor was she thrilled about the ghastly blemishes on her skin.

She'd planned to greet him coolly but when he tapped on the door, she had to calm her nerves by counting to ten before letting him in.

'Meg, you look marvellous.' He took off his hat and put it on the dresser next to her hairbrush. 'I bought you some oranges.'

He tipped three into her cupped hands.

'Thank you, I'll share them with the girls.'

'No, you enjoy them.' He hesitated briefly. 'We don't want awkward questions.'

She shrugged her shoulders. 'I suppose not.' She arranged the fruit in a bowl on her bedside table. 'Did you borrow a motorcar?'

'A lorry – less likely to attract attention. There are masses on the roads.'

She was disappointed, but said cheerfully, 'Are we set then?'

'Once you're disguised.' He pulled a plain gown and a length of cloth from his kit.

'Not in a million years!'

'It's too risky otherwise. You choose – tea with the girls or an adventure with me?'

His eyes settled on hers. Something shifted inside. 'You,' she said.

As he slipped the tunic over her head, she sucked in her stomach and thrust back her shoulders.

'Now for your hair,' he said as he gathered it up. 'We'll make a native out of you yet.'

He wound the cloth so skilfully around her head that she wondered if he'd been practising on his own. His breath smelled of peppermints.

They left through the backdoor, nipping into an alleyway that teemed with Jews in long gabardine coats. She was staring at their olive skin, black ringlets and dark eyes when a leech seller in loose pantaloons and a baggy shirt bumped against her.

'Don't hang about, Meg,' Wallace said. 'We're in Pickpocket Alley.'

She clutched her new handbag tightly as if it contained Queen Mary's jewels.

He directed her to a lorry parked in a side road. Her robe caught on the door handle as she climbed in and she had to untangle it while holding her headgear in place. Her hair must be flatter than a tin tray, but there was no point fretting about it. They only had two hours.

Gripping the steering wheel as if it were a surgical instrument, Wallace skirted the Upper Town and headed along the coast, passing minarets and whitewashed walls, climbing high above the Aegean. From this distance, Meg could pretend the sea was a soft turquoise blanket with satin edges. A less tranquil image was threatening to intrude when three Jewish girls stepped unexpectedly off the pavement. Wallace jammed on the brakes. 'Attractive little misses,' he said as they crossed the street.

Meg sized up their body-hugging corsets and full skirts, their sleek dark hair hanging from green beaded caps, shaped like upturned saucers. 'I'd look good in their clothes.' She tugged at her tunic. 'This makes me look like a giant candle.'

Wallace roared with laughter.

'Keep your eyes on the road, please. We don't want an accident.'

He reached over and patted the fabric bunched over her knees. 'Seriously, MD, they're not a patch on you.'

'A compliment a day will keep other men away.'

More laughter filled the cab.

He changed gears as they climbed a hill. 'Tell me what you enjoy.'

She talked about the best films and shows she'd seen until he drove down into a cove surrounded by a stand of tall, slim trees. Their greenish-blue leaves were the same colour as the eyes of a self-obsessed chap she'd gone out with for a while. He'd expected her to solve his problems. Just as well she hadn't settled for him. She ran her hand over her cheek and found another piece of loose skin.

Another memory swooped in. When she was seven years old, Ma had bound her arms and ankles with twine and tied them to the legs of the kitchen table. Using a scalding-hot poker, she'd branded crosses onto the soles of her feet. Her skin had stunk of burnt meat. She remembered the pain, remembered passing out, remembered Pa coming up from the stables, untying her and locking her in the back bedroom. Her aunt and uncle were on holiday in Timaru. She hadn't known if she'd see them again.

Stepping down from the lorry, she walked around to Wallace's side and leant on the bonnet. An unfamiliar fragrance wafted towards her. 'What's that smell?'

Wallace had got out to stand beside her. 'Cypress. The ancient Egyptians made their coffins from trees like these.'

She didn't want to think about dead people, not with Wallace only inches away. His oiled hair smelled of coconut and gleamed in the sun. He circled her wrist until his thumb and forefinger touched. Banding her, she thought.

'Meg, if anyone approaches, put your head down and don't speak. I'll say you're my driver, that we have a problem with the lorry, right?'

'Fine.' When had he thought up that excuse?

He kissed the tip of her nose. 'Are you ready for a surprise?'

She nodded, not trusting herself to speak.

Scrambling into the back of the lorry, he pulled out a wicker hamper. 'Pumpkin pastries, cheese pie, almond cake, melon. Do any appeal?'

'All of them,' she said.

He draped a red napkin across her lap. 'Tuck in, dear girl.'

She reached for a large slice of pie, then, not wanting to appear greedy, withdrew her hand.

As if reading her thoughts, he said, 'I admire women with a healthy appetite.'

He ate quickly, hungrily.

When a sesame seed stuck to her top lip he dabbed it with his finger, then placed it on his tongue. She remembered a screen star doing something similar. Had Wallace seen the same film? 'I—'

'Hush.'

He tasted of ripe melon. She wanted him to keep kissing her lips, her neck, her shoulders, and the hollow in her arm. Instead, he slipped his fingers down the yoke of her tunic. Why didn't he hold her, make her feel safe? If she didn't please him he mightn't take her out again, but she wasn't ready to go the whole way. She let his hands run across her shoulders until it felt as though he was holding her over a low flame. Then she told him to stop.

IT WAS THURSDAY now, the 28th of October. Addie had stayed in bed with a high temperature – a delayed reaction, according to Netta, to seven hours in seawater. Addie knew worry was the main factor but she didn't have the strength to argue, although she rallied sufficiently to convince Netta to put the posy she'd brought her in a vase and leave to meet Dora for lunch. As the latch on the door clicked shut, Addie picked up a monograph the hotelier had lent her, outlining the history of Salonika and settled down for a quiet read.

She was well into chapter two when Iris popped in to see her. Despite a badly bruised hand, she began straightening the bedclothes. 'That's better. How are you, Addie?'

'I'm fine, Iris, thanks.' She lay back on the freshly plumped up pillows. 'But what about you? You must have been in the water for ages.'

Iris's voice shook. 'I thought I was the only survivor. I was terrified. I'm not used to being alone.'

'It won't be over until we're all back together again.'

'We mustn't give up hope.' Iris flattened the edge of Addie's top sheet. 'Where's Meg, by the way?' Addie shrugged. 'Well,' Iris continued, 'you rest. I'll call by again in an hour or two.'

Addie was reading chapter three when Meg bounced through the door carrying a cup of beef tea. 'Guess what?' she said, rocking on the balls of her feet.

Did Meg have news of their friends? 'Tell me.'

'He took me up the coast for a picnic.'

Her hope died away. 'Who? Not Wallace! You didn't! Meg! It's dangerous to leave the hotel. You heard the CO. There are fights breaking out in streets not far from here.'

'That's why he disguised me as a native. He thought of everything. I'll treasure this day for the rest of my life. Have you been in bed the whole time? Where's the thermometer?'

'It's only a temperature. I've been reading.'

Meg wrinkled her nose. 'Tell me one interesting fact.'

'Well, fish were once so plentiful in Salonika that the local astrologers believed their city lay under the sign of Pisces. Our soldiers are finding all sorts of artefacts as they dig trenches. I want to see them.'

'The artefacts or the soldiers?' said Meg with a grin.

Addie ignored the joke. 'Does Wallace know where we'll end up?'

'I don't care as long as we're together. Do you believe in fate? I do. Wallace is mine. When he looks at me, I go hot all over. Do you know what I mean?'

Addie laughed. 'Me?' She fanned her face with the monograph. 'I once had a raging fever due to pneumonia.'

'Oh, you're impossible.' Meg pretended to slap her. 'I meant over a man.'

'Smart chaps weren't thick on the ground in Riverton.'

'So you do think he's a cut above the rest. He could fix you up with a chum.'

'Stop it. You're as bad as my mother. Anyway, we won't be here long.'

Meg pulled up a chair. 'Promise to keep your trap shut and I'll tell you everything about our picnic.'

This could take hours, Addie thought, as she settled into a more comfortable position.

BY FRIDAY it was time to leave, time to go back across the Aegean to Alexandria – this time on a hospital ship. Addie's temperature had returned to normal and there was a little colour in her cheeks. Even so, Meg insisted she wrap up for the journey. You should never risk a chill in the kidneys.

Wallace was waiting at the top of the gangplank, cap off, looking serious but not stern. He raised his hand. She glanced at Addie and they stopped walking and waited for him to speak.

'You need to be strong, girls,' he said quietly. He placed his hands either side of his head as if he had a headache. 'I'm afraid I have distressing news.'

Meg gripped Addie's arm.

'What's wrong?' Meg spoke more loudly than she'd intended.

He stepped closer. 'The bodies of Sisters Isdell and Rogers have been found in a lifeboat, along with four soldiers.'

Meg staggered slightly and Addie put her arm around her waist. 'Are you sure?' Addie said. 'Helena and Margaret!'

Wallace straightened his tie. 'Yes. I'm so sorry.'

Addie's voice dropped to a whisper. 'Please don't let it be true.'

'Who found them?' asked Netta.

'A search party from a warship,' said Wallace. 'Sister Rogers was wearing a wristwatch with her name engraved on the back, and a chap found a disc with Sister Isdell's number on it, and her nursing medal.'

'Where were they?' Meg managed.

'In a boat drifting upside down some distance from shore,' Wallace said. 'All six lifebelts were tied to a thwart.'

If she thought of Helena and Margaret struggling to keep their heads out of the water, fighting to stay alive, Meg knew she would scream the place down.

'Where are they now?'

'In Zagora – they were buried near where they were found, very respectfully. Please accept my condolences. I realise it comes as a terrible blow.'

Meg felt as if she'd stepped into a lift that was dropping too fast.

She grasped Addie's trembling hand. 'We'll remember them in our own way.'

Early into the sad, strange return journey, Meg dropped some flowers into the Aegean while Addie said a few words for those lost, who included Isabel and Marion. If she died, Meg thought, few mourners from Tuatapere would pay their respects. Certainly not the boy in her Standard Six class whom she'd kicked in the shin for calling her mother crazy. They'd both been sent to the headmaster, who'd got out his strap and given them six of the best. She hadn't cried then, and she wouldn't cry now. Not even Wallace would make her cry.

If she'd been in Alexandria under different circumstances, she'd have sashayed down the wide avenues and visited the fancy tearooms, not slouched around the hotel ruining her posture. When a senior army clerk arrived with five pounds for each nurse and instructions to stock up in preparation for hardships and cold weather, she was glad to have something to do.

Iris went for woollens and checked them constantly – to make sure they wouldn't disappear like her possessions on the *Marquette*, Meg thought, as she half-heartedly bargained over the price of a pot of face cream.

Addie refused to let her replace her necklace. 'Not under the circumstances,' she said, stopping in front of a large shop mirror.

Meg stared at their reflected images. Addie's hair had lost its auburn highlights; hers looked like a dish-mop. Flakes of skin continued to come off when she rubbed her blotchy cheeks. You'd have thought the two of them had shut their eyes for an instant and aged ten years, although the chap who'd dropped in the money and told them about the inquiry into the sinking reckoned she and Addie didn't look half as bad as the poor nurses who'd given evidence.

October 26th, H.M.S. *Talbot*, Salonika Harbour. Facts: T.S. *Marquette* carried 95 crew, 646 ranks and ratings, including 36 nurses and 12 officers; 14 lifeboats (8 at davits and 6 inboard); sinking on October 23rd at approximately 9.20 a.m. due to a submarine attack on the starboard side, close to the bulkhead between No. 1 and 2 holds; the *Lynx*, *Mortier* and *Tirailleur* picked up survivors. Witnesses called, cautioned and questioned. Lowering and getting away of boats effectively / not effectively carried out; the Officer of the Watch stopped / did not stop the engines; the Captain was on the bridge / not on the bridge when the torpedo struck. Only one detail agreed upon: nurses acted with discipline, courage and selflessness. Verbatim: 'Their fine example, combined with their cheery encouragement, undoubtedly prevented many men from giving in.' Oversight: the court failed to obtain a report from the officer responsible for placing the unit on a transport rather than a hospital ship. Two battered and bruised nurses delivered concise first-hand accounts, referring to, but not dwelling on, three separate acts of male cowardice. Once the nurses' part was over, they were given afternoon tea then the Commander instructed his blue-jackets to cheer while he accompanied them to the door.

Eight

'A SHODDY SHINE is unacceptable,' the new matron told Dora, as they lined up for inspection in the hotel foyer. 'Polish those shoes again, Staff Nurse. And straighten your shoulders.'

This matron, with her piercing blue eyes, had forged her reputation in the hell of Belgium where, it was rumoured, she'd single-handedly escorted seventy women and children through enemy lines. A war correspondent had dubbed her 'Matron of Valour'. There was talk of her receiving a medal.

As she made her way down the line, Matron declared that she would never ask them to do anything she wasn't prepared to do herself. Their role was to care for the wounded; hers was to ensure they had adequate support and facilities. By the time a car called to take her to a meeting, she had won them over.

Free to do as she pleased until dinner, Addie invited Netta to take a walk through the hotel gardens since Meg had gone to her room to style her hair, wanting to look her best for Wallace. There was talk that he wasn't as available as he made out. Addie hoped Meg wouldn't get hurt.

As they passed lime-green succulents and orange lilies staging a riotous show beneath rows of palms, a scent reminiscent of jasmine drew rapturous praise from Netta.

'It's a liana. Stand guard while I take a cutting.'

'Please don't.' Addie looked around nervously. 'You'll land us in trouble.'

But Netta had already pulled a pair of scissors from her handbag and was advancing stealthily towards the foliage. Not wanting to witness the crime, Addie continued down the winding dirt path.

Netta soon caught up with her. 'Look out for plants I can grow in jars,' she said, swinging her handbag in the direction of an expansive border. 'Next time I'll bring my diary and take down the botanical names.'

Addie laughed. 'Just as well we don't have to hand them in to get marked.'

If Addie had declined Netta's offer of a fruit squash after their walk, she wouldn't be trying to scrub a stain out of her uniform with a nailbrush and soap. She checked the time: their second inspection was due in twenty minutes.

She was last to arrive in the foyer, where everyone was standing shoulder to shoulder, as if attempting to fill the gaps left by the dead. Meg beckoned her over. 'Did you get it out?' she whispered.

'Not completely,' Addie said, arranging the folds of her skirt to hide the damp patch.

A desk clerk sidled past, his sandals slapping on the tiled floor. Nearby caged birds sang plaintively. How cruel to deny them a full stretch of their wings, she thought, as Matron strode through the door and paused in front of her. Convinced the slightest movement would uncover the stain, she lifted her head cautiously and was relieved when Matron moved on.

This woman had the ability to command in all sorts of ways. Dora was curbing the amount she ate and Iris no longer guarded her possessions. Even Meg seemed more settled, and most days Addie was able to push the Aegean tragedy to the back of her mind. Sadly, though, she couldn't see the Germans or Turks laying down their arms. Her lot weren't likely to either.

'You're all recovering well,' Matron said, 'and you've made an effort to smarten up. Thank you. I'm proud of you. If it was up to me, I'd give you another week's rest but unfortunately, you're needed elsewhere.'

Addie held her breath as Meg asked for the name of their new destination.

'There's a shortage of accommodation at Lembet, where No. 1 is going, so for now, Dutton, you and Harrington and Smith will join Captains Madison and Ramsay at 15th General, not far from here.'

Good, thought Addie; she and Meg were staying together, and Netta too.

'The rest of you are down for transport duty,' continued Matron. She paused to let the news sink in. 'Hospital ships mainly. You'll most likely be on the Mudros run.'

Dora clutched Addie's arm. Addie didn't blame her for feeling nervous. Such a posting meant travelling back and forth across the Aegean to Lemnos, where she'd heard conditions were diabolical both for the wounded and for the Canadian and Australian nurses caring for them. 'Our boys will be pleased to see you,' she murmured.

Iris whispered, 'We'll be fine. Hospital ships rarely come under attack.'

But what about the *Anglia*? Addie thought. It had been transporting injured officers and soldiers from Calais to Dover when it struck a mine and went down a mile off the Kentish coast. Mines couldn't differentiate between hospital and transport ships. And who would perform nursing duties at No. 1? Surely, the officials weren't going to rely on orderlies.

'Our duty is to serve those in need wherever they might be,' Matron said firmly. 'Gather up your belongings and start packing.'

Addie gave a clock she'd won in a hotel raffle to the young girl who'd been cleaning her room. She showed her how to alter the time and set the alarm. 'It will go off in three minutes,' she said. The girl opened the window and held the clock aloft.

Below in the crowded street, a body on a shallow wooden frame, concealed by a shawl and carried on the shoulders of six men, moved forward swiftly. Three men, ululating at the top of their voices, preceded the bier. 'Each man is paid for his vocal labours,' explained the girl. 'Number of howlers signifies importance of dead person.' Behind them, women with dyed hands and indigo faces tore at their garments and wailed monotonously. This funeral procession was nothing like the sedate Presbyterian affairs Addie had gone to in Riverton and Invercargill.

When the alarm went off, the girl shook the clock, trying to silence it. Addie showed her which knob to press. There was a rusty tinge to the sky as though it were a sheet of metal left to discolour in the rain. 'Do you need anything else?' she asked. 'Something that would give you pleasure?'

The girl shook her head. 'The lifespan of happiness is shorter than that of a flower,' she said and she left the room before Addie could ask why she made beds when she could have been a translator.

⫷⫸

THE 15TH, a well-equipped government hospital currently under the care of the Royal Army Medical Corps, was a place of canvas – large numbers of patients had cots in marquees and their nurses slept in smaller tents. The one assigned to Meg and Addie by a harried quartermaster was patched and had a torn door flap. Meg was vexed to boiling point. Wallace had yet to arrive, and she had a crick in her neck from checking over her shoulder for him. After they unpacked, Addie suggested they inspect the nurses' sitting room, which turned out to be a run-down outbuilding filled with a few rickety armchairs, a scratched table and droves of fat Egyptian flies. Matron was already inside, sniffing in disgust.

'We can make it more homely,' Addie said, looking around. 'We could find some curtains for the windows and put something over the chairs.'

'You're here to nurse, Harrington, not decorate,' Matron said. She ran a finger along a window ledge. 'Dutton, make sure this place gets a thorough scrub.'

'I'll see to it, Matron.'

'You've certainly greased your way into her good books,' Addie said as they walked back across the sun-hardened earth to their tent. 'You could be an actress, Meg.'

'I told you acting comes in handy. Matron finds me useful, unlike my home-decorating friend.' Seeing Addie frown, she said, 'Sorry, but I need to stay on side. I don't want her interfering with me and Wallace.'

'You can only push your luck so far.'

'She has her eye on you, not me. Learn to act, Addie. Think of it as trying on lots of clothes until you find the perfect outfit for every occasion. Speaking of which, I need a new dress. There must be a dressmaker nearby. Once I've seen Wallace, we'll sneak off. I'll watch your back.'

'That doesn't make me feel any safer.' Addie gave an exaggerated grimace.

'If the wind changes, you'll stay that way. Then how will you get a boyfriend? Seriously, if you ever come face to face with Fritz, tell them you have a German grandfather. They won't harm you if they think you're one of them. That's what I plan to do.'

WORD SPREAD through the hospital that Wallace had arrived with a bag of mail, the first news from home for weeks. Addie

110

ran all the way to the mess. As she squeezed through the door, she heard Netta reading out a sentence from her grandmother's letter: 'Every Sunday I place fresh flowers in your room and pray for your safety.' The envelope in Meg's hand must have come from her aunt. Her mother never wrote.

Addie collected her bundle of mail, and a parcel of new books, and wandered off to find a private spot, settling for the cab of a parked truck. The first envelope bore her mother's flowery handwriting. She held it against her face for a moment before sliding her finger under the upper fold. 'I can't believe the Germans attacked a ship with you onboard. Don't travel by sea from now on. Erin has mumps. Your father recently purchased a pedigree bull. I'm making a signature quilt with members of the baking guild. We pray for you, Adelina. Do you have enough to eat? Are you getting sufficient sleep? I hope your bronchitis hasn't started up. I spend half my days and most of my nights worrying about you.'

'The newspapers are full of stories about the torpedo,' wrote her father. 'We were relieved to get official word that you were safe. Please think about coming home. I could pull a few strings. You only have to put up your hand.'

Christmas was only a month away – the start of summer back home. Mother would have doused her fruitcake in brandy and Father fattened a turkey. In a fortnight, Erin would pull a box of gold and silver baubles from the hall cupboard and decorate the tree. But she'd never be home in time, even if she did get permission, and then she'd hardly be through the door before her parents would start haranguing her to marry someone they'd dredged up at the local A&P show.

Addie's ward contained the usual mixture, from mild typhoids through to serious head cases. One day merged into another. When the sun shone, she told Blue and Davies, a new orderly, to tie back the sides of the marquee and let in fresh air.

Tarpaulins doubled as flooring and luckily were easy to scrub since dysentery was rampant.

The previous day, Davies, who had a slight stutter, had been removing a full bedpan when he tripped on a discarded boot and slid precariously through the open tent flap, yelling, 'Sh-sh-shit! Sh-sh-shit! Sh-sh-shit!' The poor fellow landed heavily on the edge of a trench dug to offer protection in a downpour and shelter in case of a bombing raid, both of which were unlikely to occur in Alexandria. She sent him to the ablution hut with instructions not to return until he was immaculate. While he was away, she scrubbed down two patients and attended to a surgical who had burst a stitch laughing.

When Davies returned, another patient, with two broken wrists, said, 'Hey, Crapper, we should catapult you and your pans over the line.'

'Enough of your cheek,' said Davies, pretending to throw a glass of water over him. 'Remember who sh-sh-shovels in your tucker.'

It was good to hear the men laugh. She was busy but not excessively so, and there was time to talk to the patients, who were mainly English, with a scattering of New Zealanders. These conversations invariably lifted her spirits, especially when they reminisced about the lush green countryside of home, such a contrast to the arid, beige terrain around them. She was tempted to slip a sketch of the hospital into her next letter until she learnt that an eagle-eyed padre had taken over as censor for a month while the regular lackadaisical post chap went on leave.

COMING OUT of the laundry, Meg overheard a bunch of orderlies planning a competition to determine who at the 15th performed the most tasks in a twenty-four hour period. Entries were to be sixty words or fewer and the prize was a bottle of brandy. She found a discarded attempt in the laundry and read it to Addie and Netta. 'Worked morning in dispensary; attended venereal patients in afternoon, gave medicines every four hours, cleaned and tidied wards. Played euchre, reread my girl's last letter, had lurid thoughts, woke with Long John Silver stiff, took myself in hand, attended reveille at 6 a.m., paraded at 6.45 a.m.'

'I can't believe one of our orderlies wrote that!' Addie exclaimed.

'He did more than write it. You lived on a farm. Didn't you watch the animals?'

'Surely men are different?'

'Not really.'

Netta tossed her head and gave a snort.

A sapper carrying a plank gave them the once over as he passed by. As soon as he was out of earshot, Addie said, 'We should start our own competition, Meg.'

But she was no longer listening. She wanted Wallace to buy a motorcycle so he could speed back to her from his trips into the city, where he was setting up a surgical society. The idea was that surgeons from several hospitals in the area would be able to visit each other and observe unusual cases. In the laboratory yesterday, she'd suggested he buy a leather helmet. Laughing, he'd pulled her towards him and trailed his fingertips down her neck, causing what felt like an electric current to surge through her.

After Netta left, Meg told Addie she intended to ride pillion, disguised as a native again.

'You might have addled Wallace's brain,' Addie said, 'but don't underestimate Matron's.'

'Do I look like a fool?'

'I worry about you.'

'No need. Get a move on or you'll be late for night duty. I'm going back to our tent.'

She made her way down the line in the dark because the CO had forbidden the use of hurricane lamps. Inside the third-to-last canvas hump, Meg tugged off her boots, then her uniform, and flopped onto her cot. Matron was the least of her worries. Top of the list was finding a headscarf to keep her hair under control when she went for a spin on the motorcycle – she was sure Wallace would get one. 'I never tire of looking at you, Meg,' he'd told her yesterday. Yet she'd gone away feeling empty. It was the same when she was growing up. No matter how much love and attention Aunt Maude and Uncle Bert gave her, each day she climbed the hill at the back of their property and stared north towards Ma and Pa's place.

※

ADDIE LIT a candle and tried to read but her attention kept straying to the latest rumours. In France, where the Germans were marching back to their homeland with the Tommies hard on their heels, women and young girls – even nuns – were said to be suffering indignities every day. Bombs had fallen on Salonika and endangered nearby Lembet – No. 1 might have to evacuate.

In theatre that morning, Wallace had urged Ramsay and Davies to bet on which rumour was more likely to be true. Once he picked up his motorcycle, the winner could ride it for a day. Meg put his cavalier attitude down to bravery, but in Addie's opinion it came from a darker need; however, she appreciated his willingness to explain unfamiliar procedures. Both she and Meg also considered Edward Ramsay generous with his knowledge. Yesterday, when Addie had asked a question about ether, he'd suggested she administer it to the next patient, whose weakened state would mean he was unlikely to struggle. She'd manoeuvred the soldier's jaw forward and, holding the mask over his face with one hand, administered the drops with the other. If she was too light, Edward had said, the patient could start moving and vomit, possibly choke. If she was too deep, he could stop breathing. Before long, her arm had ached

114

from repeating the same movement but she'd had to stay alert to pick up the slightest change in the patient's condition. There was more to giving anaesthetic than she'd thought.

Throughout December, boys arrived, mostly via the camps but also from the Dardanelles, with fluctuating fevers, stomach cramps and yellow watery stools. They went straight to the typhoid ward, which Netta oversaw. Those who failed to recover were evacuated to hospital ships that took them for further treatment in England, but the cots in the marquees never stayed empty for long. An Australian patient had five shrapnel wounds, two serious. His mate in the next cot, who had lost his genitals, covered his eyes in embarrassment when Addie changed his dressings. 'What's the point?' he asked. She worried he might take his own life if she failed to come up with a reasonable answer. It wasn't enough to insert a catheter, and prescribe enemas – number nines the orderlies called them – to overcome a diet of army biscuits and bully beef.

Last night a chap had arrived with what she thought was a dark cloth covering the upper half of his face. When she got closer, she realised there was no cloth, just a cavernous black hole where his eyes and nose should have been. He'd seized her arm and slurred, 'Only a scratch, save the others.' Struggling to stay composed, she'd given him morphine. One of the men who brought him in had said they were losing ground. Addie envied those who continued to believe their side would win, men like Edward Ramsay, who stayed calm no matter what unravelled around him.

My childhood turned me into the precise, self-contained sort of chap that I am. I can administer chloroform and ether, any time, any place. None of it comes down to bravery; just my way of containing the chaos. I dread losing control so I concentrate fully on whatever is in front of me. A tactic I developed as a boy. Picture an English estate transplanted to the Canterbury Plains: Father ambling through an avenue of oaks, a book under his arm and archaeological theories stirring in his head; Mother carving statues in her studio, a thin Cuban cigar between her crimson lips, stopping intermittently to read about her current subject. My whereabouts, no, my existence, slipped her distracted mind, even when I stopped eating. Mrs Harvey, our housekeeper, a pragmatic woman, deposited mugs of banana custard in strategic places, believing enough would slip down my wayward gullet to ward off starvation and rickets. I read up on Egyptian pharaohs and sculpture, talking about them incessantly whenever I could catch Father and Mother's attention, but they remained elusive, my presence immaterial to them, my care left to an assortment of home tutors who dispensed unrelated chunks of Latin, French, trigonometry, classics and history. I also spent hours in our home library reading up on anatomy because I wanted to understand the workings of the human body. Eventually I went down to Dunedin to take up a place at the Medical School. There I developed an interest in anaesthesia.

Nine

BLUE AND DAVIES lifted another boy onto the table; Wallace's eighth amputation for the day. When the soldier had come in late last night, Meg had irrigated his putrefied lacerations, which were writhing with maggots. Despite the morphia she'd dispensed half an hour ago, the boy's eyes remained open. He should have been enjoying a picnic with his girl back home, not facing the knife. She laid her palm on his forehead as Edward Ramsay administered the chloroform. The soldier's eyelids flickered, then his jaw slackened and his chest rose and fell, steady as clockwork.

Wallace probed the area around the knee. 'Scalpel, Sister.'

He made his first incision an inch above the adductor tubercle. If all went well it would be over in fifteen minutes. She watched him complete the circular incision and dissect a cuff of skin. Then he divided the muscle in a way that allowed for padding. If you left enough of a flap to cover the stump you could avoid puckering, which Wallace believed reduced the chance of friction and therefore infection. Too many butchers chopped without thinking. She mopped his brow..

'How's he doing, Ramsay?'

'Steady.'

Wallace separated the remainder of the muscle circularly down to the bone. ' Swab, Sister. Hurry, I can't see! Blue, pull on the ankle. I need the leg taut. Elevate the periosteum.'

'Scraper or raspatory, sir?'

'Scraper, Sister.'

He divided and separated the periosteum, ready to part the bone at a slightly higher point. As well as sawing, he had to attend to major blood vessels and cut the principal nerves. Once this stage was over, she passed him a file, which he used to smooth the bone to ensure the stump had the best chance of healing.

Until the patient went to Blighty, she would do her best to prevent infection, though it wasn't easy in a place where insects outnumbered people. Another of her cases, poor chap, believed blowflies entered through his eyes and expanded inside him. If he directed them towards the light, they shrank. Any lapse of concentration and they would enter the eyes of other patients. 'My work is crucial,' he'd told her yesterday. 'I daren't stop to eat.'

Wallace wasn't eating properly either, or getting enough sleep, judging by the dark pouches under his eyes. He kept stopping to stretch, which meant his back was playing up. No other surgeon worked at his pace. 'Time for a break,' she said, as he checked the stump a final time.

'Sister, tell Davies to dispose of the limb. We don't want this boy waking up on the stretcher with his leg sitting on his chest like the last poor blighter. And get Davies to take this bucket out while you're at it.' He prodded it with the tip of his boot.

Inside were yards of bloodied gauze and chunks of discarded flesh. 'Yes, sir.'

'Don't stay away long,' he said. 'I need you for something else.'

In the Red Cross room, Wallace ran his hands along her shoulders.

'Can you feel it?' she asked, referring to the prickling sensation under her skin.

'I feel whatever you do.'

She dropped her head onto his shoulder. As he stroked her face, she asked when they could get away again. He was working on it, he told her. There could be a chance once he had set up the surgical society.

'Can theatre nurses belong?'

'Sorry, Meg, it's just for surgeons. Anyway, I can teach you whatever you want to know.'

IN THE WEEK before Christmas severe winds, sleet and snow struck the Balkans and soldiers began to arrive in Alexandria with tales of water in the trenches rising over their boot tops, their blankets and greatcoats freezing, ice forming in their moustaches, the hairs in their nostrils snapping like glass. When Addie removed their leggings, she almost retched. The stench was similar to dank swamp grass.

Many of the men had black feet. Few could bear the weight of a blanket; their skin sloughed off, sometimes taking entire toes. She applied boracic powder and had Davies wrap the affected areas in cotton wool, which he had to use sparingly as supplies were low.

Only Matron appeared unfazed, summoning a group of off-duty nurses to the sitting room on the 22nd and handing them brown paper parcels inscribed 'To a New Zealand Nurse', compliments of lady volunteers at the Wellington City Council.

Addie poked her package. 'Something feels interesting.'

'We need combs,' said Netta. 'They ask for them as soon as they come out of the anaesthetic. I had to tell a young lad last night, before I removed his bandages, that his hands were gone. He asked me to part his hair with a comb his mother had given him. When I'd finished we both bawled our eyes out.'

Addie had already opened her family's presents and given the cakes of soap and tins of honey to her patients. Her mother had also enclosed a photograph of a neighbour's nephew who lived in Winton: 'A fine young man with a condition unlikely to pose a problem for a trained nurse but serious enough to prevent him fighting in this ghastly war. Would you consider writing to him?'

She made the mistake of showing his photo to Meg when she popped in to see her in the ward.

'We could raffle him,' said Meg. Before Addie could stop her, Meg had pinned the photo to the wall of the marquee. 'Any bids, boys? Surely he would suit a sister or a cousin.'

A convalescent had tossed a couple of darts, one of which landed left of a weak jawbone while the other quivered on the tip of a beaky nose. Addie had given the dart-thrower a withering glare and rescued the photograph. Throughout the day, she'd picked at it furtively, and on the way back to quarters, tossed the tiny pieces into an unruly evening breeze.

***

EITHER HER PARENTS had forgotten to send her a gift or Ma was ill again. Aunt Maude and Uncle Bert had given her an embroidered silk housecoat, a food hamper and Christmas decorations, lanterns and tinsel, which she'd hung in the ward. After the patients fell asleep, she filled their Christmas pillowcases with tins of sardines, chocolate and oranges.

Pa preferred useful presents. Like the tractor seat cover she'd knitted him as a kid and a mug she'd painted with yellow daises. One Christmas he'd pinned a card she'd decorated with pictures of horses cut from a catalogue to his stable wall. This year she'd posted him a tiny gold statue of a stallion, a tea tray to her mother, a pretty shawl to her aunt and a painting of camels to her uncle. She'd bought a silk cravat for Wallace, a diary bound in black morocco for Addie, a flowerpot for

Netta, and chocolates to give Dora and Iris when they returned from transport duties. In case no one gave her a present, she'd wrapped up a beaded purse for herself.

On Christmas morning Meg was helping Dora stack the breakfast dishes when Wallace arrived, draped in her red cape and sporting clumps of cotton wool over his ears.

'Santa needs a helper, Sister. Want to volunteer?'

She took a strand of tinsel from the tree and wound it over her veil. 'Where do you want me?'

'Helping everyone open their festive pillowcases for now,' he said, a smile playing at the corners of his mouth. 'Come on, boys. Show us what you have.'

A boy pulled out a pair of silk bloomers and turned beetroot-red from his neck to his forehead.

'How did those get in there?' she said. 'Davies?'

'No idea, Sister.'

The patients were still larking about when Addie poked her head through the tent flap. Never one to miss an opportunity, Blue snatched the bloomers from the boy and held them above her head as if they were mistletoe. Desperate to escape his puckered lips, she tripped on a rumpled section of tarpaulin and fell into Edward Ramsay's arms. A string of catcalls alerted Matron, who burst through the tent flap and barked, 'Harrington, get back to your patients.' Checking her watch, she added, 'And why haven't you started dressing rounds, Dutton?'

Normally the rumble of a dressing trolley would dampen the boys' spirits but today no one complained. One hip case sang 'Hark the Herald Angels Sing' during the worst of his treatment. Meg admired people who put on a brave face.

MID-AFTERNOON, after a traditional Christmas lunch, Ahmad, their Egyptian kitchen worker, who enjoyed making treats for the convalescents, carried over a tray of dolma – grape leaves stuffed with rice, onions, tomatoes and parsley. Addie invited him to serve the patients. 'Big pleasure,' he beamed. A chest case gave him a cigar in exchange for two portions. Ahmad sniffed the tip appreciatively: 'A hundred blessings to you.'

At dusk, Addie lit a dozen candles and arranged them on saucers in the middle of a central table where they cast a pool of soft light over the nativity scene Iris had set up. For a moment Addie almost forgot where she was. Back home Mother would be in the kitchen and Erin and Father would be sneaking nuts and chocolates from fancy dishes in the front room. She gazed around the ward. On both sides, able-bodied convalescents sat beside bed-bound patients playing cards or filling in crosswords. Occasional laughter broke out but the mood was generally pensive. Thinking they might enjoy a tune, she put 'Smoke Clouds Set Me Yearning' on the gramophone, which made everyone overly sombre until Blue swapped it for a dance tune and encouraged those who could walk to set aside their sticks and flush out partners.

A Londoner from Netta's convalescent ward came up to Addie and before she could think of an excuse, she was in his arms, gliding across the tarpaulin. Although it was too noisy to catch every word, she heard him say he was an artist, which could be true, since she'd seen him with a drawing pad. His name was Hugh Phillips. It suited him. He had nicely shaped ears that lay flat against his head.

She had three more dances with him and one with Edward before choosing to sit out the next set. While she caught her breath, Wallace and Meg took to the floor and livened things up with a racy version of the Bunny Hug. Hugh was smoking not far away and Edward stayed close by too.

'Pretending she's a screen star is all very well,' said a nurse who hadn't been asked to dance, 'but the only way women get ahead is through hard work.'

'Isn't that what Meg's doing?' asked Addie.

'Our two blazing stars do seem compatible,' Edward said.

She was about to ask what he knew of Wallace's personal life when the bane of the ward banged his tin mug on the frame of his cot. His rage often peaked at dusk. She fetched a morphia tablet, which he knocked from her hand.

'Pills won't give me back my legs.'

'I'll make you a nice cup of tea,' she said.

'Make it two beers, Sister,' said Edward, who had pulled up a chair next to the man's cot.

When she returned with a bottle and two mugs, they were discussing artificial limbs.

'We can send you to London for fittings,' said Edward. 'You could be back on the dance floor in no time.'

The soldier shook his head. 'Smart girls won't give me a second glance.'

'Some value a generous heart, don't they, Sister Harrington?'

She agreed hesitantly, aware Hugh was listening.

Edward said, 'Would you like a shandy, Sister?'

'Or fresh air?' Hugh offered her his arm.

His eyes were the shade of glacial ice and they were staring directly at her. Although Edward's offer was tempting, she followed Hugh outside, thinking this was an ideal opportunity to pick up characteristics to bestow on the imaginary boyfriend she'd been thinking of fabricating to placate her parents. He needed to sound authentic: her mother was no slouch in the romance department.

A light breeze was blowing. As they walked the length of the compound, Hugh talked of the carnage he'd experienced and the trouble he'd had getting adequate art supplies to depict these images. 'The public need to see the human cost of war.'

'It can't be easy to find time to draw when you're with your regiment,' she said.

'I'm a better artist than a soldier.' He waved an imaginary brush in the air, then looked at her again. 'Your distinctive eyes make you stand out.'

His frankness surprised her and she turned away as if something in the distance had caught her attention.

He cleared his throat and moved closer to her. 'The boys refer to you as an angel.'

She lowered her eyes and said quietly, 'They say that about all of us.'

'I'm sure they favour you more.' Netta could be heard calling them for cocoa. As Addie went to leave, Hugh said, 'You have a fine set of bones.' Thank goodness she was taking them inside.

⁂

MORE SAND than usual coating her uniform and hair, Meg crept into the tent, relieved Addie was asleep, although she'd wanted to thank her again for her Christmas present, a gorgeous tangerine headscarf and a manicure set. Netta had surprised her with a pot of rouge. Wallace's gift was an ivory compact. 'So you can see what I see,' he'd said.

He'd arranged for her to assist him regularly. Early in the morning, they'd worked on a chap who'd arrived with a fractured limb which had been splinted with the slats of a Johnnie Walker whisky case and secured with baling twine. After helping Wallace to splint the leg properly, Davies had suspended it from a stout beam that ran three feet above the patient's bed. Just as he finished, there was a loud crack and the beam twisted and heaved like a consumptive trying to dislodge phlegm. Instinctively she hunched over the patient to steady his limb. Two, maybe three seconds later, a section of the beam glanced off her shoulder and sent her reeling backwards. The patient screamed as she dropped his leg. She caught her hip on the corner of a trolley as she went down and instruments clattered to the floor.

'Damn! Sister, are you all right?' Wallace rushed to her side.

'Sh-sh-she's unharmed, s-s-sir,' said Davies, helping her up. 'Right, S-S-Sister?'

'Absolutely.' She dusted herself off and resumed her position. Elsewhere in the ward, fracture patients were gazing intently at the beams above them.

The face of the patient they had been working on had turned deathly white and his fractured left limb rested at an awkward angle. As she reached over to straighten it, the tibia in his healthy right leg shot like a startled albino snake through the skin around his calf.

Wallace yelled at Davies to fetch a stretcher and a couple of sappers before turning to her. 'Sister, are you hurt?'

'No permanent damage. There might be a few bruises.'

'I'll see to them shortly. Can you help me take this chap to surgery first?'

Pain nipped at her shoulder as she eased the patient onto the stretcher Davies had brought in. 'What on earth caused the beam to snap?'

Wallace snorted. 'If enemy armies aren't attacking us the damned termites take over.'

In the privacy of the Red Cross room, he inspected her tender shoulder. In due course, he said, 'Everything's where it should be,' and kissed her for the third time. 'Better not lift anything heavy for a week or two. If you need someone to rub liniment into that bruised tissue, I'm your man.'

Her man was exactly what she wanted him to be, and hearing him confirm it made her feel warm and safe.

He placed a hand under her chin and tilted her face upwards until their eyes met. 'Meg, are you sure you feel all right?'

'There's nothing wrong that another kiss won't put right.'

He bailed her up against the closed door and undid the rest of the buttons on her uniform, skilfully exposing more than her shoulders.

Outside she could hear men running past – probably more sappers on their way to the fracture ward.

Wallace slid his hands up her neck and wound a strand of her hair around his finger. 'Shush,' he whispered in her ear. 'We'd better wait here until things quieten down.'

AT THE FAR END of the compound, two canvas tents served as the nurses' bath huts. A tap produced hot water worked by a geyser on a primus stove. Addie was second in line. She'd worked twenty hours straight, tending hundreds of walkers and who knows how many stretcher cases. Her hands throbbed from cutting off blood-caked uniforms. The pins she pulled from her hair stank of pus and blood. She put them in her dressing-gown pocket.

'All yours, Addie,' said Netta, leaving the bath tent with a towel wrapped turban-style around her head.

'Thanks. Sweet dreams.'

She dropped her gown on the wicker chair beside the tub and bent over to feel the water. It was lukewarm and a layer of scum floated on the surface. She scooped up the greasy film and flicked it onto the sandy floor, then climbed in. Other than a rumble of wheels in the distance, and a swirl of discontented wind, it was quiet. She eased herself back into the water, sliding down until it spilled over her concave stomach and protruding hipbones. Her skin was smooth, despite irregular applications of lanolin, though a bruise glistened on her left knee. Her legs were long and well formed. A good body, she thought. Even so, she couldn't imagine it pressed against Hugh.

Something grazed her buttocks. She shifted slightly and fished about until she found a sliver of soap the shape of a pea pod. Wringing out her flannel, she dripped the excess water over her breasts and blew softly on the rivulets that encircled her stiffening nipples. She ran the soap across them, felt a spark of heat. The light from the gas lamp next to the tub illuminated the canvas wall, revealing a rough texture and something else. She looked again. Something glinted back at her. Everything slowed, then magnified. A gasp became a thousand cries; a slight rustle, a lion's roar; a pair of feet scurrying across the sand, a marching army. She opened her mouth but panic choked her. She kept trying until one scream fell on top of another, then another.

Netta burst in, brandishing a flywhisk. 'Addie, what's wrong?'

By now, she was standing upright in the tub, clutching a towel to her bare body. 'Over there!'

'What? Where? I can't see a thing.'

She shook her fist at the wall. 'Someone was peeping.'

Meg dashed in. 'How ghastly, you poor thing. Netta, chuck me her dressing gown. Are you sure, Addie?'

'I'm not making it up. I saw an eye blink.'

'You weren't harmed?' said Meg. 'He didn't . . .?'

'No, but I feel sick.'

'I'm not surprised,' said Netta. 'We must report it. Last night I felt uneasy in here.'

Neidman, a ruddy-faced lieutenant, and Watkins, a top-rate runner until a hunk of shrapnel shattered his kneecap and turned him into a pen pusher, swept their torches across the sand.

Watkins waved his arm towards the bath tent. 'Who would do such a vile thing?'

'A filthy Gyppo,' said Neidman. 'Look.' He pointed to a section of the tent.

A shaft of light danced around the edge of a slit in the canvas, giving it a macabre, almost carnival appearance. Watkins stabbed the sand beneath it with the toe of his boot. The two men interviewed everyone in the compound, including the Egyptian water carrier, who at the time had been in the kitchen playing cards with a convalescent, and two nurses who also reported unsettling incidents – a section of the bath hut canvas that seemed prone to wind shifts, a headscarf found in the vicinity a week before.

The investigators decided an unknown native was responsible and recommended in their report that suitable males patrol the perimeters of the tent whenever the nurses carried out their ablutions. Matron crossed out 'males' and wrote 'females'. 'Since you haven't uncovered proof of native involvement you can't be sure it wasn't an insider.'

'The eye wasn't dark,' Addie repeated for the third time. She trembled despite the warm night.

'Noted,' said Watkins, 'but fear plays strange tricks.'

'Meaning?' Meg asked.

'Nothing,' said Watkins, fiddling with his lapels. 'Time you got back to your duties.'

Matron explained that *she* would instruct her nurses where they should go and when.

Addie's cot creaked as she tossed and turned. She didn't feel the terror she'd experienced when the *Marquette* sank, but she kept thinking about what would have happened if the beast had slashed the canvas. 'Take a morphia tablet,' Meg pleaded ten minutes later. 'Heaps of people do.'

'Not me.'

It was one thing to fret about the war dragging on but quite another to know that a man, maybe someone she knew, had deliberately used her nakedness to satisfy his debased and vile needs. Everyone was a suspect, apart from Wallace and Edward, and her regular orderlies, who were as decent as the day was long. What if she looked up from her dinner plate in the mess one evening and saw the same eyes staring at her from across the table? She had to stop thinking like this. It would do her no good. She wanted to light a candle and read, but Meg might wake up and complain. Shivering with frustration and anxiety, she wrapped herself in a blanket and lifted what remained of the tent flap. Beyond the glittery, starry darkness, circled planets that scientists believed couldn't support life. Beauty always had dark sides and courageous people concealed weaknesses. She mustn't let one nasty incident overwhelm her. Nothing would happen if she walked to the end of the row of tents and back.

She'd only gone a couple of yards when a shadow appeared. She jumped.

Edward raised his hands in the air and froze. 'Steady, Sister.' His voice was calm and soothing. 'You've had enough of a shock for one day.'

Edward wasn't wearing his glasses.

'Is there anything I can do to help?' he asked. 'Maybe keep you company for a while?'

'I keep imagining what might have happened.'

He handed her the mug of cocoa he held. 'I was light on milk and heavy on brandy. Drink up. It will do you more good than it will me.'

⁕

EARLY IN APRIL the papers were full of news from the Western Front where the Germans were renewing their assault north-west of Verdun and gaining ground over the French.

As planned, Meg met Wallace in the lab. He seemed out of sorts. 'What's wrong?'

He flicked the ash off his cigarette into a glass jar and stared at the growing mound.

'Please tell me.'

He gave a slight cough and hunched his back as if he was preparing to carry a heavy load. 'I've received orders to take two weeks' leave in England in a month or so.'

He couldn't go, not without her. She knocked against his hip playfully. 'A certain surgeon could say I needed urgent treatment in London.'

He adjusted his cap. 'If Matron got a whiff, she'd send you packing. We can't risk it.'

She pushed on, desperate now. 'We could go at slightly different times but make sure we overlap. Don't you want to go on the razzle with me?'

He tossed his cigarette butt into the jar where it flared briefly before fading into the ash. 'You're too damned attractive to let loose in Trafalgar Square. You'd stop the traffic.'

She masked her disappointment behind a cheery smile.

'We'll get another chance,' Wallace said. 'What do you want me to bring you back?'

She didn't want gifts, she wanted him. A bolt from the lock on the door dug through her uniform into her back but the pain was strangely comforting. Matron hadn't given her and Wallace as much as a sideways glance. If she wore a plain gold ring, they could stay in a hotel together, come and go as they pleased. 'What if . . .?'

'Don't doubt my love, Meg.'

Did he say love? 'I'll miss you,' she said.

As she walked away, feeling empty and uneasy, a memory flashed into her mind of a winter morning fifteen years ago when Ma had chucked her wedding band in the river while she, Meg, had hidden in scrub on the bank, terrified she'd be next. That afternoon Uncle Bert had taken them to his place, where Aunt Maude cared for Ma and her for weeks.

A lull in the fighting meant patient numbers fell to a trickle. Meg swung from boredom to crotchetiness and back. Just when she was getting mad again at Wallace for not finding a way to take to her to London, Matron handed her a list of names. 'Sister Dutton, now we've time on our hands, I want you to accompany these nurses to Aboukir.' They all knew about this elegant, roomy home, lent to the Red Cross so weary sisters could have some respite from the war. 'I want you to make sure everyone gets plenty of rest. When you come back we should know where we're going next.'

Wallace had organised it, Meg thought, so he could spend time with her before he skedaddled to England. 'I'll do my best, Matron.'

'It was worth you giving that peeping Tom an eyeful,' she said to Addie at dinner.

'I didn't *give* him anything,' Addie said indignantly.

'Sorry.' Trust her to say the wrong thing.

Addie put down her knife and fork.

'There's apple turnover for pudding,' Meg said. 'Your favourite.'

Addie dabbed her mouth with a napkin and stood up. 'Excuse me.'

'I'll come with you.'

'No, please stay here.'

That depraved creature had a lot to answer for. So did she, and her big mouth. She'd do anything to make Addie feel better. Even throttle the peeper with her bare hands.

They think it's a native. Ha! Let them. I got an eyeful so I'm happy. Beats life as a runner. A month before I copped it in the knee, I trod on a bloated belly. It burst open, covered me with muck. Give me a bare-breasted nurse any day. Some have knobs big enough to hang your cap on. Feasted for three nights before the skinny girlie screamed her head off. I deserved a treat after the Dardanelles. Piss-hard snaking up stony paths, bullets splattering around me, shrapnel bursting, howitzers barking. Bloody hell, even when I made a shelter with my trenching tool, I couldn't sleep, not with eighteen-pounders firing continuously on the hill behind me. The shells make a rapping, tearing noise, and then there's a tremendous thump. In the gully, Turkos, Fritz and Tommies lie puffed up like toadstools. Stretcher-bearers from all sides stagger among them, but you never know if they're above-board. Sometimes Fritz carries machine guns under his stretcher blankets. And the cunning buggers have mastered our bugle call. I once cut a pretender's throat with a knife I nabbed off a corpse, took his cigarettes too, and his playing cards. But my best mementos came from spying on those nurses. Closest I'll get to humping anyone. Our side's had it. The Maoris reckon the owl of death is flying over us.

Ten

'SO HE HANDS OVER his big house to the Red Cross and swans off,' Netta said from the back of their taxi. 'He must be wealthy then.'

Addie didn't care if the owner of Aboukir was mogul of the century as long as she got a few days without work or worry. She reached over and tapped Netta's handbag, which was in her lap. 'Don't forget generous.'

'We're allowed to use his tennis court and his yacht. There's even a houseboat,' said Meg, 'and donkeys.'

Netta swatted Meg's arm with a newspaper. 'You won't get me on a bum-biter.'

'It can't bite what you sit on,' Meg retorted.

The taxi dropped them at the station, where they waited on hard benches until their train steamed up, pulling five carriages. An elderly guard on the platform rang a big brass bell.

'Find our compartment, Netta,' Meg shouted. 'Jump on, Addie. Quick!'

Two sharp blasts of the engine whistle and a smoky haze obscured the waving crowd. As she sat down, Addie smoothed the wrinkles in her dress before realising that, once again, she was doing what her mother would do. A final whistle and the train rocked gently down the track.

A brown paper bag of sandwiches, which Meg lobbed at the netting baggage rack, fell short and landed on Netta's head, where it perched like a rooster until she shook it off.

Their laughter attracted the attention of an English-speaking conductor, who opened the door. 'Ladies, you have a problem?'

Netta told him they were transferring a nurse to a special hospital. 'You needn't worry. We can manage.'

He looked doubtful.

'Really,' Netta stressed.

The conductor sighed and returned to his duties.

Addie found her thoughts drifting but forced herself to listen to Meg telling a story about two upper-class English officers, both convalescents. One collected square-inch pieces of tin, the other paintings of young women riding side-saddle. Obsessions, she mused, took many forms. When she couldn't get her hands on a book, she read road signs, instructions, labels.

To shut out the glare from the sinking sun, she reached up and adjusted the leather strip securing the blind. Golden light floated over the landscape. Somewhere out there, boys were losing their sight or their limbs; others, their dreams or their lives. A week ago, Netta had nursed a violinist whose right arm was gone. He wouldn't have minded if it had been a leg, he said. Across from him, there'd been a mountain climber with two good hands but nothing below the knees.

'Addie,' Meg said, nudging her, 'are you thinking of the beastly peeper? I hope they catch him soon and string him up.'

At first Addie had harboured similar thoughts, but now she considered hanging too high a price to pay for misplaced curiosity or an unbalanced mind. 'I'm fine, really,' she said and smiled.

On the opposite seat, Netta opened a tin of candied orange peel and handed her a piece. The pungent tang burst unexpectedly onto her tongue.

The train finally crawled to a stop. As Addie pulled her holdall from the rack, the door opened and porters rushed up. The heat was stupefying. She'd never choose to live in this part of the world, so overcrowded and terribly noisy – and parts were filthy. She was grateful when Meg took her arm and propelled her through the crowd on the platform onto the street, where they hailed a gharry.

Their driver's bare feet were cracked like poorly kept leather. Halfway down the dusty road, Addie noticed a small boy urinating against the bole of a tree, aiming higher and higher with each flick of his hand. If he didn't pay attention he'd wet his own face. A bit further on, a holy man was calling believers to prayer. She drifted into a listless trance, and only came to life when an expansive cove came into view ringed by a rocky coastline. Running into the bay was a promontory with the remnants of a castle and perhaps a small fort. There'd been battles here between Nelson and Bonaparte's fleets but today the sparkling blue water was calm and empty. All that concerned her was an insect that had settled on her wrist.

Eventually they pulled into a driveway made from crushed shells and flanked by poinsettias in earthenware pots. The house was large and handsome, with shady balconies and grey-green palms running the length of a wide verandah. Flute music wafted through an open downstairs window. Someone drew back a curtain and retied it.

Meg was shoving her. 'Quick, Addie, grab your handbag. We're here.'

An elderly man in a white robe belted with a red tie and wearing a skull-hugging fez bowed to them. 'Aboukir welcomes you,' he said. 'My name is Hassan. Please be coming inside.' He clapped his hands and two boys appeared to retrieve their luggage while Iris paid the drivers.

Hassan said, 'Come, I be showing your rooms. Then you eat. We have excellent cooks. Please be enjoying afternoon tea. I recommend cake.' He patted his ample midriff.

Addie followed him through an ornately carved front door and along a passageway where orange-scented flowers in large pottery vases adorned two elegant sideboards. Gold-framed pictures hung on a far wall: boats on the Nile, desert camps, harem scenes. She stopped near the staircase to study a large oil painting of a market. At its centre were three Englishwomen on horseback dressed in waistcoats, high boots, white cloaks and loose-fitting trousers cinched with ornate belts from which sabres protruded. Their expressions ranged from haughty to bold to resolute. Copper-brown dragomen in braided jackets stood behind their fair-skinned charges.

From the landing Hassan gave a discreet cough. The others were already going into their rooms. Addie hurried up the stairs, thinking Englishwomen who rode into the desert with complete strangers had to be remarkably brave or terribly foolhardy. She was puzzling over their motives when Hassan broke her concentration. 'You like, yes?'

There was a hint of sandalwood in the room, which was spacious and elegantly furnished: a chest decorated with pieces of mother-of-pearl and ivory at the foot of the bed, matching side-tables, a wooden writing desk and a straight-backed chair under the window. The furnishings were mostly cream, although there was a large red armchair in one corner. Filmy net curtains surrounded the bed. 'It's lovely, very peaceful, thank you.' Hassan bowed and shut the door behind him. Addie ran her hand over the embroidered counterpane, wishing a similar touch could magically restore sanity to the world.

⋙

MEG POKED her mattress. It was softer than previous ones, and there was a large wardrobe, plus an oil lamp. She picked up a melon from a bowl. Using the small knife beside it, she cut off a slice and nibbled, juice trickling down her chin. She searched through her luggage for a handkerchief. Three blissful days

136

lay ahead and no bed bugs to spoil the nights. She'd lost count of the times she'd stuck her cot legs in saucers of kerosene or swathed her head in a towel to prevent Egypt's nasty pests taking up residence while she slept. Best of all, she had enough water to give her hair a decent shampoo and have a long bath. Afterwards she'd rub loads of lanolin into her skin. When Wallace arrived, he could take her on a moonlight picnic at the base of a pyramid. Everyone went sphinxing these days.

On the washstand, she laid out a brush and comb set and a lipstick she'd bought in Alexandria. Aunt Maude had introduced her to face-paint when she turned seventeen. 'Mind how you apply it. A light touch attracts the right kind of man. Any sign of one?' No one in Tuatapere interested her. 'Not yet,' she'd said. Aunt Maude had given her a hug. 'Mr Right will turn up.' Meg pressed Wallace's compact to her lips and kept it there until Addie knocked on the door and asked if she wanted to go for a walk.

'Give me a tick.'

She poured water from the jug on her dresser into a bowl and washed her face and under her arms, then she dabbed her nose and cheeks with a powder puff and put on her lipstick. Wallace admired women who made the most of their looks. He knew the names of all the female screen stars. Unlike the cheeky sapper who'd been chasing Dora before she went on transport duty, Wallace was refined. 'I'm brushing my hair,' she called to Addie. Each stroke took her deeper into a fantasy: Wallace asking Pa for her hand, dressing up in white silk and lace, dancing around the Tuatapere Town Hall, everyone, including Ma, envious.

THE AFTERNOON WIND was as strong as the salt-laden southerlies that flattened the macrocarpa on the back road to Orepuki. As Addie battled to stay upright she strayed into the path of a veiled woman balancing a water jug on her head. 'Forgive me. I wasn't watching where I was going.' The woman didn't acknowledge her apology. Addie supposed her husband had forbidden her to speak; Iris had mentioned that Egyptian men expected their wives to be subservient.

Lost in thought, Addie bumped into a donkey laden with baskets of the pink-skinned oranges she enjoyed as a treat.

'Anyone would think you were shickered,' Meg said as she steered her out of harm's way. 'According to Wallace, the better class of women wear white yashmaks.'

'You two spend a lot of time talking.' Addie's eyes were on a child teaching a dog to sit. 'Erin spent hours training her pets.'

'Did you hear about his latest miracle?'

Addie sighed slightly. 'No.'

'Remember that corporal with massive abdominal injuries? The day before we left, he was sitting up drinking fluids.'

Addie paused and looked intently at a basket of spice before saying ruefully, 'Some of us think you're the miracle worker, Meg, landing Captain Madison in less than two months. What did you promise him?'

Meg placed her hands on her hips. 'Addie! My personality is quite sufficient.'

Addie grinned. 'Don't forget your looks. No one wears our uniform with such flair.'

'Come with me to the bazaar. I want to buy dress fabric. Guess which colour Wallace thinks I would suit?'

'I have no idea.'

'Burnt orange.'

Addie gripped her handbag as a huddle of beggars circled her. 'A friend of Mother's believes men say whatever women want to hear during courtship. Six of her daughters married bounders.'

'Wallace isn't a slippery character.'

Addie took a deep breath. 'Does he mention a wife?'

'Not to me,' Meg snapped and walked off.

At least she'd placed a little doubt in Meg's mind. There wasn't much more she could do. These days, couples courted at breakneck speed or delayed things indefinitely. She and Hugh had fallen into the latter category: they had only been alone once since the night of the dance. Shortly after the peeper incident, when she was too nervous to return alone to her quarters, she'd allowed him to escort her. On the way, she'd tripped on a loose bootlace and he'd knelt down and fastened it for her, briefly resting his hand on her ankle. He was due to return to the front in two weeks.

Hurrying to catch up with Meg, she said, 'Did Wallace mention anything about Hugh?'

'Only that he intended publishing a book on war wounds. That badly burned fellow Wallace operated on a fortnight ago should be on the cover. Did you see him?' Addie shook her head. 'He looked dreadful. Wallace sat with him when things were quiet. Hugh sometimes kept him company. Not very talkative, is he?'

Addie thought for a moment. 'He is when he's interested in the topic.'

JERKING HER FINGER in the direction of a municipal building, Meg said, 'That gold trim must have cost a packet.' She thought of Aunt Maude dressing for a ball, choosing which sparkly necklace to wear, Uncle Bert fastening the clasp, his hands lingering on her shoulders. Meg wanted their kind of love.

'Mafeesh faloose,' she told a bead-seller who was rattling his tray at her. 'Wallace reckons no one will bother us if we say we've run out of money.' Addie sighed again, something Meg heard her do a lot lately. She needed cheering up. 'Dora and her sapper went to a fortune-teller who predicted they'd have eight children. We should go. I'll flag down a gharry.'

'What about your dress material?'

'Oh, it can wait.'

The driver explained that his aunt, an esteemed fortune-teller, had a stall near the bazaar. Heaps of soldiers visited her because she knew which of them would live. Her fame was spreading. At this time of day, though, there would be no queue.

The aunt, who had hooded eyes and a cavernous mouth, sat cross-legged on a brown leather stool at the back of a long narrow room, trickling grains of rice through her knobbly hands. A smoky aroma of paprika hung in the air. A flimsy curtain behind her fluttered unexpectedly as if stroked by a ghost and a young man appeared in the room. He had a lopsided shoulder, suggesting a deformity of the spine.

'Please, come forward,' he said to Addie.

'Go on,' Meg said. 'I don't mind if you're first.'

He waited for Addie to sit on the floor. 'I will translate,' he said. 'If you do as the wise one tells you, your life will be enriched one thousand times.'

The fortune-teller had a full-throated voice and words poured from her. Moving confidently between the two languages, the man presented her statements to Addie as though they were gifts.

'You are woman of quiet courage. You are not driven by greed.'

'Water is a constant pleasure. Not of late, too much came. Smoke was your saviour.'

No surprise there, thought Meg. Their rescue *was* in the newspapers.

'Reading is good but it does not give you all the answers.'

She got *that* right, Meg thought smugly.

'Do not marry in haste or you will fail to notice the compassionate one.'

Interesting. Who could he be?

'A long life is foretold. You will know much love.'

A painful cramp gripped Meg's left foot and she pressed her shoe into the dirt floor, disturbing a clutch of discarded snakeskins. Puffs of dust rose into the air.

Finally, the man said, 'You may rise.'

Addie got to her feet, bowed to the woman and placed three coins in a bowl. 'Thank you.'

Keen to hear she would also receive love, Meg stepped forward, but the woman spoke forcefully to the man, who said, 'She says you are not ready to listen.'

Meg whipped round, her eyes blazing. 'I don't believe in hocus-pocus anyway!'

'Insh'Allah,' said the man. 'If God wills.'

A shiny motorcycle rested on a stand outside the house at Aboukir. Two pairs of goggles dangled from the handlebar, yellow daisies peeped from a canvas side-bag and an army-issue towel covered the front seat. Hooked over the headlight was a leather helmet. Meg brought it up to her face. Yes, there was a faint trace of coconut. 'Race you down to the water, Addie.'

'It mightn't be a good idea to—'

Meg didn't want to listen to doubts: Wallace was waiting. She pulled up her skirt and ran down the narrow path.

He was on the deck of the houseboat, legs apart, hands clasped behind his back, staring across the water. Like a film star, she thought. 'Wallace!'

He glanced over his shoulder. 'Meg! By Jove, you look splendid.'

As she leapt onto the deck, he gathered her up and spun her around until neither of them could walk without staggering. They giggled like school kids – and kissed like them.

'You came on the motorcycle,' she said between breaths.

He made his thumbs and forefingers into circles and held them like goggles up to his eyes. 'I persuaded Hugh Phillips to join me. He knows a thing or two about engines.'

'Hugh's here. Good. He can amuse Addie. Did the ride mess up your hair? No. I suppose you can't ruin an army cut. Don't expect me to wear goggles when we go for a spin.'

He planted a kiss on her forehead. 'Slow down, MD, or you'll rupture something.'

Only my heart, she thought.

Their lips were almost touching when Hugh came out of the cabin.

'You struck it lucky with this place, Sister,' he said, indicating the bay with a sweep of his arm.

'No need for formalities here. Call me Meg.'

'We rode through town looking for you,' said Wallace. 'Where were you?'

'Oh, sightseeing.' She turned her head to look at Addie, who was dawdling down the path. 'Hurry, Hugh's waiting.' Some old crone didn't need to predict what she already knew. Her future stood beside her.

'HOW WAS your journey from Alex, Addie?' Hugh said.

She took his outstretched hand and stepped onto the house-boat. He had a firm grip. She tilted her head towards Wallace, who was a few feet away whispering to Meg. 'I doubt it was as fast as yours.'

Hugh smiled conspiratorially. 'Shall we go below?'

She nodded.

His fingertips rested for a brief moment on her back. 'Down we go then.'

As he guided her through the opening, she wondered what the touch had meant and whether she should have responded in some way, but these thoughts abated as she entered the cabin.

She admired the leather ottomans, a plush green sofa adorned with a silk shawl, several low tables and a piano, and walked over to a telescope. A bird wheeled through the air, perfect, she thought, until she adjusted the settings and noticed a single leg tucked against its torso. She couldn't think of anything to say, but if she didn't speak soon Hugh would think her an idiot. 'Good quality,' she said decisively, tapping the stand of the telescope.

'You don't mind my coming?'

She wondered if he was nervous because he kept fingering his neatly trimmed moustache.

'Not if you came freely.'

'Wallace is in charge of operating theatres, not soldier artists.'

'Yes, I suppose he is.'

Unsure what to say next, she flicked through a pile of maps and charts on top of the piano, then studied paintings of battle scenes on the walls and ended up angling her head at a shelf of books: Hardy, Wilde, Zola. 'It's a shame I won't have a chance to read them.'

'Reading isn't everything, remember?' Meg came through the door, Wallace's hands inches from her hips. 'Why don't you two take a sailboat out?' She glanced at Wallace and Hugh. 'Addie knows how to sail. Her father taught her.'

Addie could hear Hugh breathing steadily behind her. 'Well,' she said, hesitantly, 'should we?'

'I'll bring my sketchpad.'

The mainsail flapped, half-filled, slackened again. She steadied the tiller and adjusted her course to make the most of the slight breeze. Waterfowl preened on the bank and light-brown seabirds fed on insects that skimmed across the surface of the water.

'You do know your way around a yacht,' said Hugh admiringly.

'Father taught Erin, my sister, and me to sail on Lake Hayes.'

'Where's that?'

'Oh, not far from Queenstown, a place where we holiday at home.' She smiled at him.

He gave her a friendly nod. 'Can't be easy for him knowing the conditions you work under.' He leant over and plucked a leaf from the water. 'Nice shape,' he said, holding it up to the sun.

Addie gripped the tiller more firmly. 'He wants me home but I can't go. There's so much to do here.'

'I'll visit your ward when we get back.'

'What for?' She noted that he hadn't sought her permission.

He held up his pencil. 'To draw soldiers who've lost limbs or suffered burns.'

'Some boys mightn't want you there,' she said cautiously. 'You could upset them.'

Hugh tossed the leaf back into the water. 'The public deserve to know the truth.'

She thought of the sanitised photographs in newspapers. He could be right. 'Don't let Matron catch you.'

'I'll do a preliminary drawing of you now.'

Realising nothing would deter him, she said, 'You'd better be quick,' and set a course back to shore.

***

AS SHE RAN HER HAND across the velvety fabric of the sofa Meg thought it felt a bit like warm skin. Wallace was sitting beside her, his long legs crossed. 'Tell me about the ride down,' she said, looking at him, head on one side. 'How fast did you go?'

He sat forward. 'Come for a ride with me tomorrow. See for yourself.'

She held up her hands in mock horror. 'What will I wear? Oh no, don't tell me!'

They laughed and moved closer. Between kisses he said, 'You look wonderful to me no matter what you wear.' He slipped a hand down the front of her dress and pressed his lips to her neck. The tip of his tongue flicked the lobe of her ear.

'Did you miss me?'

He arched his eyebrows. 'Why do you think I'm here?'

She gazed up at him. 'What if we . . . you know . . . then you transfer to another hospital?'

'I'll say you're the best nursing sister in Egypt and I need you to come too. Meet me tonight. Come alone.'

'Do you really think I'm the best?'

'I think about you all the time.'

Back in her room at Aboukir, Meg stood in front of the mirror and rubbed lanolin across her shoulders. She slipped on her best frillies, the ones with lace panels up both sides. They felt sleek and stylish. Next, she applied perfume behind her ears and in the crook of her elbows, where the skin was baby-soft. Her new dress, bought after she and Addie saw the fortune-teller, showed off her hourglass figure. She picked up her lipstick and applied it generously, then smacked her lips together and put on a second coat. The house was quiet. The others had gone to bed, their bellies full of yellow pilaf and cream tarts. After listing her usual concerns, Addie had promised to cover for her. He was a surgeon, for goodness' sake. No one was more honourable.

The moon hung like an ivory disc in the dusky sky. The scent of a lily caught in her throat. She halted briefly as something stirred in the foliage, but even a viper couldn't stop her. She came through a clearing and stepped onto the path that led to the mooring. He was standing on the deck gazing at the sky. The water barely slapped against the prow as she stepped quietly onto the vessel, then crept up behind him and slipped her arms around his chest.

He turned to face her. 'I thought you'd run off with a colonel.'

'I couldn't get away. The girls wanted to talk.'

'Well you're here now.'

He took her in his arms and said her name slowly as if etching it into his skin.

She said, 'Wallace, it might not be . . .'

'I think about you every minute of every day, Meg.' He took her hand. 'Come through to the cabin. You'll be warmer there.'

Inside the cabin, she looked into his eyes while he traced the shape of her body with his hands. She felt his mouth on her breast as she stepped out of her clothes. She trembled with excitement as he led her to the sofa.

'Leave is an entitlement,' Evelyn writes to me. 'You're owed two weeks, Wallace. Take them or else.' As usual, her timing is impeccable. Just when it's the last thing I want, the ice queen, with her instinct for knowing the unknowable, orders me home to escort her to a rally. No longer content to give them money, she wants to join the radical suffragettes. 'Power is everything,' she told me the day we met. I should have made a dash for it then but, as always, her social status trapped me as laudanum snares an addict. When we were courting I fabricated a past – parents killed in an accident two months after my birth, raised by an aunt who squandered my inheritance, a man of lofty principles who became a surgeon thanks to a scholarship and burning ambition. To please her, I cultivate the illusion that I favour women holding public positions. But my father was a scrap merchant, and my mother an alcoholic who once traded my ten-year-old body to her deviant brother for a bottle of gin. Evelyn doesn't love me. With Meg, I have a chance.

Eleven

THREE WEEKS after she returned from Aboukir, Addie was sitting on a bench in the hotel garden studying Hugh's latest sketch, dated and signed, of metal-grey skulls with minuscule razor nicks of white. He couldn't have witnessed the deaths but he may have come across an old battle site or – she could hardly bear to think it – a group of civilians killed some time ago by an advancing regiment. Their farewell had been awkward; she hadn't known what to say and he couldn't decide where to put his lips. In the end, he'd kissed her hastily on the cheek and climbed into the truck. He was gone before she realised that she'd forgotten to give him the box of pastels she'd bought to ease his return to army life. It would have to follow him by post.

In the distance, someone was calling her name. She got to her feet as Netta came into view. 'Take your time,' she called. 'I'm not going anywhere.'

'Yes, you are,' said Netta. 'We're to take over the auxiliary hospital at Pont de Koubbeh in Cairo. They have a high rate of sickness. Iris and Dora are joining us. They got back today.'

'That's good news. I've missed them.' Addie rolled up Hugh's sketch.

Netta tapped the tubular shape in Addie's hand. 'Is that from your chap?'

'He's just a friend,' she said, more sharply than she'd intended. To discourage more questions, she returned to the bench and picked up the rest of her mail. Netta followed behind her.

'Friends don't send parcels as often as he does.'

Addie flicked an insect off her arm. 'He hasn't any family.'

'Then you can't blame him for wanting to start one of his own.'

'I'd never give up nursing,' she said with conviction.

'You have to if you marry. It's regulations.'

Addie wound a length of string around the sketch and knotted it securely. 'Netta, you tell Iris and Dora the news. I'll find Meg.'

She never wanted to be at sixes and sevens over Hugh, as Meg was with Wallace. In Hugh's drawing of them at Aboukir, there were charcoal blobs where Meg's eyes should have been, as though she was sightless. Standing behind, slightly to her left, Wallace was barely visible among the foliage of a plane tree. Hugh called the drawing 'Camouflage'.

Iris and Dora entertained them with hair-raising transport tales as they travelled to the new camp in open lorries along dusty, heavily potholed roads. The drivers had to stop regularly to fill the radiators with water, making them hiss like steam engines. Seated on a wooden bench in the back of the vehicle, Addie was sipping bitter chlorinated water from her canteen to counteract the heat and wondering if Hugh had taken to trench life more easily the second time, when suddenly the lorry lurched to one side and she tumbled to the floor.

'This vehicle is a disgrace. I'm sure it transported coal before us,' said Iris as she helped Addie off the lorry and onto the ground. 'Don't be surprised if we get chest complaints.'

'Anything's possible,' said Addie, wiping her hands on her handkerchief as the remaining nurses climbed down so the driver could change the rear left tyre.

Dora scratched her nose, leaving a smudge of coal dust on the tip. 'Why are you so quiet, Meg? Aren't you feeling well?'

Meg made a face. 'We're either on a ship, a train or a lorry. Since leaving Wellington I'm sure we've covered more miles than there are grains of sand in this dull-as-ditch-water desert.'

No one spoke until Dora said quietly, 'We have to go where the war takes us.'

In the midst of wiping dust off her boots with a rag, Iris added, 'And our hardships are nothing compared with what our boys go through.'

'I didn't say they were!' Meg protested.

Sometimes Iris got on Addie's wick too. Staying abreast of nursing developments was admirable, but acting high and mighty because she'd been on transport duty was another matter altogether.

'Can't you work faster?' Meg jabbed the driver's puncture kit with her toe.

'Keep your hair on, Sister. The war won't end today. If anything, it's heating up.'

A sign on an arch fixed to two pillars welcomed them to Pont de Koubbeh. To her relief, Addie could see a sizeable stone building with deep verandahs overlooking a large quadrangle covered in marquees. The place had an organised appearance, which generally meant adequate staff and proper equipment, along with nourishing food for the patients. An hour later she found Meg in their quarters thumping a mattress. 'What's bothering you?'

'Knots,' Meg said, landing another blow.

Wallace being on leave, Addie thought, pulling a letter from her pocket that she'd collected from a post tent next to the hospital. 'Hugh managed to get this one past the censor en route to his new posting.' She waved the letter in the air. 'It's full of rumours he's heard about a terrible new gas that's destroying our boys in France.'

Meg flopped onto her battered lump of kapok and clasped her hands behind her head. 'Go on, if you must.'

Addie began to read about men turning blue in the face, struggling for breath, drowning in the fluid rising higher and higher in their lungs. Her voice cracked but she read on, stopping when she saw Hugh's next words: *They must be terrified, Addie. I could be over there soon. Say a prayer for me.*

'Complete madness!' Meg pulled the pillow from behind her head and gave it a violent shake. 'Wallace should tell Haig and his cronies to roll up their war maps.'

Addie repressed a groan. 'Nothing will change until British women get the vote, like us.'

'Men detest girls who wear their brains on their sleeves. Reserve that spot for your heart, Addie.' Meg tapped a finger against the side of her head. 'And keep quiet about your blue-stocking views or you'll end up a spinster. What else does Hugh say?'

Addie hadn't considered herself a bluestocking, but perhaps she was. She ran her eyes over Hugh's letter again, skipping the paragraphs about books and art. 'He also met a chap who'd conducted an experiment at a clearing station south of Ypres. Apparently he got a volunteer to cover a pad with butter muslin that had been soaked in lime and then hold it over his mouth and nose during a gas attack.'

'That wouldn't offer much protection.'

'Well, he had to inhale ammonia fumes to regulate his breathing when he came in but the chap in charge thought the mask worked well enough. Now they're making thousands of them.'

Meg sat up. 'A change of wind could send the gas all over the show and harm civilians too. Wallace would be furious if that happened.' She gazed into space for a moment. 'I haven't heard from him. What do you think is going on, Addie?'

Addie slipped Hugh's letter into the envelope and dropped it into her holdall. 'You're best to ask Wallace when he gets back. I'm ready for bed.'

Like Hugh, she was determined to make the most of her life once the army had finished with her. A refreshing candidness had begun to permeate their letters and she'd agreed to visit England after the war. They'd see how things developed.

WHEN AN OUTBREAK of meningitis hit the camp, Meg took charge of the isolation hut. Aspirin was ineffective for the terrible headaches and soaring temperatures, and only surgical cases got morphia. There was nothing in between. She went down one side of the ward and up the other, checking the condition of each patient. Foam bubbled from a fellow's nostrils. 'Don't let me die, Sister!'

'I won't,' she replied, placing a damp cloth on his forehead. And she would do everything in her power to save him, work day and night if necessary, as Wallace would have done if he were here.

She'd met him every night at Aboukir. While her pals rested and wrote letters home, she and Wallace had escaped on his motorcycle, careering along dirt tracks until they found a deserted cove where they made love on a rug he kept in his saddlebag. Their first night on the boat had been tender, their nights under the stars wild and passionate. They'd come to know each other's bodies as well as they did their own.

The meningitis cases usually arrived howling in pain and she could do little to ease their misery. The chap she'd promised to save died in agony. As soon as Blue stretchered him out, Davies wheeled in a replacement. It carried on like this for weeks.

Everyone was exhausted when the crisis finally ended, a situation not lost on the CO, who called a special meeting. 'Half of you take next week off and the rest the following one. Blue, Davies, help Ramsay escort the first group to Luxor.'

As arranged, Meg met members of her party for afternoon tea in the garden of their hotel on the east bank of the Nile, an eye-catching spot that would have been a darned sight better if Wallace were present.

Iris handed her a pamphlet. 'I've booked everyone on this tour, Meg.'

Maybe a doddery old attendant at Wallace's club had forgotten to post his letters. She should stop worrying. 'Let me see.'

Iris drummed her fleshy fingers on the table. 'Make it quick.' She tapped them again. 'Girls, remember to make detailed notes. They'll come in handy when you write a letter to Miss Maclean for *Kai Tiaki*.'

'I will,' said Dora sweetly. 'Does the fare include afternoon tea?'

Iris said, 'No, but a three-course dinner is planned for tonight.'

'Listen to this,' Meg said. 'Philae is the burial place of Osiris, a god slain and dismembered by Typhon, then resuscitated by his singing sisters.' She looked at Addie. 'What do you think?'

'There are plans to submerge the island,' Addie replied. 'We could be the last to see it.'

'Wars should vanish, not islands,' Meg said.

'Your surgeon has done a vanishing act, if you ask me.' Iris snatched the pamphlet back and put it in her handbag.

'I didn't!' Meg reached over and pulled a hairclip from Iris's prim bun.

'Get your hands off me!' Iris screeched. 'I've a good mind to report you.'

'I vote for a picnic,' Edward said. 'Who wants to help me organise one?'

Meg stood up and threw the hairclip back at Iris. 'Do whatever you want.'

She sprinted down a path that took her deep into the lush hotel gardens, repeating under her breath, 'Iris is jealous, nothing is wrong', until she almost believed it.

AS THE FELUCCA glided down the slow-flowing Nile, Addie thought of the women who lived in the small villages ringed by clusters of carob trees on the riverbank. Did any of them hanker after a different life? In the distance, purple mountains appeared as reflections in the pewter-grey water, reminding her of the schist outcrops of Central Otago. Her parents and Erin would holiday there without her this year.

The guide, who had an excellent command of English, directed his rowers to the southern end of a dilapidated mooring where they secured the felucca. Following his instructions, she left the boat, climbed a steep bank and entered an irregular-shaped courtyard that led to the temple.

'Who built these?' Edward asked, running his hand across a honeycombed colonnade.

The guide stroked his long black beard. 'Coptic villagers from early Christian times, but the Ptolemies were here before them.'

'So this small island has a long history,' said Edward.

The guide nodded. 'Yet it is destined to disappear.'

'The pens of ill-informed men often change the course of history,' said Edward.

Addie hadn't realised they shared similar views on such matters. It was on the tip of her tongue to say society in general would improve when women the world over got the vote, but she remembered Meg's warning about bluestockings and stayed quiet.

Halfway through the guide's next history lesson Meg meandered off. Although she would have preferred to stay and listen so she could talk intelligently about the island to Edward at dinner, Addie felt obliged to follow.

The ceiling in the next room was decorated with coralline pink and soft green paintings of lotuses.

'Beautiful,' Addie said, gazing up from the doorway.

Meg stared at the flowers for some time. 'Tell Hugh his drawings need colour.'

'You tell him!'

At dinner that evening, Addie sat beside Edward. The waiter poured them each a glass of wine, then a second. Edward turned out to be quite a raconteur and she enjoyed his self-deprecating sense of humour. Davies got a spark up as well, declaring Egypt more a memorial to the past than a country for the living. 'Do you agree, Dora?' Addie asked, her voice wobbling slightly.

'Well, it does have lots of tombs,' Dora said as she piled bite-sized pieces of meat covered in plum sauce on her plate. 'Apparently American visitors like to photograph them.'

It was odd, Addie thought, that the Americans hadn't yet entered the war, despite complaints from their businessmen of increasingly perilous transatlantic shipping routes. Their women had been quicker off the mark. Newspapers sometimes carried stories about Red Cross nurses from New York and Chicago working in French hospitals, and one enterprising female reporter had motored to the Western Front in a fur coat and jewels and wired her report back to the *Washington Post*. American socialites also took trips to the battlefields so they could give talks about their experiences. Addie wanted to discuss this peculiar form of tourism with Edward but he was laughing at something Meg had said.

BACK AT CAMP, the oppressive khamsin, a hot tormenting wind, joined forces with a heat wave, causing severe sandstorms. In the middle of the night, Dora rushed into Meg and Addie's more substantial tent, clutching a sheet. 'My tent pegs have been tugged clean out. Could I bunk down with you until morning?'

Meg made her a temporary bed on the floor.

'Thanks,' said Dora. 'I'll be glad when this wretched wind stops. I can't get the sand out of my hair, or my teeth.'

Meg handed her a pillow without speaking.

During the worst of the hot winds, the temperature reached 116 degrees in the shade. Meg instructed her orderlies to dip their thermometers in cool water and check the readings before using them on patients.

Although she had plenty of work to do, her mind steamed like a copper on washday. Jealous thoughts merged with disturbing images: Wallace in a club, at the theatre, dining out, smiling at women on the street – and making love to a wife. She wheeled her trolley into the storeroom and took a furtive swig from a bottle of medicinal brandy, swirling the fiery liquid around her mouth. He'd made an odd comment before he left: 'You deserve a less complicated man, Meg.' Was he married, as Addie suspected, or was he referring to another snag, one she could help him overcome? Had she been foolish to give herself to him?

He occupied her mind from the time she got up until she went to sleep, and then he populated her dreams. In last night's, she'd travelled through bombed countryside, then reached a building that was a cross between a church and a hunting lodge. She'd pushed open the large wooden door. Across the vestibule, down five steps, on a sturdy platform, lay an open coffin. When she walked over and peered in, there was Wallace floating in clear, bubbling liquid. She remembered screaming and him opening his arms and indicating that she should join him. When she woke, she described the dream to Addie, who said, 'Obviously stewing in his own juices.' But Meg had thought he was in danger and that only she could save him.

A rat was gnawing at the wire cage she baited to keep the numbers down in the ward, where the rodents came for splatters of blood on the floor. Davies removed the creature while she attended to a fellow with rabies who was particularly restless this morning. When Davies returned, she got him to help her

156

bed-sponge the patient, thinking cool water might settle him. They'd just started on his chest when he drenched them in watery mucus and saliva. Because they both had scratches on their arms from restraining a head case, Wallace's replacement believed they were in danger of contagion and sent them to the CO, who said, 'No amount of washing in carbolic will remove the threat. You need treatment at the Pasteur Centre in Cairo.'

She'd thought you could only contract rabies through a bite. When she asked the CO if he was sure of his facts he turned puce and she thought his heart was going to give out. Once he recovered, he ordered her and Davies to pack while he organised a lorry and a driver. What rotten luck. Wallace was due back tomorrow. She'd have to leave a note for him with Addie, saying what she lacked the courage to say to his face. If he knew she loved him, he might give her a sapphire engagement ring to match her eyes.

❧

NOW STATIONED somewhere in France, Hugh was writing Addie longer and more intimate letters. She collected another pile from the mail tent, opening the top one as she walked back to quarters. Whatever he'd written on the last page had upset the censor because there were more black lines than words. Something about a battle he'd come through, judging by the few still visible. Whole rows, heads, legs, arms, yards of mud. Last night she'd wept when a stretcher-bearer told her of finding a dead young Tommy in the arms of a dead German. 'We had to prise them apart with our rifle butts.' Only last month, Father had written to tell her that the families of eleven of the seventeen boys in her Standard Four class had been informed of their sons' deaths.

Yesterday Edward had shown her a letter from his cousin in London, a friend of Edith and Osbert Sitwell, who'd enclosed a copy of Rupert Brooke's poem, 'Peace'. When she'd quoted the line 'And the worst friend and enemy is but Death' to Meg, she'd said, 'You could say the same of love.' Addie had replied, 'I don't know much about that sort of thing.'

'You're not supposed to *know*,' Meg answered, 'you're supposed to *feel*.'

WHEN MEG RETURNED to camp, Wallace came to the nurses' sitting room on the pretext that he needed her to go with him to the moribund ward. Iris, who'd been about to hive off to the mail tent, sat down again, while Netta muttered something about watering plants and hightailed it through the door.

'We should get going, Sister Dutton,' Wallace said, giving her a sheepish smile.

Did he expect her to pick up where they'd left off without telling her why he hadn't written? If they could talk in private, she'd drag the answer out of him, but that wasn't going to happen, judging from the determined set of his jaw. Meg flung her cape over her shoulders and stamped out.

As they walked through camp, people kept stopping Wallace to ask his advice. She wanted to tell them he had a bigger problem of his own to deal with. An hour passed before he whispered, 'Sorry, Meg. You deserve better.'

'I agree,' she said and stormed off alone.

That evening she persuaded Addie to dine with her under the stars so she wouldn't do her block when she saw Wallace in the mess. If he wanted her back, he would jolly well have to do more than tell her she was too good for him.

The following day he came unexpectedly to her ward. Finding a kitchen worker handing out fruit to the patients, he grabbed the startled chap by the scruff of the neck and manhandled him outside. Then he grumped at Blue for failing to dispose of fouled linen fast enough.

'He's all yours, Sister Dutton,' Blue said as he grabbed a pile of towels and scarpered.

While Wallace conducted a medical round, she sneaked quick looks at him. His hair was untidy and beads of perspiration dotted his forehead. He walked as if he had stiff joints.

'Are you unwell?' she asked after he finished and was nearing the tent flap.

'I'm fine,' he replied brusquely.

She thought he was going to walk off without saying another word but he turned and whispered in a silken tone, 'Better now you're back. Meet me after dark in the pumphouse.'

He'd combed his hair and changed his jacket but she could smell alcohol on his breath.

'Wallace, you seem . . . different . . . not yourself.'

'Did those injections hurt you, my beautiful girl?'

He came closer, stopping just short of touching her. His eyes were dark and mournful. Her anger fell away. 'Wallace . . .'

'Let me look at your tummy. I want to make sure you have no blemishes.' He pulled a blanket from his kitbag. 'Here, lie on this.'

He barely glanced at her as she took off her uniform, and brushed aside her hand when she attempted to pull his head towards hers. Then, without speaking, he directed the torchlight methodically over her body. Although she was no longer contagious, he wasn't interested in making love. Had she done something wrong the last time they were intimate? Desperate for him to be fully hers again, she said, 'Did you miss me while you were in London?'

He shifted the torchlight from her thighs to her face. It was impossible to tell what he was thinking because she couldn't see his expression. He ignored her question. She tried again, this time in a joking tone. 'Not even a little?'

The light in his hand wavered. 'I caught a play one night. The lead actress wasn't a patch on you.'

159

Her next question went through him like air. Had he gone mad in a different way to her mother, Lois, her debility cases? Minutes ticked by. Neither of them spoke. Finally, she said, 'What was the play about?'

He dropped his head. 'It's cold, and late. We can't stay here.'

She gathered up her clothes. 'Wallace, tell me what's wrong. Please.'

'Don't waste your time on me.'

He left her to dress alone.

THREE MONTHS passed before Addie and the others received instructions to pack again. This time the unit was heading for Southampton, then France. She put Hugh's drawings and letters, and her books, at the bottom of her suitcase, followed by her clothes and diary. If she died and Matron shipped her belongings home, Mother was sure to go through everything. She considered throwing her diary overboard, or at least wrapping it in brown paper and writing a fictitious name and address on the cover, but that would mean repeating the exercise every time she wanted to write in it.

She solved her dilemma on June the 1st while rattling along in a fast goods train that was transporting perishables. 'Notes for a Novel, 1916', she wrote on the diary cover.

Meg shook a thermos in front of her. 'Want a drink?'

'What?'

'I asked if you wanted a drink.'

'No thanks.'

Meg poured her one anyway.

'What's up?' Addie said.

'Wallace is acting oddly. Whenever we're alone, he goes out of his way to pick a fight. Anyone would think he wants to drive me away. Then just when I make up my mind to ditch him, he looks at me with such longing that I doubt my decision and we're back squabbling again.' She tightened the top of her thermos. 'I worry he'll transfer permanently to a British hospital. He *is* one of them, after all. We have no claim on him.'

You have no claim, Addie thought. 'I'm sure he wants to stay with our unit.'

In Alexandria, on board the *Dover Castle*, the dinner bell rang while Addie was stowing her luggage. When she reached the saloon, Edward directed her to his end of the table, where he'd kept her a place.

'Beats camp fare,' said Iris, who was sitting opposite. She held up a chicken leg.

'There's custard for afters,' Dora said. 'Real eggs, full milk – heavenly.'

'Sherry, Sister Harrington?' asked a steward who had cheeks mottled like windfall apples.

Her grandmother had taken a medicinal port every night of her adult life, holding the first sip in her mouth for a full minute, swirling around the second for pure pleasure, and giving herself fully to the sleep-inducing third. Addie held out her glass.

The ship dropped anchor at Gibraltar to take on supplies. There was no time to go ashore, so Addie had to take in the sights from the deck with Meg and Iris. 'I couldn't imagine living here.'

'Great convict settlement,' Iris said. 'No one could escape unless they had a boat.'

'It looks more like a holiday spot to me,' said Meg. 'I wish we were back at Aboukir.'

Iris harrumphed and moved off.

Meg tapped Addie on the arm. 'Have you noticed anything different about Wallace?'

'Well, he virtually emptied a decanter of port single-handed last night.'

'I can't make him out. He blows hot and cold.'

'Do you know why? Has he said anything?'

'All he does is talk. Not about anything important, though.' She jammed her hands in her pockets. 'I'm going to bed.'

'I won't be far behind you,' Addie said. 'I just want to see the rock light up first.' It would be something to tell Hugh in her next letter.

At dusk, the ship steamed off. Once the lights faded from view, she headed towards her companionway. Halfway there, she spotted Wallace partially hidden behind a bulkhead, staring out to sea, head bowed, shoulders quivering. She veered away before he noticed her. Everyone she knew struggled with doubts and fears. She wondered what Hugh was going through.

I draw what I see: blackened tree stumps splattered with human tissue, fragments of bones protruding from red-crusted earth. Some men get a taste for killing. You can see it in their eyes. They won't stop when the final whistle blows. The rest of us struggle to contain our disgust. It's one thing to feel windy, but to shirk the job is unmanly. They shoot chaps for cowardice. We're doomed either way. A generation can't die without the worm turning. It turned in me the day a fool of an officer ordered us over the top during heavy artillery fire. Thirty seconds later, shrapnel killed three of my friends. I avoided forming close attachments after that, so I was surprised to find myself walking out with a certain sister, both of us awkward, unlike the surgeon and the siren. Not sure if I'm falling for Addie. Affection in wartime can easily be mistaken for some other emotion.

FRANCE,
1916–1918

Twelve

A REGIMENT of fresh-faced soldiers poured down the gang-plank at Le Havre, talking excitedly. Their banter dropped to a steady hum as they spilled onto the quayside and stood alongside recently unloaded cases of ammunition. Although Meg admired their eagerness, she couldn't cheer them on. So many of them would be dead by the end of the month, and the same fate awaited German lads. Before long, no country would have enough men to father the next generation.

The rest of her chums were in the sitting room having after-noon tea, and only she was topside with Matron to watch this latest batch of boys line up like school kids ready to take to a rugby field for a friendly game. You'd have thought they were overly confident, judging by the amount of tomfoolery going on, but every now and then one would glance over his shoulder towards the ocean as if weighing up his chances of seeing his family again.

'When do we disembark, Matron?'

'Noon tomorrow, once the paperwork has been completed. They want us to make our way to a makeshift hospital near the wharf. Expect to find the wards in a dreadful state. I was told twenty thousand men went through in the last nine days.'

'Shouldn't we go straight away?'

'We have our orders,' Matron said.

Although Meg wanted to remind her that soldiers could die in an instant, that children became orphans overnight, that life knocked you down as often as it raised you up, she kept quiet. Matron had earned her respect. Not just because of her war record, which would impress anyone, but because she believed the woman beside her had been through worse than the fires of Belgium. More than once, she'd glimpsed heartache in Matron's eyes. Another reason to think before she spoke, she decided, and waited in silence for her frustration to ease.

WHEN THE CO finally permitted Matron to escort her unit ashore, Addie joined a queue inside the port office to have her photograph taken for a special passport. Tacked to the walls were notices in French that she was unable to read. Since the queue was moving slowly, she studied the layout of the room, and by the time Meg and Netta had caught up with her she'd memorised the entire contents of the counter.

'Is he a decent photographer?' Meg asked when she arrived, loosening her hairpins and rearranging her hair.

'He better be. I don't want poppy eyes,' said Netta.

Addie laughed. 'Try turning your head slightly to the side.'

Every five years Mother insisted on a Harrington family portrait, which usually entailed endless fussing at home and excruciating hours in a studio. Her father loathed it. He tried every trick in the book to put the event off yet he proudly hung the portraits in the hallway of the family home. Another was due this year, but in a recent letter he'd said that they'd decided to postpone the deed until she was safely home.

Once the army photographer was satisfied, she walked with her friends along a cobbled street to the hospital. Her first impressions of France were an improvement on Egypt. There were proper pavements for a start, less rubbish in the gutters, and the buildings along the waterfront were sturdier and better kept. People on the streets were more like her in appearance and demeanour. Learning their language might test her, but as long as she picked up important medical terms, she should manage. Meg was already saying 'Bonjour' to every person she met. The daytime temperature was cool, verging on chilly. Addie fastened the top button of her cloak.

The pitiful state of the patients and their filthy surroundings made it difficult to know where to begin. All three hundred beds contained boys injured by snipers' bullets, rifle grenades, shrapnel, bayonets, nail-studded coshes. No matter where Addie looked, putrid green pus seeped from wounds. Fortunately, Matron assigned her two Voluntary Aid Detachment workers. She got the VADs to scrub the place with carbolic, including the corridor where twenty patients lay on pallets of straw because the hospital had run out of cots.

Edward was the closest thing she had to a surgeon. Together they removed enough shrapnel from a lance corporal's face and upper body to fill an enamel basin. A serrated chunk had blinded the lad's left eye. Another piece had taken his nose and shattered his left cheekbone. The moment she applied a lint pad to a gash on his shoulder, he raised his head and coughed. As she slipped her arms under his back to support him, he vomited up blood. When she lowered him back down, a clump of matted brown hair came away in her hand, tissue attached. There was no time to compose herself. The next fellow had an unsightly chest wound and, beside him, the leg of another chap was open to the bone.

MEG'S VISION was blurred and her brain showed signs of going the same way. Apart from two meal breaks and three lavatory stops, she'd been in theatre with Wallace and Edward for seventeen hours. Her legs ached and her back had taken on a permanent kink. 'Tea, Sister Dutton,' said Davies, bringing in three mugs. She gulped down the sugary brew and asked him and Blue to stretcher in the next chap. Podgy-faced, scared stiff, he'd taken a hit in the groin. She tried to reassure him as Edward put him under, but before she could hand Wallace the scalpel, blood spurted from the soldier's wound – more than she could swab. For some reason Wallace didn't pitch in, but kept backing away from the table, as if in shock.

'No pulse,' Edward said. 'We've lost him.'

Wallace roared, 'What do you expect? I can't save my bloody self!'

He peeled off his gloves and stormed out.

She went to follow but Edward moved between her and the door. 'Give him a few minutes, Sister.'

'Who made you an expert on Wallace?'

Edward raised his hands as if surrendering but he didn't move out of the way. 'We could get something to eat first. Talk to him afterwards. By then he might have cooled down.'

Meg groaned. 'You're right. Sometimes I'm a bit rash.'

'Only sometimes?'

She threw a cloth at him.

During the next lull, Wallace said he wanted to discuss a head case with her. 'Me,' he joked as they ducked behind a row of vehicles and headed for a bunch of trees partially concealing a barn. He held the sides of a creaking ladder as she climbed up to the loft. Once again, he carried a torch. When she asked what he had in mind, he said, 'I need to see a healthy body. Please let me look at yours.' His voice sounded husky, as if he had a cold.

Unnerved once more, yet desperate to please him, she removed her outer clothing, followed by her undergarments, and tried not to think of the bugs lurking in the musty straw. She had to find out what was going on. He was turning into a different person.

She held out her hand and their palms touched. He groaned; recoiled. 'Wallace, please tell me what's wrong. I want to help.'

He ran a beam of light across her stomach, traced the curve of her thigh, the dip to her knee, her shins and feet. 'Keep your eyes open, Meg,' he said, 'and breathe. I need to hear you breathe.'

'I am, Wallace, listen.' She moved closer. He backed away. Fearing he might flee altogether, she said, 'It's all right. I'll lie down again.'

He knelt before her as if taking benediction, her body his altar.

It was ages before he switched off the torch. She reached for him again, stroked his neck and talked to him lovingly. He slid down beside her, less agitated now, and she took his face in her hands. They said what they'd never admitted to each other: that their childhoods had blighted them. She told him about the night Ma had shaved off her hair and written in ink all over her scalp. He told her what his uncle had done to him, how the old goat's crotch had smelt of mouldy cheese. He'd caught a whiff of something similar in theatre today – that was why he'd fled. He ran a finger around her wrist. 'You're the only good thing in my life. Forgive me, please?' She was too afraid to ask him for what. 'Everything and anything,' she whispered. He kissed her forehead. She closed her eyes. Instead of kissing her on the lips, he rested his nose on hers. Their breath mingled. Nothing will separate us, she thought. Not the pile of paper-white limbs stacked beside the door, which Davies should have burnt in the incinerator, nor the big guns booming day and night, nor a woman back in London.

IN MID-JULY, slightly over a year since they'd left Wellington, the unit moved to Amiens to take over a hospital in the convent of Sainte Famille and a nearby girls' school. A handful of English nurses agreed to stay on until extra New Zealand replacements arrived. Unlike Iris, Addie believed their presence would ease, rather than hamper, the changeover, owing to their experience and familiarity with the area.

'Don't expect them to take an active part,' Matron told Addie as she handed over the accommodation register. 'They tend to observe and supervise. I'm not in favour of this approach even though I went through the same training.'

Addie put down her pen. 'How did that come about?'

'English mother,' Matron said briefly and returned to her papers.

Matron's prediction proved correct. The English nurses were highly knowledgeable, but they left day-to-day tasks to their orderlies and the VADS, watching over them like hawks and pouncing if anyone deviated from the rules.

When nineteen replacements from home turned up, among them was Joan Watson, whom Addie had nursed with in Invercargill and considered a terrible gossip.

Reluctantly she offered to make Joan a hot drink. While waiting for the kettle to boil, she steered the conversation towards ordinary matters. 'Everyone's doing their bit.'

'They certainly are. As soon as a fleece is halfway decent, my uncles get out their shears,' Joan said as she spooned sugar into an empty cup. 'Walk through Gore and all you hear is the clickety-click of my aunts' knitting needles churning out balaclavas, mittens and socks. Even Nana's neighbour, Mrs Why-wait-for-your-husband-to-come-home-when-the-doctor-does-housecalls, has taken it up.'

'Our boys need woollies,' Addie said. She poured Joan's tea. 'What's your job here?'

'I'm theatre sister for the convent block.'

'Ah, with three hundred and fifty beds you'll be run off your feet.' Joan would have no time to interfere in people's affairs. 'We have the same number of beds in the lycée.' She paused momentarily. Her favourite patient had died at dawn but she mustn't think of him. Joan would surely taunt her if she wept. 'Did you come from Boulogne?'

'Yes, and what a trip it turned out to be. The usual four hours took twelve because of a kerfuffle in a village close to a section of rail track. At first, I thought our troops' bomb drills had caused the smoke and commotion. I only learnt later that there'd been a battle. Things were grim on the food front too. All I had was a measly bag of fruit, hardly enough to fatten a sparrow. Talking of which, remind me to tell you about a certain sister's unexpected departure from Southland Hospital.' She mimicked the shape of a swollen belly. 'I have no complaints about my charming French travelling companions though. The brave poilus offered to share their rations. Naturally, I turned the poor chaps down, but when the train stopped at a station they leapt off and bought me turnips from a couple of farmers. They needed a jolly good wash under a tap – the veggies, not the farmers.'

Joan laughed at her own joke.

There would be little to amuse her in Amiens. Whenever the guns roared, the place filled to bursting point. Addie was about to run over the class of injuries Joan could expect to face when Meg raced in and lifted the lid of the serving pan. 'Oh no, yesterday's stew. It was bad then.' Nevertheless, she filled her plate and sat down. Addie introduced Joan in a cautious tone that she hoped Meg would decipher and therefore control her tongue. If Joan got a whisper of her and Wallace, she would destroy their reputations in a flash.

'I hear the bombing is bad up here,' Joan said. 'How does anyone sleep?'

'Stuff cotton wool in your ears,' Meg said. 'I keep a stash in my pocket.' She stabbed a piece of meat with her fork. 'Help me eat this muck or the cooks will keep serving it up.'

Joan put her hand over her plate. 'I ate earlier. So Addie, tell me about this place.'

'We're only fifteen miles from the front so we receive high numbers of injured soldiers. Sometimes I doubt we have enough boys left to fight. Listening to the guns can be hard on the nerves. I often feel that anything could happen. The Germans could travel down the Somme on barges and we wouldn't know until it was too late.'

'They'd better not trample over Netta's garden. She'd take to them with her scissors,' Meg said. 'Have you met her, Joan? She has a green thumb.'

'If you mean the redhead guarding the Japanese anemones, then yes, I have.'

Iris came through the door. She dipped her head in Joan's direction and sat down next to Addie, who gave her a plate of stew.

'One of my patients swears the scent from Netta's roses reduces the stench of gas in his nostrils,' Iris said. 'She brings him a fresh bunch every day. The poor chap's stump burns and tingles and the pain prevents him sleeping most nights. She hates to see him suffer.'

'You'll suffer if you eat this stew, Iris. Chuck me over the salt and pepper,' said Meg. 'I need to make it edible.'

Iris waggled both shakers. 'You're out of luck.' She picked up the sauce bottle. 'See if you can get something out of this.'

Meg hit the bottom with her fist. A splodge of brown gunk landed on her stew. 'Sounds like Netta's sweet on him.'

'She wheels him outside regularly. Quiet fellow, always has a crossword on the go, not silly upstairs. Nice manners, never complains when I change his dressings.' Iris poured herself a cup of tea. 'Netta was humming this morning while she brushed her hair.'

Meg laughed. 'She'll sing if he kisses her! You might too, Addie, when Hugh comes back.'

Joan sat bolt upright, eyebrows twitching.

Staring into her teacup, Addie said, 'I doubt it.' Then she raised her head and added firmly, 'We have no lifts, Joan. Our orderlies have to carry patients between three levels. It's far from ideal.' She caught Meg's eye. 'Tell Joan how we've brightened the place up.'

Meg licked the last of the sauce off her knife. 'We ditched the dingy old army blankets and replaced them with pretty blue coverlets supplied by the Red Cross.' She stacked her cutlery and plate on the bench. 'If you want my advice, stay out of Matron's way. She doesn't miss much.'

'I heard she pulled off a stunner in Belgium with the help of her lover.'

Meg gaped at Joan. 'I haven't heard anything about a lover.'

Iris's eyes widened. 'Doesn't anyone put nursing first?'

'He was shot on their way out,' Joan continued. 'A Belgian, so it would never have worked. Continentals make amusing travelling companions but I wouldn't want one as a husband.'

Addie squirmed in her chair. 'We have forty extra beds in the gymnasium for medical and light surgicals. If something's done about the water and drainage systems, we'll be set.'

IT WAS FOUR-THIRTY in the morning. Although Meg had come off duty at midnight, she'd barely slept. There was an orange glow in the sky. Star shells were exploding and she could hear the rumble of guns. There must be a battle under way in a neighbouring town. No. 1 was virtually acting as a clearing station, with the English sending their serious cases to them. Three operating tables went day and night. Wallace had a chap assisting from the scheme he'd set up with the major general. They were short of instruments so no matter where you went in camp, you could hear Davies sharpening scalpels on a grinding stone. She threw back her bedcovers, thinking she might as well get up and lend a hand.

Hundreds of new patients had come in. Many waited on bare ground, three-quarters of them without labels. In the lantern light, she spotted an orderly pushing a trolley stacked with boots and kits. Behind him, Iris lugged a tray of dressings towards rows of shattered men.

Meg sprinted up to her. 'Set me to work.'

'Check the tourniquets,' Iris said. 'Thanks for coming back.'

When the medics ran out of supplies at the aid posts, they used everyday objects to prevent soldiers bleeding to death. Sadly, the bootlace tied around one chap's leg had done more damage than good. Not even Wallace could save it. The same soldier had a nasty wound to his arm. 'Keep the pressure on,' she told him as she applied a dressing. 'I need to attend to your mate.' She crouched down. A blood-gorged young rat scampered from a gaping wound in the soldier's buttock. Bile rising in her throat, she stuffed in a dressing. Her next theatre duty was five minutes away so there was time to check on a boy who had a hunk of shrapnel protruding from his chest. His eyes were molten grey saucers threaded with red spikes. Nothing could turn back the ferocious tide of death that was running at him full tilt. She blew softly across his lashes and whispered, 'You'll be home soon.'

An Australian nurse, who'd come down on the evening barge, along with ten spines, seven abdomens, four knees, nine heads and a lung case, had a septic cut on her hand and a pain in her chest. 'I can't stay long,' she told Meg. 'It's a human abattoir up there. We have more dead than wounded.'

When Wallace finished in theatre, Meg asked him to check the barge nurse.

'Pneumonia,' he confirmed. 'Find her a bed, Sister.'

All she could offer was a space on a tarpaulin. 'I'll find you something better soon.'

'The boys come first,' said the nurse. 'Dose me up so I canget back.' Phlegm gurgled in her chest and the last scrap of colour drained from her face.

Meg sponged her forehead. 'You're not up to it. I'll go in your place.'

When she found Wallace in the lab and outlined her plan, he put down the glass container he was examining and ran both hands through his hair. 'Are you mad? Matron will never agree.'

'It's only until the Australians can organise a replacement. Come with me. Say the aid post needs us both.' If he agreed, she might discover what else, other than the endless backbreaking surgery, was troubling him. 'Please.'

He shook his fist at her, half-joking, half-serious. 'You'll be the death of me.'

She slipped into his arms and he let her stay.

'We can talk.'

He stroked her back. 'I'll arrange it with Matron. God help me.'

From a distance, the charred tree trunks lining the riverbank looked like sentries. Meg moved along the wooden seat towards Wallace, who took off his scarf and wrapped it around her ice-cold hands. A lone owl called. She said, 'The Maoris think owls are a sign of death.'

'Shut up, voices carry,' whispered one of the pole men.

No one wanted to be on the river longer than necessary. Even on a night like this, when clouds obscured the moon, a barge could easily be mistaken for an armed vessel. Last month, one had taken a direct hit and twenty-eight men from the same regiment had died, along with two orderlies. A hallucinating head case was the sole survivor. 'Feed the darkness,' he'd sobbed when another party brought him in. 'Make friends with it or you'll never be free.'

The sleeve of her coat brushed against Wallace's jacket. He leant into her and she was half-pie thinking of sneaking a kiss when a haunting tune sung in German travelled across the water. Putting her mouth to his ear, she whispered, 'What do you suppose the words mean?'

'Something like, "your fate is calling you".'

Everything will work out, she thought, nestling into his shoulder.

The pole men dug in harder. As they rounded a bend in the river, the singing faded.

'Any regrets?' Wallace asked as they approached the aid post.

'Not about us.'

He squeezed her arm. 'Thank you for your letter. It bucked me up no end.'

Before she could ask if he'd written a reply, a chap tossed a coil of rope over a wooden stake and the barge shuddered to a halt. Another fellow clumped along duckboards holding a lamp at hip height so that its faint beam travelled the length of the vessel. When Wallace offered his arm she took it like the wife she hoped to become. If she wasn't the problem, what was? She'd seen Blue watching him lately. When she got back, she'd ask what he thought.

Think of a middle-aged man, medium height, steady temperament, with enough muscles for heavy lifting and you get me. I joined to escape farm work beneath the Hawkdun Range and a missus too busy to pay me any attention. In the early days, we'd have gone down to the stream and found a private spot. After the kiddies came, it was an elbow in the ribs if I strayed over to her side of the bed. She spoils them rotten. Still, I fuss over my patients in much the same way. Settle them when they're anxious, dish up their meals, wash them, empty their bedpans, hump dirty linen to the laundry, bring over X-rays, top up supplies. I don't gossip much. Keep most of the heartaches to myself too. A week ago, a strapping chap, newly hitched, came in clutching his intestines as if they were a bunch of flowers. I cut away the rest of his uniform and took him to theatre. We had a rush on that night and not enough anaesthetists to sling the slumber juice. So Madison ordered me to hold a gauze-covered wire cup over the fellow's nose and mouth and drop on ether since we were out of chloroform. He wouldn't go under, even though the place was thick with the stuff. I asked Madison what to do. He yelled, 'Bloody well try harder!' I dripped on more. The chap stopped breathing. I called for Madison's help again. He yelled, 'Pull him around for goodness' sake! I'm busy tying off my bloke's arteries.' I shook my fellow but I couldn't bring him back. Afterwards Madison ordered me to keep quiet about the whole thing. I can't understand why Sister Dutton still thinks he's the cat's pyjamas. He's not the surgeon or the man he used to be. Ramsay watches him closely. Sister Harrington, a damn fine sister, does too. She gets flustered if a man teases her, even me. Her hair is auburn, the same colour as my wife's.

Thirteen

NO MANNERS, Addie thought, as she walked towards four English officers in her care. An hour ago, she'd removed a pus-clogged drain from a major general's leg while he swore outrageously. The procedure could be painful but his language was beyond the pale. She'd almost had the drain out when he yelled, 'Don't use your blasted colonial torture on me!' and knocked her tray to the floor so she'd had to start again. It was a dreadful waste of sterilised equipment. To make matters worse, a two-pip lieutenant with a shattered shoulder called out, 'Sister, do you know any Maori chiefs? I hear they fancy a bit of whitey.' Feigning a need for more lint, she left the ward in a fury, a decision she regretted once she was standing outside in polar temperatures. She didn't have Meg's charm or Iris's distance or Dora's sweetness, and competence wasn't enough for these men. She needed something else. Whatever it was, she wouldn't find it here. She had to go back in even if they bayed for more blood, which was all she expected from a pack of fox hunters.

Show no apprehension, she thought, walking up to a brigadier's cot. The tuft of hair sticking up near his crown implied a boyish quality, but the taut lips and bristling moustache suggested a more malevolent nature. Adopting a clipped tone, not unlike his own, she said, 'How are you today, sir?' and placed her tray on his dresser.

He thrust out his chest. 'Like a prize bull, full of fuck and rearing to go.'

His cronies howled with laughter. The brigadier had lost a leg. She pulled down his bedcovers and said, 'Roll up your pyjama leg please, sir.' Lips curled back, he grudgingly complied. She eased the gauze off his stump with a pair of tweezers and inspected the lumpy knoll of purple skin. 'Healing nicely. You can leave for England as planned this afternoon.' Relieved, she applied a bandage to his stump for the last time.

Her next challenge was the Honourable Captain Charles Cunningham, who peeled back his bedcovers, slowly, suggestively, until they sat low on his bony hips. When not showing off, he was wheedling extra food from VADs and morphine from gullible nurses. Whenever she dressed his wounds he complained about Ettie Rout and her campaign against venereal disease: 'She's forever poking her nose in where it's not wanted.'

At least Miss Rout has one, Addie thought, glancing at the damage to his. Shrapnel had also skinned off an eyelid and removed a piece of his left cheek. A perverse pleasure ran through her as his wink descended into a wonky grimace. Feeling unworthy of her nursing medal, she instructed a VAD to put an extra spoon of sugar in his tea.

The Englishman waggled his hips again. 'What we do is none of that woman's concern.'

Addie placed two fingers on the underside of his wrist where the skin had the consistency of tripe. His pulse was full and bounding. 'Her intentions are worthy.'

'She can shove her kits up her bum.'

Picking up a needle from the kidney dish on her trolley, Addie said, 'Syphilis is no laughing matter.' She jabbed the charted dose into his rubbery skin.

'Ouch, a VAD could do better. Bring me one immediately.'

She swabbed his buttock and picked up her tray. 'They're not trained to give injections. Do you even know what VAD stands for?'

He pumped his fist under the bedclothes. 'Virgins Awaiting Deflowering!'

Addie narrowed her eyes. 'Their organisation accepts volunteers from your own class. These girls could be your sisters.'

God knows how many boys this oaf had sent to their deaths. It must be a burden to be born into privilege but have no common sense.

※

COAL SMOKE inflamed the lungs of Meg's bronchial cases but she kept the stove burning. Thick snow was falling and last night, while she wrote up her ward notes, the ink had frozen in her fountain pen, then exploded. The orderly on duty was fagged out so she'd cleaned up the mess. This morning there was no water and Davies had to heat ice from the fire buckets to make the patients' cocoa. He used the leftover water to scrub the floor. Unfortunately, the damp surface froze and she went for a skate. The frosted wool of the balaclava she'd swapped for her veil crackled when her head hit the deck. The blue lips of her patients opened wide in sympathy and alarm.

Mid-morning she went to the mess to refill their hot-water bottles. Onion soup was bubbling in big saucepans on the stove. Hunched over a table, greatcoat fastened to his neck, a chinless clerk was sorting the pays. Perhaps she should ask him to make a copy of Wallace's personnel record. She was considering the consequences when another pen pusher came in and beat her to the spare chair. She gathered up the hotties, stuffed a bread roll into her pocket and charged out the door.

A bitter wind stung her cheeks. Hunching over, half-shutting her eyes as she crossed the frosty ground, she didn't see Celeste,

180

their laundrywoman, until they almost collided.

'Ma soeur,' Celeste said, 'j'ai besoin d'un marteau' and she smacked her right fist into the palm of her left hand. 'Pour casser la glace sur les draps dans la baignoire.' She pumped her arms up and down, before rubbing her knuckles together.

Meg's French had been improving and she managed to work out that Celeste wanted a hammer to break the ice in her washtub.

She pointed towards the ward. 'Davies keeps a hammer by the fire bucket.'

Celeste nodded, then pulled a handkerchief from her coat sleeve and blew her nose.

Meg handed her a hot-water bottle. 'Warm your hands for a while.'

Since Celeste's husband had died last October, she'd been living with her grandmother and an aunt. You often saw the old ducks outside the hospital entrance, prodding the snow with their gardening forks, searching for lumps of coal. 'Sorry I can't spare you any fuel – charbon. We don't have enough to keep the patients warm. No one knows when the next load will arrive. The roads could be closed for weeks.'

Celeste pressed the hot-water bottle to the tears threatening to ice over on her cheeks.

Meg was about to apologise again when she heard an old man cough. He was leaning against a post at the entrance to camp. An elderly woman was banging her fist on the back of his frost-covered black cape. Beside them, a child in a brown overcoat blew into her hands. The red pompom on her hat glistened with ice. Meg walked over and handed her a hot-water bottle. Some clerk would have a fit when he tallied up at the end of the week but she didn't care. The little girl had smoky violet eyes.

Remembering the roll in her pocket, she fished it out and broke it into three portions. After the child ate her share, she picked up a nail someone had dropped in the snow and drew a female stick figure with a cross above her head and a man with a gun. A dead mother and a soldier father, Meg guessed.

'Grand-père? Grand-mère?' she said, pointing to the elderly couple.

'Oui, oui,' said the child.

Meg tapped the gate. 'Reviens ici, demain – come back here, tomorrow. Understand?'

The child rubbed her coat where it fell loosely over her stomach.

'Oui,' Meg said, 'you come here.'

She could spare a few rations. No one would care if she dropped a couple of pounds. Wallace had lost weight and she thought he looked better for it. Best of all, he was paying attention to her again. Last night while they sat together at the dining table, he'd pressed his thigh against hers.

Fresh snow covered the lintel above the entrance to the ward and she had to prise the door open. Before she went in, Davies emerged holding two buckets of stained linen. 'Leave those with me,' she said. 'Grab your hammer and help Celeste in the laundry.'

At dawn, the temperature plummeted inside the hut Meg shared with Addie. Meg had slept in her uniform to stop it freezing on the hanger and ending up like Addie's cape, which hung stiff as a board on the back of the door. If she didn't move soon she'd end up in the same state.

She was up and outside within five minutes. The salmon-pink sky promised more snow. Conditions in the trenches would be ghastly.

In the kitchen, she purchased a tin of milk powder and three eggs. With shoulders rounded against the wind, she clattered across to the camp entrance, where she found three Xs drawn in the snow. The child must be playing a game. As she searched for her among the outbuildings, she spied a newspaper under a bench. Wrapped up inside she found a wooden peg doll with a smiley mouth, small nose, two round eyes and black-laced boots like hers drawn on the tips of the prongs. She slipped the doll into her coat pocket. In its place, she left the food parcel. Beside the original message, she drew three new kisses and a question mark.

Rats filched the eggs overnight and left teeth marks on the tin of milk powder. There were no fresh boot prints in the snow. Either the child had misunderstood or she and her grandparents had moved on.

On her next free half-day, Meg combed a stretch of country-side. A farmer's wife remembered giving the girl a carrot. They were passing through, the old man had told her, on their way to find his son. Her husband had refused them shelter because the old woman was coughing up blood. He had to think of his livestock.

Back at camp, Meg waited for Wallace to finish his ward round. At dusk, she followed him into the sterilising room and begged him to wire through the family's details to a stuffed shirt or at least ask a clerk to make enquiries.

Midway through her story, Wallace said, 'You set off alone to find her? Anything could have happened.' He kissed her forehead. 'My brave darling, no wonder I adore you.'

'Meet me in the barn,' she said, pressing her cheek against his.

Fingering her back as if it were a cello, he said, 'We can't afford to catch a chill.'

'We won't if we keep each other warm.'

'I love you too much to put you at risk. Please believe me.'

Because his eyes moistened, she did.

During the next lull, three days before her second army Christmas, she traipsed into town with Iris, Addie and Dora to buy gifts. Shop awnings which had collapsed under the weight of the snow lay sprawled across the pavements like rumpled drunks. Ice had formed on the clapper of the bell above the door of the emporium so there was no jangle when she went inside to buy whistles and mouth organs. Two doors down, Iris picked up pipes from a barber, and Addie, shaving brushes. Dora got chocolates off a black-marketeer who also sold fir trees. They chose the best specimen and dragged it back to camp.

Once the patients were asleep, Blue shoved the tree in a tub and carried it to the main ward. Leaving Dora in charge, Meg dashed back to the hut to fetch her peg doll, which she fixed to the tip of the highest branch. Instead of asking for a happy future with Wallace, as she'd intended, at the last moment she wished the little girl would find her father.

During quiet periods, she helped Addie make paper-chain decorations. As she glued together the ends of the final one, she thought of Wallace banding her on their picnic and she leaned over and whispered, 'I want to have his baby.'

Addie blushed and blinked furiously. 'You'd better get married first.'

'Do you want children?'

'Not for a while. Maybe once I have a nice home and the right sort of situation.'

'You mean the right man.'

She finished the last chain and flung it over Addie's shoulders.

Christmas Eve wasn't half as much fun as it had been the previous year, even though she wound up the gramophone and organised a sing-along, followed by skits and carols. No one was in the mood for dancing. During 'Oh Come All Ye Faithful' the ward went quiet. She wondered if everyone was thinking, as she was, of war-hungry politicians stuffing turkeys down their deceitful gullets miles away from the guns. If she had her way, she'd put them to work in the moribund ward. That would teach them to sing a different tune.

Iris must have had a similar thought because she said, 'I wish we could parcel up peace and hang it on our tree.'

'I'd settle for mistletoe,' said Netta, gazing at Colin.

Meg smacked her lips together. 'Start the ball rolling then.'

'You could get lucky as well, Sister,' Wallace said as he stumbled through the door, waving a sprig of mistletoe at her.

He was becoming a boozer like her father. She walked to the bedside of a nice-looking captain who'd been giving her the glad eye all week. His shoulder was healing nicely, as was his leg wound. She said loudly, so Wallace could hear, 'Another week, Captain Harrison, and you'll be up dancing with me.' The captain offered her a chocolate from his Christmas box. She joked and laughed with him until Wallace left.

A YOUNG chest case under Addie's care – an only son, groomed to take over the family haberdashery business – died unexpectedly before Christmas lunch. Blue stacked his body in the pumphouse, alongside five from Joan's ward and three from Meg's. Burials had ceased after two gravediggers snapped their shovels trying to turn over the frozen ground.

Addie put on a bright smile and instructed the orderlies to serve up roast potatoes, parsnips and chicken. The patients ate in silence, then pulled up their blankets and waited for plum pudding. She gave the first spoonful to a lad who'd lost both arms in a skirmish less than ten miles up the road. Straight away he found a sixpence. She waited for him to position it between his front teeth so she could pull it out and put it in the money jar on his dresser.

'Mum will have to feed me when I get home,' he said.

It was some time before anyone started to eat again.

'What did Colin give you?' Addie asked Netta as they cleared away the plates.

'He dried leaves between the pages of a Bible, then strung them on silk thread.'

'What a wonderful gift.' A chap like Colin shouldn't have to fire a gun.

'Are you going to open Hugh's present? I hope it's not another drawing.'

Addie picked up a small parcel from under the tree. 'It's not the usual shape.' She untied the string and held up an attractive hairbrush with a mother-of-pearl handle.

'He must think a lot of you,' said Joan, raising her eyebrows.

A bunch of patients called out, 'We do too, Sister.'

To hide her embarrassment Addie passed around a box of chocolates her parents had sent, grateful she didn't have to share them with the obnoxious British officers – though perhaps even they had been through unimaginable horrors.

A censor had blocked out every third or fourth word in Hugh's recent letters, making it impossible to work out where he was or what battles he'd fought in. Thinking he needed a lift, she'd sent him a sketchpad she found in a second-hand shop. The first few pages had pastel drawings of shoppers in outdoor markets.

Fortunately, Meg rushed in and spoiled Joan's chance to pry any further. Addie picked up Meg's present from under the tree and handed it to her.

Meg ripped off the paper and held up a charm bracelet. 'You're the best friend in the entire world. I love it! Help me put it on. I'll never take it off.'

Addie pushed the clasp together for her. 'Matron won't let you wear it on duty.'

'I'll find a way. Open my present.' Meg handed her a tinsel-covered box. 'It's a bottle of perfume like the one I accidentally broke. Read the card.'

A lump formed in her throat. Meg had written, 'Dearest Sister-in-arms. I will treasure you forever. Best love, Meg.'

AT ELEVEN-THIRTY on New Year's Eve, after another long stint in theatre, Meg was in the mess, sitting beside Wallace and opposite Edward, eating cold vegetable soup. She felt like a wreck and assumed she looked like one. So when Wallace took her hand from her lap and held it in his, she gave an audible gasp.

'Water, Sister?' Edward pushed a full glass towards her.

It reeked of chlorine. She closed her eyes and tossed it down.

'If you don't need me, Madison,' Edward said, standing up, 'I'll check our last spine case and hit the sack. We're due back in theatre in four hours.'

'Good chap,' said Wallace distractedly.

She was tempted to quiz him on why he'd given her a pen for Christmas and not a ring to secure their future, but she dropped the idea in case he had one in his pocket. 'Have you something to ask me?' she said hopefully.

He gave her hand a squeeze.

'Meg, I've volunteered to go up the line again.'

Ah, paying her back for flirting with Captain Harrison. She'd only meant to scare him, not drive him away. 'Do you want to die?'

He let go her hand.

'What's going on, Wallace? Tell me!'

He tugged at the cuff of his jacket. 'I wish things were different. None of this is your fault.' His voice faltered slightly. 'You're a better person than me, darling girl. Best you don't give me another thought.'

'Wallace, I meant every word in my letter. We can face anything together.'

She leaned over to kiss the side of his neck. He flinched.

Throughout January 1917, the worst winter for years according to Celeste, Meg was on theatre duty. Between operations, she plunged her gloved hands into buckets of disinfectant. The surgeons did the same. No one talked unless requesting an instrument. Their efforts went into cutting, sawing, stitching, swabbing. Her glands were up and a slight rash had come and gone, along with a sore throat, but no cough. Wallace found reasons to be with her but never in an intimate way.

In February, there was heavy fighting and not enough stretcher-bearers or safe periods to pick up the injured, who sometimes lay for days in heavily manured soil, which led to infections and gas gangrene. A Tommy in Meg's care, whose thigh had rotted almost to the bone and smelled like fly-blown mutton, asked if he could talk to her about a private matter. She pulled a chair up to his cot.

'Sister, my fiancée fell pregnant during my last leave. Can you send for her so the padre can marry us?'

If this boy could think of marriage, why couldn't Wallace? 'I'll get Captain Madison to come and see you shortly.' The boy's romantic ideals might rub off on Wallace.

'Tap it with your finger, Sister,' Wallace said during his rounds, directing her to a piece of intact skin on the Tommy's thigh. It made a crackling noise like crumpled paper.

'Make him comfortable, Sister,' he said and walked away.

She followed him to the door, where he took her elbow and steered her outside. 'The lad has twenty-four hours if he's lucky; three days, if he's not. His fiancée won't arrive in time even if she does get permission.'

'But they have a child on the way. Can't the padre cut through the red tape?'

'Meg, millions of children grow up without fathers.'

'I'm thinking of writing to mine. Do you suppose he'd tell me the truth if he thought I wasn't coming back?'

Wallace gripped her arm tighter. 'Are you unwell?'

She shook her head. 'I'm fine. But I need to know why he didn't want me.'

As still more gangrenous cases arrived, the lost causes went straight to the moribund ward; anyone with a chance came

Meg's way. She loaded the dressing cart with an irrigation outfit and jars of Dakin's bactericidal solution, intending to administer the new Carrel treatment. You fixed a glass container to the head of a patient's cot, ran a long rubber tube into a glass cylinder that had up to five nozzles and packed them into various sections of a suppurating wound. Once you clamped the rubber tube to drip in the right quantity of Dakin's, you were in business. The treatment could be painful and patients were unable to move without tipping over their drip pan, but wounds tended to heal within a fortnight.

After one shift Meg returned to her hut at midnight. If she finished a letter to Aunt Maude and Uncle Bert before she went to sleep, she could catch this week's post. She picked up the fountain pen Wallace had given her and began to write. 'A runner found my German patient in one of our shell holes and took him prisoner. His right arm is badly infected. A family man, judging by the photo he showed me – young twins and a fat-cheeked wife. He doesn't complain when the treatment burns his healthy tissue, as well as killing his gas gangrene germs. He's always stoical and polite. He has a good singing voice.'

She put down the pen and rubbed her hands together to ease the stiffness that often struck her fingers. Then she added two sentences: 'Can you please tell me why my parents didn't want me? Whatever the reason is, I need to know.'

There was no birdsong, only the sound of whirring generators and the crunch of frosted gravel as she walked at daybreak with Netta to the main block to drop her letter in the postbag.

Netta tugged on her coat sleeve. 'You didn't hear a word.'

'Sorry. Tell me again.'

A twig was sticking out of Netta's hair: she must have been tending her plants in the drying room. Wallace caught her there recently, and when he didn't report her she crowned him Sir Bee's-Knees, a vast improvement on Dr Swank, the nickname she'd given him in Egypt.

'I said if you have to nurse Fritz, then please don't treat him with respect.'

'He's my patient. I give him the same level of care our chaps receive.'

Whenever the Dakin's solution dripped into his wounds, her German sang 'Jesu, bleibet meine Freude', a Bach chorale, the padre informed her. Sometimes she believed he was the singer on the Somme.

'A German blew my Colin's leg off. How do you know it wasn't him?'

'Your Colin! Netta, are you two serious?'

'We're walking out, that's all.'

Wheeling out, she thought. 'Good for you. We could all go up in smoke tomorrow.'

Their next lull coincided with a rise in temperature. Overnight the valley rolled up its icy carpet and the appearance of small speckled violets gave the meadows a bluish hue. During another lonely walk, Meg noticed spring flowers lifting their spindly necks to the sun, and at the edge of the woods the green tips of bulbs poked through the sleepy earth. Sometimes these stirrings of new life filled her with hope, then a memory would intrude. It was sixteen years since she'd plucked silver catkins from a willow tree near Pa's stable and pretended they were toys he'd made her.

Perhaps she credited Wallace, too, with more than he was capable of giving her. She was deep in thought when he called her name. For an instant, she believed he would take her into the woods, then she recalled that he no longer touched her unless others were present, and then only sneakily. 'Glorious day,' she said cheerfully.

'Nothing comes close to you.' He watched a stick-insect crawl along a lower branch before asking how she was.

'Perfect. And you?'

He looked down at the ground. 'I'm in the pink.'

'I have permission to go into Amiens. Can you get away?'

He dug his shoe into the boggy track. 'I have reports to write.'

'Don't you want . . .?'

'Say a prayer for me in the cathedral please, Meg.'

He'd never shown the slightest interest in religion and the padre had long since given up on him. 'I don't understand. Why won't you come with me?'

He slumped against the trunk of the willow. They would have quarrelled had she not hoisted up her dress and raced down the lane, clumps of mud flying off the heels of her boots.

In the ancient walled city of Amiens, the cathedral of Notre-Dame wore sandbags around its base like a skirt. Light spilled through the stained-glass windows onto the black headscarves of the bowed women inside. Knees creaked, shoes squeaked, but otherwise the place was quiet. Behind the high altar was the statue of a weeping cherub; one hand on an hourglass, the opposite elbow resting on a skull. As Meg slid into a pew she gave the crucifix and the holy statues a cursory glance, then turned her attention to the pretty cushions, gold candlesticks and ornate goblets. The pleasant scent of beeswax candles compensated for the musty smell of hymnbooks, but nothing could distract her for long or lighten her mood.

She knelt on a footrest, clasped her hands under her chin and lifted her eyes to the vaulted ceiling, but no matter how hard she tried to concentrate on the beauty of the cathedral, questions kept swirling through her mind. Why had her parents given her away? What chance had Wallace of finding peace? Would she ever feel truly happy? But she was unable to entrust her uncertainties to a God she didn't believe in.

APRIL BROUGHT mild weather and clumps of lily of the valley, which Addie picked to perfume the rapidly emptying wards.

For once, she had time on her hands and could fit in a visit to Amiens with friends.

While Netta and Iris went to a handicraft stall, she and Meg bought fresh bread from a young woman who had a tray strapped to her shoulders. The rolls tasted gritty, as though the baker had bulked up the flour with sweepings from his floor. Addie spat a mouthful discreetly into her handkerchief but Meg carried on eating hers. Judging from the dreamy expression on Meg's face, Addie knew her friend was miles away. She prodded Meg's arm with a finger. 'Meg, do you want to go boating on the Somme? Colin lost his leg near here.'

'It's hardly going to be propped up against a fence post waiting for Netta to collect it.'

'Meg! She wants to see the spot.'

'I'd sooner have coffee and cake at a café. My feet are killing me.'

'If we put a penny aside each time we complained about our feet, we could have afternoon tea every month in the best hotels for the rest of our lives.'

Meg rubbed her calf. 'Blast, now I've got cramp.'

'You need salt.'

'I need a dose of something. Speaking of which, Iris reckons Ettie Rout's kits are finally official.' Meg sat on a bench and unlaced her boot. 'Who would have believed that condoms and crystals could lick syphilis?' She flexed her foot. 'Addie, aren't you curious about that side of things?'

'A little, I suppose.'

'I'll tell you everything when we find a café that sells reasonable coffee.' Meg loathed the chicory concoction they got at camp but it wasn't sporting to grumble when French families had to survive on watery cabbage soup.

A poodle in a knitted coat trotted past, attached by a lead to an elderly owner swinging an ebony walking stick.

'Follow him,' Meg said. 'I bet he knows his way around town.'

Halfway down the street, the Frenchman entered a small

eatery, canine companion in tow. Addie followed the pair inside. The dog's coat would be something to tell her mother about in a letter. She hoped Meg wouldn't talk too loudly as the tables were close. But she needn't have worried. As a waitress was taking their order Netta and Iris spotted them through the window and came in to join them.

Netta held up a clump of parsley. 'I'm going to plant it in the hospital garden.'

'Isn't there an old wives' tale about parsley and falling pregnant?' Meg said as she stirred a teaspoon of sugar into her coffee.

Iris said, 'Tell them, Netta.'

Netta gave a shy smile. 'Colin has asked me to marry him. We'll set a date once he can walk down the aisle on his artificial leg.'

Addie reached over and squeezed her hand. 'That's wonderful news. Congratulations. The delay will give you time to organise bridesmaids and bouquets.'

'And find a church that's still standing,' Meg said.

Netta picked off a head of parsley and chucked it at her. 'Be happy for me, Meg.'

At that point, it occurred to Addie that she'd never thought of walking down the aisle with Hugh. 'How do you know when you're in love?' she asked.

Netta and Meg spoke together: 'You don't need to ask.'

On Friday the same week, Matron instructed Addie to accompany Wallace and Edward to a British clearing station eight miles from Vimy Ridge, where the Canadians were sustaining high casualties. She'd hardly had time to pack her kit before Edward came to collect her.

The road was rutted and strewn with splintered posts and rubble. No. 1's driver had a heavy foot and no consideration for the bone-weary soldiers struggling through the same quagmire, splattering their boots and leggings with thick grey slush.

Further along they spent quarter of an hour stuck behind a column of mule-drawn ammunition wagons that were inching forward, their drivers stopping every few yards to cover bomb craters with wooden boards and then manoeuvre the animals across. Despite the men's best efforts, a wagon pulling a heavy howitzer sank into a pit. No. 1's driver tooted impatiently then, without warning, veered into a field and bumped across the uneven ground, returning to the road at a nearby junction where wrecked carts and abandoned supply wagons cluttered the verges. As the boom of the big guns grew louder Addie folded her arms across her chest, hoping to calm her galloping heart.

All month her diary entries began the same way: 'Another harrowing twenty-four hours.' The continual roar of guns left her with a perpetual ringing in her ears. A dark covering of smoke obscured the sky. Every hour she checked which cases needed fresh dressings and labels and instructed the orderlies to feed and water those able to travel by train to base hospitals. Out of the forty Canadians they'd kept back yesterday, five had died before dusk, another three at midnight and six at dawn.

By the time the day's last critical left the operating table, Wallace looked exhausted and his joints were obviously aching. Edward had to help him to the door. 'Catch some shut-eye, Madison. I'll walk Addie back to her hut.'

'No, you get along,' Wallace said. 'I want a word with Sister Harrington.'

Her neck and head ached. She wanted only to lie down.

'Is that all right, Addie?' Edward said.

She gave him a half-hearted shrug: Wallace was her senior officer. Edward dropped back but he didn't go inside.

Wallace lowered his voice. 'You're as good as Meg in theatre.'

She raised her eyebrows. Why was he buttering her up? She waited.

194

Wallace adjusted his tie. 'Will you and Meg work together after the war?'

She refused to let him off the hook. 'Not if Meg marries.'

Following an uncomfortable silence, Wallace said, 'I do love her, you know.'

She wanted to shake him. 'You don't behave as if you do.'

Wallace rested a hand on her shoulder. Was Edward watching? She shifted slightly.

'Addie, I might not be around much longer. A big push is coming that will involve your lot. It could take you further north. Watch out for her, please.'

If he hadn't driven an ambulance to an aid post close to the line last night, lights off, in the middle of a raging battle, and brought back men, then operated on and saved them, she would have kept berating him. Instead she said, 'You know I will.'

I have plenty of the right stuff, but none of it bloody works. Seems I have two choices: a miserable demeaning death or a quick honourable demise via a German sniper. If I choose the latter, I need to pick a heavy battle. Then I can sink unseen into French soil and have my shame die with me. Think I'll go out with the stretcher-bearers tonight. Have a practice run. Pick a spot, near a tree. An elm, if there's one left standing. What a blasted catastrophe. So many boys need me. No point talking to the padre – I'm beyond redemption. Damn difficult to be near Meg and not succumb. For the first time in my life, I care about someone more than myself. I'd no idea this was on the cards when we got together. If I tell her, she'll be devastated. Worse, she might want to stand by me. Then the Evelyn complication will arise. Besides, there's no war pension for chaps like me. A lethal ping is best.

Fourteen

THE LONGER Wallace stayed at the clearing station, the more Meg's doubts grew. If he wasn't with her, she didn't believe he loved her. Uncle Bert once told her that wood pigeons mated for life. A pair had roosted in a stand of native bush behind Pa's stable. When airborne they sounded like woollen blankets flapping on a clothesline. They were always together, as she and Wallace should have been.

She was no longer feeling off-colour: whatever she'd picked up was gone. For a while, she'd feared becoming ill like her mother. She never knew what triggered Ma's collapses, though sometimes she thought Pa was the problem. Other times, she believed she was the cause. Her aunt and uncle took good care of her but it always came back to the same thing: her parents hadn't wanted her and now she was terrified Wallace would abandon her too.

He and Edward should never have allowed Addie to go with them. If the Germans broke through, she was unlikely to fib and play the grandfather card. Edward would have to size up the situation and do what he could to protect her.

When the trio returned late Sunday afternoon, washed out, bags under their eyes, Matron ordered Addie to bed for a well-earned rest. Meg longed to do the same to Wallace, who tapped his finger on his lips three times as he walked past the open door of her ward. That meant he loved her. She tapped back. Two stuffed shirts were escorting him to headquarters for a briefing. If Wallace had said he had important matters to attend to first, she could have been inside the Red Cross office with him after her duty, not cooling her heels outside.

Shortly after she caught up with Addie, who'd slept for twenty-one hours, two things happened: the weather picked up and patient numbers dropped. A situation that would have allowed her and Wallace to slip away unnoticed, had rats not taken over the area. Bold with hunger, they devoured anything that resembled food and you couldn't move without tripping over them. Their quivering pointed faces gave her the willies. At sunrise, a mother rushed into camp screaming in broken English that a rat had gnawed her infant son's feet while he slept beside her in a barn. Meg left the squalling baby and his mother with Dora and reported for duty.

Inside the ward, another wretched rodent was clawing frantically at the mesh over the trap and frothing at the mouth.

'You'd think the sanitation men could do something,' she grumbled to Blue, who disposed of the rat and replaced the bait.

'They come for the crumbs in my moustache,' said an abdominal case.

'More like the muck leaking into the bucket Sister Dutton has under your cot,' said his neighbour. 'You bloody pus-bag.'

'My drains will come out. You're stuck with your miserable personality. You'll expect mourners at your funeral next.'

She tidied the abdominal patient's bedclothes and fluffed up his pillow. 'Does anyone know a quicker way to catch rats?'

A chest case meowed. His mates went to pieces.

She wagged her finger at them. 'Behave or I won't bring you cocoa.'

A chap with blistered hands said, 'You have to help me, Sister. I can't hold a mug.'

'Davies can see to you tonight. I'm staying this side with the handsome chaps.'

More laughter – enough, she hoped, to stave off the night terrors of two nineteen-year-olds who resisted sleep in case they relived past battles. She had to rub their backs to get them to nod off. Just as well she had strong hands. She couldn't say the same of her heart, which went haywire whenever she thought of Wallace. Sometimes she thought it would stop altogether.

SEATED ON a wooden bench in Netta's hospital garden, Addie opened her mother's latest letter and skimmed over the usual news, slowing down when she reached the last page. 'Erin punched a boy's nose at school and made it bleed when he tried to kiss her. I thought it served him right but the headmaster didn't see it that way. Your father is threatening to send her to boarding school. Erin is kicking up bobsy-die.'

A boy had kissed her little sister! That was more than Hugh had attempted with her, but maybe he expected greater encouragement. She was staring into space when Iris arrived, as red in the face as the geranium at their feet. Addie cleared a space for her on the bench. 'Sit down. Tell me what's happened?'

'New orders,' said Iris, puffing like a steam kettle. 'We're to travel by train to Calais, then proceed inland to a place called Hazebrouck.' She scraped her boots along the rail under the bench to clear off the worst of the mud.

Addie picked a geranium flower and crushed it between her fingers. She was so tired of moving. 'How long do you think we'll be there?'

'Things will speed up now America has entered the fray. Their boys are determined to make Germany pay for sinking the *Lusitania*. We could hang up our military capes soon.'

Addie stood up. 'Thanks for letting me know.'

Unlike Iris, she wasn't interested in rising through the ranks, preferring to work alongside people, not manage them. On her way back to the hut, she weighed up the likelihood of their unit staying in the next place. Not high, she thought, opening the door.

'We're moving again.' Meg was pulling a pair of stockings off their indoor clothesline. 'These are yours.' She tossed them to her. 'Should I remind Matron that I'm Wallace's regular theatre sister?'

'She isn't trying to separate the two of you. There is a war on, remember.'

Meg rammed a fist into her kit to make more room for her belongings. 'Have you heard from Hugh? He could be on the move too. Who knows where we'll be in six months.'

'Hang on while I fetch his latest sketch. I'd value your opinion.'

She handed a roll of paper to Meg, who spread it flat on the table. The pastel drawing depicted a bombed church with thighbones as pillars; shattered faces instead of stained glass windows; human hair woven around the altar; eyes lined along the pulpit drawn with the pastels she had sent him. 'I haven't come up with a title,' he'd written; nothing else.

Meg studied the image. 'Addie, take a closer look at the eyes.'

They were two-toned! 'I don't love him.' As the words left her mouth, she knew they were true.

'I'm not surprised. This drawing would put anyone off.'

Addie took a deep breath and straightened her back. 'He rarely asks what I think.' Her mouth was set in a straight line. She turned to face Meg, arms rigid at her sides. 'He's not my type.'

Meg dropped her kit on the floor and shrugged. 'Who is?'

Addie picked up a pillow and flicked it across Meg's hip.

'Don't tease. I have to finish with him. Is it kinder to write or wait until I see him next?'

'What are you actually ending?'

Opportunities, she thought, nothing more. 'Just plans we made for after the war. He was going to introduce me to a few people and show me where Charles Dickens grew up.'

'You could hire a tour guide with bookish connections if that's all you want.'

Addie gave a weak laugh.

'Pity I don't have a stash of red plonk. We could have toasted your brief career as an artist's muse. Which reminds me, Matron found Netta and Colin in a clinch.'

'Really!'

'Colin claimed Netta tripped on a bag of soiled linen and landed in his lap.'

Addie picked up her new family photograph from the box beside her bed and packed it between the folds of her dressing gown. 'Where are the love-birds?'

'In Amiens buying an engagement ring,' said Meg. She paused for a moment. 'I thought I'd be first,' she said softly.

Executing a deft sidestep – a Wallacism, as she'd come to think of them – Addie said, 'You deserve to be.'

They both left with No. 1 on the last day of May to take over the No. 12 Casualty Clearing Station at Hazebrouck, a hospital of more than a thousand beds in what had originally been a three-storey girls' boarding school. The sappers cleared an additional outbuilding and set up tents in the grounds to accommodate the high number of wounded expected to arrive towards the end of the month. Since most beds were currently empty, they had time to settle in. They were to sleep in a large house that smelt musty. As soon as she entered her room, Addie placed her kit and suitcase beside the army cot and flung open the wide sash windows. Not far away an overgrown walled garden waited for someone like Netta to restore it. Fortunately, their quarters were within walking distance of the wards.

Once she'd unpacked and made her bed, she rolled up her sleeves and went outside to help Netta tidy the main herbaceous border. The warm twilight reminded her of an idyllic summer evening when she and her family had steamed up Lake Wakatipu on the *Earnslaw*, admiring the views of the Remarkables from the comfort of Prussian velvet seats. She'd been away from home for almost two years. When she pulled on a thistle, it came away easily from the chalky soil. A good omen, she thought, as Netta dragged a sack in her direction.

'Dump your rubbish in here, Addie. You know, we could make something of this garden. Brick walls retain the heat.' Her voice fell. 'But we'll probably have to move before we reap the rewards.'

Addie nodded sagely. 'Those who come after us can enjoy what we create.'

'Netta, Addie,' called Meg from behind a clump of bergamot, 'a grateful ex-patient sent me a box of gramophone records. Do you want to come inside and play them?'

'Not right away,' Netta said. 'I feel closer to Colin in the garden.'

He'd left for England that morning to be fitted with a new leg, which meant Netta was unlikely to see him again for weeks, maybe months.

Meg hitched up her skirt and leapfrogged over a bush. 'I bet you miss him.'

'We intend writing every day. Addie, you go in if you want.'

Reluctant to leave the peace of the garden, she said, 'We can listen to them later. Meg, pick up a trowel and help us.'

YESTERDAY WALLACE had taken Meg to a café in town. When he'd chosen a secluded table, her hopes had soared. After the waitress had taken their order and left to prepare their coffee and omelettes, he'd asked if Meg wanted anything else, like a glass of water or an extra serviette. She'd said he was all she needed. He'd smiled but there'd been no spark in his eyes. She'd waited for him to brighten up, to show real emotion, but his head had drooped and his shoulders were slumped. He must be more worn-out than she'd realised. When she'd reached over and touched his arm, he'd looked up and said sadly that he would love her from the grave. She'd said she would love him more if he stopped harping on about death. He hadn't laughed. To her surprise he'd pulled from his jacket pocket a heart-shaped silver locket containing a lock of hair. 'Mine,' he'd murmured. 'Add a snip of your own tonight.' She'd rubbed her cheek against his hand, felt the skin over his knuckles tighten as he fastened the clasp around her neck. Kissing her lightly on the shoulder, he'd whispered, 'You've made me happier than I deserve to be.'

If that was the case, why go to another aid post, and this time alone? There was no point acting the devoted beau one minute and running off the next. She'd reminded him that a big push was under way near Messines and stacks of boys would be rolling in. He'd begged her to unpin her hair so he could run his hands through it, as he had at Aboukir. She'd despaired as he'd removed her hairclips, told her he didn't want to leave, said he had no choice.

You damn well did, she thought now, and tossed a clump of weeds over her shoulder.

'Watch it!' yelled Netta.

It was fine for her. She still had Colin, or at least most of him.

Meg had been right about Messines: droves of wounded were arriving in field ambulances. It was impossible to reason with the jabbering head cases, and the American brain surgeon filling in for Wallace couldn't tell her if they would improve or worsen. She sent Dora to fetch the padre, thinking he could calm them, but he was presiding over burial after burial and had no idea when he could come.

Overnight she received twelve extra head patients and sixty surgicals. She was so exhausted that she nodded off while restacking a trolley and banged her head on the metal edge. There was no time to apply a cold compress. A head case had picked a fight with another fist-flailing maniac and she had to drag them apart and persuade them to return to their beds. It was another six hours before she got a break.

She hardly had her head down in the makeshift sleeping space off the ward when a German plane flew over and anti-aircraft and machine guns let loose. She sat bolt upright, thinking she might have been having a nightmare, but the noise grew louder. Her breakfast tray and half-empty tea mug crashed off a table. She placed her hands over her ears – if the hideous din didn't let up she'd grow deaf. A hunk of shrapnel sliced through a gumboot that was propped against her door and bullets whacked into the floor. Although her feet refused to move, her brain registered danger. She grabbed an enamel bowl from the top of a locker and stuck it on her head. There was no way she'd end up a head case, she thought, laughing hysterically.

More bombs rained down the following night, terrifying her patients. Matron instructed her to apply the latest classification system. 'Label anyone suffering from hallucinations or unable to speak, hear or see, NYDN, not yet diagnosed, non-efficient. I'll arrange for the worst to go to England.'

'Yes, Matron,' she said.

She probably gave one or two shirkers NYDN labels, not wanting to send a genuine case back to the front. Better to believe a liar than doubt a madman.

It was another clear, balmy night, the kind that usually attracted enemy planes, but before Meg knew it, Addie was shaking her awake. 'Meg, Meg. Davies came in on the last barge with a wireless chap. Twenty patients have been killed at Wallace's aid post, but no medical officers, thank goodness.'

She grabbed Addie's wrist. 'Are you sure? Is he safe? Are you sure?'

'Davies has a message from Wallace. You're not to worry if he can't get back.'

'Who's worried!' she yelled.

THEY FACED a new horror in July – mustard gas. Sufferers arrived with inflamed eyes and blistered throats, scorched lips and noses, lungs irritated to the point of collapse, plum-coloured burns. Addie asked a soldier whose features were barely distinguishable how men could do this to one another.

'We follow orders.' He scratched off a flake of singed flesh. 'Am I going to die?'

She picked up a needle from her tray. 'I'll give you an injection to relieve the swelling around your eyes and I'll soothe your throat with a spray of menthol oil.' He wouldn't learn from her that on the second or third day after this type of gas attack, bronchitis commonly developed, often leading to fatal pneumonia. When he complained of stinging eyes, she bathed them with bicarbonate of soda, which would help for a while.

It would be ages before she could get back to him. Over sixty gas-affected women and children had come in. The little ones were crying, 'Ça pique! Ça brûle! It stings! It burns!' Since it was too dangerous to send for a translator while fumes lingered, she recited 'Pat-a-cake, pat-a-cake, baker's man' in an effort to calm the children while she rinsed their eyes. Newly blinded mothers ran their fingers over unclaimed infants as though skin was a code they could crack. No one could outrun this gas. It travelled on the wind.

Once she'd done everything possible to help the civilians, Addie left Dora in charge and made her way to the kitchen, concerned there mightn't be enough soup to feed five dozen extra mouths. To her relief the head cook was already bulking up the day's concoction with lentils while his assistant halved bread rolls and a store clerk signed over custard powder, milk and tinned fruit to another cook, who was planning to make wholesome puddings.

Reassured, she continued to the main ward where she was due to accompany a visiting major on an inspection. She outlined their current cases as they went through the door. Across the room, she saw a mild gas patient fiddling with the neck of his hot-water bottle. By the time they reached him, he had a thermometer in his mouth.

The major took it out and read it. 'This boy has a very high temperature.'

Unable to witness his own deceit, the patient turned his face to the side.

'He's not ready to be discharged, sir,' said Addie, and of course he wasn't.

Shirkers used every trick in the book to cadge an extra day or two. Last week two offenders had soaked cigarettes in vinegar to spike their temperature and bring on a state of temporary unconsciousness. They were lucky not to die.

A few patients with severe injuries had to stay in hospital for months. Some wrote to their mothers who, in turn, wrote to her, thinking she could get them sent home: 'He is a dreamer, not a fighter', 'I need him on the farm being unwell myself', 'His sister is going astray', 'His three brothers have already given their lives.'

In her replies, she commended the women for raising sensitive boys and explained why she couldn't override army rules. Yesterday she'd readmitted a lad described not long ago by his mother as 'thoughtful and kind'. Sent back to the front, this time he'd sustained serious injuries from a melanite shell packed with scrap iron. Although unconscious, he might recover, unlike the chaps from a field artillery brigade decimated by dum-dums. She'd already closed nine pairs of eyes.

As soon as the major had left, convalescents from another brigade gathered around the table in the middle of the ward to play a sometimes macabre card game called Odds and Oddities, in which points were awarded for severity of wounds and the likelihood of death. They'd drawn crude symbols on scraps of cardboard. A lucky card, called 'Sure Thing', depicted a nurse showing a slim ankle. If a player got her, he lived.

'Yikes, what a deck,' said Dora.

She was shuffling for an armless player who hadn't yet mastered a suitable technique with his toes. The patients treated Dora like a much-loved kid sister, and even rough chaps swallowed their expletives when she irrigated their wounds.

For this reason, Addie asked her to inject hydrogen peroxide into a sergeant's mucky shoulder. As expected, it fizzed madly. The card players raised their voices to drown out the poor chap's groans. If the area healed, she'd get Dora to dress it with lint soaked in spirit lotion, a less intense treatment. He was unlikely, though, to regain much use of his arm since the muscles were in a terrible state.

Two beds down a twenty-three-year-old was dying from a secondary haemorrhage, a common enough complication with big sloughing wounds. Iris had been looking after him until she picked up an infection through a minuscule scratch on her wrist. A medical officer had to open up her arm and insert a drain, which meant the ward was one sister down – and more gas cases were on the way.

If I'm sent back to the trenches Fritz will get me this time for sure, but if I scarper I'll be shot for deserting, which leaves two options: harming myself (haven't got the stomach for it) or extending my stay in hospital. This afternoon Sister Harrington caught me heating my thermometer. I pray she didn't think too badly of me. It's not as if I haven't given soldiering a chance. Not everyone's suited. I freeze whenever the call comes to go over the top. My mate, Owen, would give me a shove but he can't anymore because he took a direct hit last week. I dragged him into a shell hole where I tried to clean him up using my hat as a washbasin. Fritz shot it out of my hands – rat-tat-tat, rat-tat-tat. Then a fence picket slammed into Owen's chest. His eyes burst open. To calm myself I listed the contents of my jacket pockets: spare bootlaces, stub of candle, pack of cards. It helped until I got to the tin whistle Mum gave me to blow if I was injured. I was scared to use it in case it attracted Fritz. Then a rabbit, his fur on fire, ran around the rim of the shell hole. I peered over the top. Uniforms stretched for miles. At first, I thought the chaps in my division had pissed or shat their pants and taken them off. Then the bundles started to writhe! A vapour rose off them. I couldn't breathe. I couldn't scream. I couldn't see.

Fifteen

IF WALLACE could tear off whenever he pleased, so could she. She'd do a stint on a hospital train and not be here when he got back. Serve him right. He shouldn't treat her like a plaything he could pick up and put down. She ripped off her apron, kicked off her shoes and said aloud, 'Why does he take risks?'

Addie turned back her covers and climbed into bed. 'You do the same, Meg.'

'I put my hand up, that's all.'

But she knew it was more than that: she'd always been reckless. How else did you make people notice you? She brushed a knot in her hair, furiously, as if the thing that terrified her lodged in its roots. Next thing she flung the brush across the room. It made a cracking sound as it hit the floor.

She undressed and put on her nightgown. If she were lucky, the train would have a decent water supply. Yesterday she'd had to choose between a pot of tea or a wash, and it was ages since she'd run a bath. You shouldn't have to skimp on toiletries when there was a man on the scene. If Wallace gave in there was no chance of her falling pregnant until they were married because she douched with sulphate of zinc. Even if they slipped up, she would simply open her heart wider and let their baby crawl in.

'I'm tired of second-guessing what's going on. Do you think he's serious about me?'

'You need to talk to him.'

'Well, I would if he was here!'

Addie picked up her book. To block the glow of the lamp, Meg stuck her head under her pillow. Half an hour later, she pulled it off and yelled, 'You'll go cross-eyed!'

Addie banged her book shut and put out the lamp. 'Satisfied?'

'Don't get sniffy. I can't sleep with the light on.'

'You've mocked me twice this week for reading. I don't stop you doing anything.'

'You do.'

Meg counted in silence the number of times she'd tried to talk to Addie about Wallace's worrying symptoms, only to have her pick up a damn book. She said again, 'You do. You read when I want to talk.'

Addie lowered her head. 'I read to escape the war. I get scared.'

Meg wanted to ask Addie what terrified her most, but because she was crotchety she said, 'I'm scared too.'

'We're even then,' said Addie.

'Don't get on your high horse with me.'

Addie climbed out of bed, pulled on her dressing gown, yanked the cord tight, threw open the door and disappeared into the night.

❧

AT DUSK on July the 31st, Addie was in the mess with Dora and Iris listening to a dishwasher claim that in a former life he'd cooked for Maximilien de Robespierre, a story Meg would have enjoyed had she not carried out her threat and applied for hospital train duty. She'd been gone a couple of weeks and

Addie was missing her terribly. Her sense of humour had helped to mend their friendship the night of their row. Addie had returned thirty minutes later to find a torch lying on her bed and a note that read 'I hereby declare that Talking is willing to shake hands with Reading and nut out a Peace Plan'. After agreeing on times to talk and times to read and to pin a red label on the door if either of them wanted a break from the other, they'd hugged and laughed, then slept until dawn. Back in the kitchen, the dishwasher was saying that a fortune-teller he frequented had called up a spirit from the revolutionary era, who predicted a bright future for him as a dealer in culinary treasures. To help the prophecy along, he was collecting ancient French recipes and old kitchen utensils.

Addie was about to ask if he thought he could earn a decent living when, without warning, she was knocked off her feet and covered in a film of thick choking dust. The dishwasher lay crumpled beside her on the floor, his blackened face a stark contrast to the whites of his eyes. Neither of them had been hurt, just shocked. He waved her on. She crawled across the lopsided floor to Dora, who was crouched under a table. The windows were shattered and a patch of sky was visible through a gaping hole in the front wall. Outside a bell clanged.

'They've broken through!' Dora screamed. 'Addie, do something!'

Acrid powder caught in Addie's throat as she opened the door.

'Quick, back inside,' said a sergeant who was running past. 'Take cover as best you can.'

Blasts sounded every seven minutes for over an hour. She and Dora took refuge behind an upturned bench. They barely spoke, but when tears began rolling down Dora's face, Addie gathered her into her arms and held her.

By nine o'clock, the bombing had become intermittent so Addie and Dora crawled over to Iris, who was sheltering behind an overturned cupboard that had once contained the crockery now in pieces in her lap and studded through her hair. Iris grabbed Dora's arm and angled her head towards the door. Addie nodded. 'I'll take a look around.'

On the outskirts of the camp, amid swirling blue and grey smoke, she could make out Frenchwomen pushing high-sided carts and wheelbarrows filled with mattresses, grandparents and infants. Running alongside this caravan of despair were young girls clutching meagre possessions; and whimpering children, notes pinned to their coats, presumably recording their names and addresses in case they got lost. A pot tied to a rope that spanned a cart clattered against a cage, causing trapped hens to squawk.

Among the mayhem army types were dashing about yelling in English for the women to clear the road, and outside headquarters a senior officer roared 'Evacuate, evacuate!' while his adjutant shouted 'Lorries, ambulances, railhead!'

Ten yards from Matron's office, Addie ran into Meg, who looked worn to a shadow. After a quick hug, Meg told her that as soon as she heard the Germans were heading this way she'd boarded the last evacuation train bound for No. 1. 'I wanted to be with you and the unit. Matron met me. We have to get everyone ready to leave.'

'I'll tell the others.' Addie rushed back to what was left of the mess.

Over the next three hours, in darkness and under continuous shelling, they evacuated six hundred patients. Drivers lined up their lorries with the assistance of sappers, who darted alongside calling out instructions. An officer insisted they place sacks over the bonnets to dim the brightness of the headlights. By midnight, the hospital was empty. Only the nurses and a few supply vehicles remained.

'We deserve commendations,' said Iris. 'Matron should mention us in dispatches.'

'Iris certainly has the chest to support a row of medals,' Addie whispered to Meg, who thrust out her own. 'All right, you do too.'

'I didn't get supper,' said Dora. 'It could be days before we eat again.'

'See if there's a loaf of bread in an oven among the rubble,' Meg said. She was rolling up the last mattress in the ward. 'Addie, I'll be back in a minute.'

'Hurry,' she said. 'We have to leave.'

'You go. I need to find Wallace.'

So it wasn't over. 'Don't be long.'

Watching Meg dash across the courtyard, veil flapping behind her like a surrender flag, brought to mind stories Addie had heard of soldiers raising white handkerchiefs and still getting shot.

Netta pulled at her cloak. 'Addie, we have to go. Wallace will look after Meg.'

'I'm coming. I just want to fetch my diary.'

MEG ROUNDED a corner and collided with Wallace, who took her in his arms and hugged her to his chest.

'Darling girl, thank goodness. I thought I'd lost you.'

His uniform smelt of smoke.

'Meg, please don't volunteer for more dangerous jobs. This is bad enough.' He looked at the devastation around them. 'I couldn't bear it if anything happened to you.' He slid his hands down the sides of her uniform. 'You've lost weight. Is something wrong?'

She flicked him a conciliatory smile. 'Not any longer.'

'Good.' He played with a curl that had escaped from her veil. 'I gave a staff nurse the fright off her life before. I pounced on her, thinking she was you. She thought I was German. Poor thing wet her pants.'

'Oh, Wallace, she didn't!' His expression was serious again. He looked older, wearier. 'What's wrong? Please tell me?'

He reached into his kit, pulled out a fat brown envelope

and broke the seal. Inside were bundles of English banknotes, several hundred at least.

'What are they for?'

Placing the envelope in her hands, he said, 'I have no need of them.'

She tried to give the package back but he refused to take it.

'Put it to a good cause.' He ran his fingers up her arm. 'Promise me.'

She rested her fingertips on his lips.

'Look after yourself, Meg. Do you hear?'

'I will. I do.' She said the words as solemnly as she would her wedding vows. But why was he saying this? Wasn't he coming with her? Knots formed in her stomach. She thought of the garnets that Aunt Maude had collected from Garden Bay near Tuatapere and lined along Meg's bedroom windowsill when she first went to live with her and Uncle Bert. Her love for Wallace was as solid and lasting as those gems. She would keep the money safe for him, for their future. 'I promise.'

'Good, that's settled.' He fiddled with the top button of her uniform. 'I have news of Hugh. Do you know where Addie is?'

'What's happened to him?'

He pulled a piece of lint from the bib of her apron and worked it back and forth between his fingers. Her mother used to pick fluff from a woollen blanket she flung over her shoulders on her worst days. Debility cases worried their socks or gloves in much the same way and got shirty if anyone tried to stop them. 'What did you say happened to Hugh?'

'I didn't, Meg. Besides, Addie needs to hear first.'

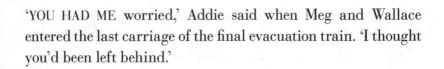

'YOU HAD ME worried,' Addie said when Meg and Wallace entered the last carriage of the final evacuation train. 'I thought you'd been left behind.'

'Come with us to the dining car,' Wallace said. 'It's quieter there.'

As he took her arm and steered her through the crowded train, she wondered if someone in her family had fallen ill, or worse. No, Matron would relay such news, not him. And judging by Meg's glum face, he hadn't popped the question.

Scrambling into a seat in the dining car, she said, 'What is it?'

She heard the words 'sorry', 'both arms gone', 'a leg too', 'he's in bad shape', but she didn't catch the name. She asked what this person had to do with her.

'Hugh, it's Hugh, Addie,' There was a serious weight to his voice. 'He's lost three limbs.'

Not his arms, she protested silently, not his hands.

As Wallace pushed her head down, she heard him say, 'Meg, fetch a cup of strong tea, two sugars.'

Take deep breaths, Addie said to herself, as the markings on the floor of the carriage blurred and merged. When she came to, she was in a seat and Wallace was sitting opposite her.

'Do you feel better, Addie?'

'Tell me everything, please.'

The furrows on his forehead deepened. 'Two bearers found him in a shell hole and brought him to the aid post, where he ended up on my table. I gave him a transfusion to reduce the shock, but the extent of his injuries means he may not make it across the Channel.'

She couldn't take it in. 'He might die?' Her eyes filled with tears. Wallace pulled a handkerchief from his jacket pocket and handed it to her.

'Not many chaps survive the loss of three limbs. He also has horrific facial burns.'

She fixed her gaze on the water jug that sat between them and thought, melted face, three stumps, no balance. 'He'd sooner die. He'll will himself to die.'

Wallace nodded. 'That can happen. A neighbour of mine in London lost his wife to tuberculosis. Three days after her

215

funeral, he dragged a rocker up to their roof terrace, faced it towards her grave and waited. Every time we fetched him down, he climbed back up. Grief carried him off five weeks later.'

She put her hands on her forehead and kept them there for a moment. 'I can't imagine loving someone that much.' Her voice sounded thin and flat.

Leaning forward, he said tenderly, 'It has been known, Addie.'

She didn't know how to respond. If she stayed silent, Wallace would consider her callous. An English nurse back in Amiens had told her about a decently brought-up girl who became hysterical when she saw the flat counterpane where her fiancé's legs should have been. She turned the water jug around so the handle faced her: Hugh would never pour another drink, never paint. 'He'll need constant care,' she said. 'I can't give that to him.' If she loved him, it might have been different. She stared at Wallace. 'You must think badly of me.'

His expression remained thoughtful. 'Our lives rarely run in straight lines. Sort out your feelings before you rush to his bedside. If he survives, and it's a big if, he'll have a lengthy recovery in hospital. You can afford to bide your time.'

She paused before saying diffidently, 'I could write to him.'

'Ah, here comes Meg with your tea.' He reached for his hat.

'Oh, Addie.' Meg bent to kiss her on the cheek. 'Here you are. It's piping hot.'

Addie held the mug up to her face and breathed in the steam.

Meg turned to Wallace and said, 'She hasn't even kissed Hugh properly.'

'Right now that's the least of her worries.' He stood up and straightened his tie. 'I'll leave the two of you to talk.'

But there's nothing to say, Addie thought, nothing at all.

'YOU TOLD ME a few weeks ago you didn't love him and he hasn't replied to your letter, so why visit him?' Meg handed Addie the hairbrush Hugh had given her.

Netta and Addie had two weeks' leave in London; Meg had been posted to a British hospital not far from Hazebrouck.

'How could he write? He can't hold a pen!'

'No, but a VAD could on his behalf.'

Needing a moment to think, Addie turned away and put her brush on a shelf that contained two new books her mother had sent over. When she swung around, her face was serious. 'Sorry, Meg, I don't mean to take my worries out on you. For all sorts of reasons I'm dreading this trip, unlike Netta, who can't wait to see Colin.'

'That's love for you.'

'Hugh mightn't want visitors.'

Meg rolled down her stockings. 'See what his ward sister thinks.' She rubbed her feet. 'How was Wallace while I was away on the hospital train?'

'He was cranky the whole time.'

Nothing made sense, and now he was back at his precious aid post. 'I'm off to the bath house. Will you be all right?'

'Don't worry about me. I'll be fine. Enjoy your soak.'

Meg gathered up her toilet bag and opened the door cautiously, but there was no sign of a Taube. On quiet nights, she could almost forget where she was, but she'd never be able to erase what had happened with Wallace in the Red Cross room the night he left.

He'd drawn the curtains, turned on the light and said, 'Let me look at you.' Reaching up to push his hair off his forehead, she'd accidentally knocked off his cap and when he bent to pick it up, she'd noticed that the bald patches on his crown had grown larger. She teased him but he didn't poke fun in return, although he could have: she had an insect bite on her left cheek and a scratch on her nose where a patient had lashed out during an irrigation. Instead, he'd got huffy and walked out.

Some chaps were touchy about losing their hair. Three months earlier, she'd nursed a boy, burnt to a crisp, who complained when Davies gave him a second-rate trim. Some mild ragging was no reason for Wallace to ruin their time together. She'd no idea when she would see him again. Worse, when she went through his symptoms, a chill settled in her bones.

❧

THROUGHOUT THE NIGHT crossing, Netta talked incessantly about Colin while Addie told herself that she mustn't let duty and compassion trap her into taking care of Hugh. After they'd disembarked, she followed Netta to the station, where they purchased second-class train tickets to London and two currant buns. A stiff breeze blew cinders into the air as they climbed into their carriage.

Grassy banks bordered the rail tracks, and beyond the fences and hedges lines of washing criss-crossed the poky backyards of grim terraced houses where children played. Then there were grubby shunting yards, stone buildings looming up behind them, and on the platform several small wooden huts with signs printed in large letters announcing 'French money exchanged here to officers and soldiers in uniform'. What about nurses? she thought as the train finally shuddered to a stop and she got a better view of Victoria Station's wonderful ornate ceiling. It was exciting to be here, but she also felt nervous.

Netta sprang out of her seat and opened the compartment door.

'Hurry up, Addie. The sooner we book into our hotel, the quicker we can catch a motor-bus to Roehampton. I wrote the street name down.' She pulled a piece of paper from her handbag and waved it at her. 'Colin said he'd wait for me at the gates of the Queen Mary.'

Addie reached for her suitcase. 'Sorry Netta. I'm just so worried about visiting Hugh.'

'Stop me if you don't want to know, but a fortnight ago Colin went to see him and copped a torrent of abuse for his trouble. A clerk from the Capitation Department also got a blast when he tried to record Hugh's details in a register. Did you tell him you were coming?'

'No. Do you think I'm doing the right thing?'

Netta screwed up her face. 'You'll know when you get there. Now get a move on.'

Stiff bowlers, caps, wide-brimmed hats bobbed up and down in front of Addie as hundreds of people – more than she'd ever seen in one place – hurried along the platform. Chauffeurs met ladies in tailored suits and fur stoles. Another group of women handing out notices looked rather pushy so she tried to get out of their way. In her haste, she almost tripped over the walking stick of a well-dressed gentleman who was checking his fob watch. 'Sorry,' she said. He tipped his hat.

'Keep up!' Netta called to her above the roar of voices and the bursts of steam from the huge engines.

When she got outside and saw a Buckingham Palace Road street sign and realised she really was in London, she wanted to yell, 'Dickens lived here!' at the top of her voice. Instead, as Netta instructed, she handed her luggage to a porter, who carried it to the bus stop. He didn't hold his hand out for a tip as the porters in Egypt had done.

Cars, trucks, horse-drawn carts and bicycles filled the road. When a big red motor-bus with advertisements splattered along its side pulled in to the kerb, people rushed towards it. The porter pushed her and Netta in the same direction. 'This is the one you need, girls,' he said, swinging their luggage on board. A female bus conductor took their fares.

Addie gazed out the window, hoping to see the palace. Like everyone else, she'd studied the English kings and queens at school, read how Anne Boleyn's life rested in the lecherous hands of Henry the Eighth. King George seemed decent enough, although plenty criticised him and Queen Mary for their lavish way of life while the rest of the nation went without. 'There it is,' she said suddenly. 'See.' She and Netta stared at the great building with its multitude of windows, at the sentries in their boxes by the elaborate gates.

Shortly afterwards their motor-bus turned into a side street lined with magnificent houses and bordering a small park. There was no sign of the slums Dickens had described. Perhaps she'd glimpse St Giles or Petticoat Lane another day. First thing tomorrow, she'd buy a map. For now, to get her bearings, she jotted down in her diary the names of the streets they travelled along.

'Hurry, Addie, we get off here,' Netta said, tugging her coat sleeve. 'We're within walking distance of our hotel.'

The hospital was close to where she and Netta were staying. If it had been miles away, she'd have had more time to think of a way to help Hugh without compromising her own hopes and dreams. Her father was setting up a work scheme for disabled soldiers, an enterprise Hugh would probably think condescending. But what if she had him all wrong and he asked for help? As the motor-bus pulled in to a stop before they reached the hospital, she rose from her seat. 'It's no good, Netta. I can't go. Say hello to Colin for me. I'll see you back at the hotel.' She dashed down the steps before Netta could stop her. When she looked back up at the window, her friend's mouth was opening and shutting like a fish.

Addie hung around the hotel for the rest of the day, sitting for a while in the lounge, watching who came in and out, studying their clothes, the way they spoke. Then she went upstairs and looked out her bedroom window. The Tower of London must be within walking distance, and the famous bridges over the Thames, and more, but it would have seemed heartless to go sightseeing after behaving in such a lily-livered manner. To avoid Netta, she retired early, undressing to the gurgle of hotel plumbing rather than gunfire. It took her ages to fall asleep.

By the time Addie came down to breakfast Netta had departed for the hospital. After eating a piece of toast, she walked to the park she'd seen from the bus and sat on a bench under the shade of an oak tree. Solemn-faced women pushed wheelchairs past her, their children lagging behind, possibly wary of the cumbersome contraptions and the damaged men trapped inside. As the sun dipped behind a church steeple, a fellow whose wife was adjusting the blanket over his lap criticised the state of her hands. Directly behind this couple, a chap without arms berated a woman pushing his chair for failing to notice a tree root snaking under the path. Shaken, Addie fled back to the hotel and picked up the novel she had been reading, but the words wriggled across the page like lice, forcing her to abandon the book and go for another walk.

On the third night, she joined Netta in the dining room.

'They can't keep up with the demand,' Netta said as she sat down. 'It could be ages before Colin and I can marry.'

'Aren't there enough ministers to take all the services?'

'I was talking about limbs. While I was there yesterday, a chap dropped in to measure Colin's foot size. He plans to come back and fit the shoe as soon as the artificial leg arrives. His doctor expects him to learn to walk on it within four to six weeks. Apparently Hugh's down for a leg too. Arms are trickier but not impossible.'

The serviette on Addie's lap floated to the floor. 'You've seen him.' A chill trickled along her spine. She picked up her teacup and put it down again. 'Netta,' she said pausing to steady her voice, 'tell me what you know, please.'

Netta buttered a slice of bread and cut it into quarters before turning to face her.

'I didn't recognise him at first. Colin had to point him out.

He was strapped into a wheelchair parked under a tree. The left side of his face looked like corned beef coated in a silvery-purple slime. I felt so sorry for him. He was once such a vigorous chap.'

Addie picked up a glass from the table and took a sip of water. 'You must think I'm heartless.'

Netta shook her head. 'No one expects you to be at his beck and call on the basis of a few letters and those gloomy drawings. It would be different if he'd asked for your hand.'

Addie made her way to her room that night even more determined not to have unreasonable expectations forced upon her. If she wrote to Hugh again, made it clear she could visit as a friend, nothing more, and if he agreed, then she'd go. Otherwise, she'd visit the galleries, museums and bookshops. Maybe persuade Netta to accompany her to *Chu-Chin-Chow*, which everyone considered a must-see.

In answer to her note, a letter arrived at the hotel four days later, written on Hugh's behalf by James Kershaw, an orderly whose details were recorded in a corner on the front of the envelope. She slipped a butter knife under the flap.

Addie –

Your proposed visit must take place under the following circumstances or not at all. Come to the main entrance on Wednesday at 2 p.m. James, my orderly, will escort you to a bench near a brick wall by the walkway. Stay seated even when you hear me on the other side. Do not under any circumstances attempt to look at me. We can talk for as long as it suits. Do not move until I am wheeled away. If this arrangement is unacceptable, return all my drawings in your keeping to James's address.

Hugh

Thank goodness she didn't have to meet him face to face.

She dressed carefully: a grey skirt, matching jacket and hat, white blouse. Sensible clothes, no frippery. She dabbed perfume on both wrists and behind her ears, made a final check in the mirror, then set off to the bus stop, where a young woman with tired eyes balanced a fractious child on her hip. Addie asked if she was also going to the hospital.

'Yes, my husband's there – what's left of him. He's due home soon.'

'How will you manage?'

'I don't know. He has night terrors and his stumps cause him no end of trouble. Little Susan deserves the daddy she knew.'

'And you, the husband.'

The motor-bus dropped them near a covered walkway that led to the main entrance of the hospital. Addie walked slowly up to the man she thought must be James and they shook hands. She resisted the urge to apologise for not coming sooner, for failing to live up to society's expectations, for having a healthy body.

'I'll bring Hugh out. Sit on the bench over there.' James pointed to a seat backing onto a brick wall. 'Don't stay long. He tires easily.'

His instructions came as a relief. She adjusted her hatpin. 'Thank you.'

Golden-brown leaves from a nearby oak drifted across the grass. She rehearsed her reasons for not making a promise she couldn't keep. When she heard a rumble of wheels and two muffled voices, she smoothed her skirt and straightened her back.

'All yours, Sister,' she heard James say from the other side of the wall.

'Hugh, is that you?' she said cautiously.

'Who else would it be?' he snapped.

She could tell from the slur in his voice that he was still on morphine. 'You've had a horrid time.'

'You don't say!'

She shifted uneasily. 'Why don't you tell me about it?' she said. 'It might help.'

'You have no idea. I enlisted to uphold my country's freedom, and lost mine.'

She mustn't fall into the trap. There had to be a way for him to draw. 'Could you learn to hold a pastel or a paintbrush in your mouth?'

'I can't manage a cigarette, let alone a brush. Do you have any more bright ideas, Sister Sunshine?' His voice had a real edge to it.

She knew it was to be expected, but his bitterness dismayed her. 'I'm sorry, I'm not expressing myself very well. Is there anything I can bring you?'

'Not a thing apart from new hands.'

She'd made things worse. 'You must think badly of me.' Her tone was apologetic.

'I've more important things to dwell on.'

'Hugh, I'm desperately sorry about your injuries, but we were never meant to become a proper couple.' She spoke quickly, leaving no space for him to interrupt. 'If I'm truthful, the idea of a romance appealed to me more than the reality, which is why I enjoyed writing to you.' When he said nothing, she could feel her courage draining away. She tried again. 'Netta told me about a place that makes facial masks. You might want to make enquiries.'

'I only want to draw.' His voice dropped and she moved closer to the wall. 'Nothing else matters. Not my face, not the pain, not you. Leave, will you! Just go! James!'

She stood up. 'I shouldn't have come. I'm so sorry.'

Patients call me the tin mask-maker. I think of myself as a sculptor who likes a challenge. One sits in front of me today. Arctic eyes, a shock of copper-brown hair. Two empty blue sleeves pinned to his shirt. Right leg amputated above the knee. No lips. A cavity rather than a nose, lumpy cheeks, shiny patches where eyebrows once grew, wire plate supporting his jaw, a perfectly trimmed moustache. I look at my notes – Ypres. Plenty of chaps have taken a hit there. Poor bugger. You see decent folk buy limbies a beer or afternoon tea if they meet them in town and happily hold their glasses if they no longer have hands, but the same Samaritans recoil from anyone who's lost a face. This fellow hasn't spoken since his orderly wheeled him in. Time to get started. I describe the lengthy process – how, once his wounds heal, I'll study, measure and compare the new him with a previous photograph. Then I'll get his face ready for moulding, protecting his moustache with Vaseline and oiling his eyelids before covering them with fragments of tissue paper. Then I'll brush on heavier and heavier layers of plaster, until they thicken, solidify and dry. I have to judge the right moment to detach and remove the steamy shell. 'The next step,' I say, 'entails making a plaster of Paris mask, a positive from the negative, to remove imperfections.' Not the wisest word to use. 'Right, that's enough for you to think about today.'

Sixteen

ON THE OUTSKIRTS of cold, dreary Wisques, near St Omer, Dora's sapper and his cronies had cleared an acre of scrub and erected tents with tarpaulin floors. Since English, American and French soldiers were arriving in dribs and drabs, Meg had a couple of hours off every afternoon, and a half-day once a week. Not that she had anything worthwhile to do with this free time. Wallace had returned from the aid post, lethargic and low.

Town was an hour's walk from camp. To get there she had to lorry-hop, a habit that would have landed her in hot water if Matron found out. Addie had almost plucked up the courage to accompany her a few days ago, but pulled out at the last minute, blaming an upset tummy. In her eyes, bending the rules was the same as breaking them.

Dora had come last Sunday, but the entire trip was a waste of time. Thick fog had rolled in, blanketing the countryside, and their lorry had spluttered along, dropping them an hour late in the square. They'd hardly finished their coffee before they needed to find a ride back. Their next driver was deaf. 'Got too close to the guns,' he'd shouted above the pelting rain.

It hadn't let up. The tent she shared with Addie had more holes than a jam strainer and they were forever covering their belongings with scraps of tarpaulin. Soon they'd have to sleep under umbrellas. Rotten weather brought out the worst in everyone. Tempers frayed over the slightest thing: she'd lost hers twice this morning. At breakfast the cook ran out of cocoa; and then she'd tripped on a boot some idiot had left out.

Her outburst was tame compared with Wallace's. First, he'd called a sapper all the names under the sun when the generator went on the blink. Then, at lunch, he'd blasted a clerk for saying a brass hat wanted to extend the hospital and cram in another thousand beds. She couldn't repeat what he'd yelled at Edward when two oxygen cylinders went missing.

Addie had a touch of the doldrums too, scribbling in her diary for hours. No one thought she'd let Hugh down. It was obvious they were never going to work as a couple, regardless of whether he was injured or not. There was no spark. Only Netta had a bounce in her step: Colin this, Colin that. Other people's happiness was hard to take. Desperate for answers, Meg bailed up Edward and Addie during a tea break in the mess. 'Do either of you know what's up with Wallace?'

'I asked him weeks ago when he was drinking like a fish,' Edward said. 'He told me it was a personal matter, nothing to do with anyone else. You're not the problem, Meg.'

'Well, what is then?'

Addie raised her hands. 'It's beyond me. Ask Netta what she thinks.'

So Meg headed to the washroom where Netta was scrubbing dirt from her fingernails. After describing Wallace's latest behaviour, Meg said, 'What do you think is going on?'

'My knowledge is limited to Colin and he's uncomplicated,' Netta said. 'Wallace is an entirely different matter. Has Iris got a theory?'

Meg didn't think it was worth bothering Iris about matters

of the heart until Netta pointed out that a straight-up-and-down person sometimes gave the best advice.

When Meg walked into the tent, Iris put down the instruction sheet she was reading for a miraculous new paste that cleared up infections. 'What's up?'

After Meg had poured out her worries, Iris shook her head from side to side. 'Give him up, Meg. Concentrate on nursing.'

'I can't,' she said. 'Wallace is my life.'

By the time their Nissen huts arrived in November, Meg couldn't have cared less which one Matron put her in, as long as Joan wasn't in the vicinity. Addie had been right – the woman feasted on gossip. The sooner Joan got the transfer she wanted the better. Meg kept reading down the list. Whew, there she was with Addie, Iris, Dora and Netta. She would have understood if they hadn't wanted to share with her. Even she knew she'd been down in the dumps too long. It was high time she decided whether to cling to hope or face despair. Sometimes she thought both paths led to the same abyss.

At Netta's suggestion, she turned a pile of packing cases into tables and chairs, bashing in nails as if she were knocking sense into Wallace. Addie made a bookcase from two planks Dora's chap had slipped her. For privacy, Iris strung up a quilt in front of their washing area. Although they had a drum with a stovepipe to heat water for hot drinks, they continued to eat their main meals in the mess. Linoleum was easier to clean than the matting in their hut.

The hard frosts turned the tarpaulin floors in the wards into skating rinks in the mornings, then cold slush for the rest of the day. Like many of the nurses, Meg was suffering terribly from swollen feet and chilblains. She often had to wear a pair of men's socks stuffed inside a pair of oversized gumboots. Her misery didn't end there.

Last night after the embers in the stove died down, ice formed on the walls inside the hut. She woke to find the folds of her blanket had stiffened where her breath had settled, yet she was in no hurry to rise. Today would be the same as yesterday. Wallace would either gawp at her like a forlorn puppy or completely ignore her. She wanted to shake him. She wanted to scream. She wanted to bury her head in his neck and smell desire.

When she finally got up, she checked a letter she'd started to Aunt Maude.

We use the largest of the Nissen huts as our mess. There's only one window, so we got the sappers to install a skylight. Netta made serge curtains to pretty things up. We bought the material with money provided by the Red Cross. Dora whipped up cushions and tablecloths from the scraps. Netta filled a vase with ivy. Better than nothing, I suppose.

You asked if we had sufficient food. I spend my entire daily allowance of 3/6 on tucker, so I'm generally well fed, although there's never enough butter and milk. We eat a lot of fried bread with golden syrup. A couple of girls have developed tummies, not me though.

Not too many gripes, nothing about Wallace – it would do. She shuffled over to the stove and relit the fire, putting the kettle on to heat water for a wash. Her feet would come right, but she was less sure of Wallace.

꧁

THEIR THIRD CHRISTMAS passed without much fanfare other than a roast dinner and carols. Everyone, including Addie, went through the motions, but she felt terribly homesick and the patients were grim-faced and despondent. The weather was abysmal day after day. A flamboyant French patient with a cabaret background and a fearsome dislike of fresh air promised to sing Addie an English tune if she closed the ward door. When she asked a VAD if she thought the lyrics would be respectable the girl rolled her well-bred eyes.

Not that Addie was feeling particularly honourable. Last Sunday she'd tried to write to Hugh and apologise for her tactless comments at the hospital. Eventually she'd cast the letter aside, convinced that every word groaned with pretentiousness. She'd not considered the weight of words before. Even the thoughts in her diary about women giving white feathers to men out of uniform, thinking they were cowards, came across as judgemental. To compensate, she showered attention on patients whose voices reminded her of Hugh's or who were amputees, incensing an American to such a degree that he lodged a complaint.

When her shift finished at midnight, rather than face Meg's moodiness, she headed for the tranquillity of the laundry room, where she sat in the dark among the stacks of linen, rigid with cold but somehow unable to move. Edward, coming in with a load of soiled linen, almost tripped over her feet. 'What the—' He turned on his torch. 'Addie. What are you doing here? You must be deathly cold. Here, take my mittens.' She could barely thank him. Her tongue had practically frozen to the roof of her mouth. He helped her pull on the warm wool. 'Can I keep you company for a while?' She must have spoken because he sat beside her on the bench and wrapped a scarf smelling faintly of chloroform around her neck.

After a while, he said, 'I was sorry to hear about your friend. It must be hard for you.'

His voice was calm and soothing.

'It's much worse for him,' she said.

'He'll receive excellent care in London.'

She blinked back her tears and said, 'I could do with a friendly shoulder.'

'Mine's happy to oblige. You can tell me anything, Addie.'

'Thank you, Edward. Everything feels jumbled, especially me.'

'In my experience, time and distance can bring clarity. Talking to friends helps too, and quieter pursuits like walking and reading.'

'At the first sign of trouble,' she said, 'I reach for a volume of poetry. If it fails to distract me, I pick up a pen and try to write about my concerns in my diary, although if anything that usually uncovers more of my failings.' An odd formality had crept in to her speech, something that often happened when she confronted disagreeable aspects of herself. 'You must think I'm strange.'

'Not at all. Poetry helps me through harrowing times. So does daydreaming. Imagination is a wonderful escape.'

'I was thinking before about its ability to distort memories. Instead of accurately recalling a yacht trip with my father and sister, Erin, to Pigeon Island, where the wind failed and we were at a standstill for hours, I pictured a storm blowing in. If I think too much about the past I find myself altering it.' She shook her head, as if to disperse the idea. 'If I'd known what we were in for, I mightn't have signed up.'

'And we would never have met,' he said quietly.

She felt her cheeks go hot. Was he saying he more than liked her? She needed time to think but he was waiting for her to speak. Since she hardly knew anything about his life before the war, she asked if he sailed.

'I learnt to walk on my parents' double-skinned kauri keeler which they moored at Akaroa, below our holiday cottage.'

'No wonder you're such a steady fellow.'

He bumped his shoulder gently against hers. 'I'm a clumsy clod really.'

'You don't go around hurting people.'

'Neither do you.'

His voice had a thoughtful quality. He was really listening to her. She told him about the American's complaint.

'Would you like me speak to Matron? She's a good stick.'

'I'll think about it, thanks.'

He gave her mittened hands a comforting squeeze. 'Imagination doesn't have to be driven by fear, Addie. We can make it work to our advantage, use it to heal what holds us back.'

She didn't know whether to leave her hands in his or withdraw them.

'These are dark times but we'll come through them. We're both resilient, Addie.'

At his use of 'we' she felt another rush of warmth spread across her cheeks. 'When we go home no one will understand what we've been through. We mightn't fit in.'

'That plays on my mind as well. I'm not your typical chap, though; not manly enough.'

'I beg to disagree.' She could hardly believe her ears: she was flirting.

'Keep that up and I won't be able to get my head through the door.'

Aware of his lean frame, his hands holding hers, her wild thoughts, she fell silent.

After a time Edward said, 'Sometimes I want nothing more than a quiet life back home. Other times I can't bear the thought of leaving France.'

Was she part of the reason? Meg would have made a joke – 'Your intentions, sir?' – but Edward was waiting for her to speak, another thing she liked about him. 'I swing back and forth too,' she said. 'It doesn't seem right to leave France in ruins. All these fine buildings, some centuries old, reduced to rubble.'

'Not to mention the people.'

Oh no, he might be thinking she preferred buildings to people. 'I admire the French and their positive outlook, despite their country's turbulent past. The same robustness is evident in their architecture.' There was that peculiar formality again.

The rhythm of his breathing didn't change. She rested her head against the wall. His was only inches away.

'I'm not surprised you see what eludes others. You often pick a change in a patient before anyone else.'

She flushed again. 'Thank you, Edward. You've helped a lot.' She took off his mittens and handed them back to him, then stood up. 'I would appreciate it if you could please talk to Matron about the complaint.' Although it was pitch black, she smiled and hoped he'd done the same.

The disgruntled American was transferred to another hospital on the same day that Joan Watson departed and four badly wounded Germans arrived at No. 1. 'None in a state to harm you, Sister Harrington,' Matron said. Addie could see that for herself. One had the hands of a musician, which made her think of Hugh and what he'd lost; another had sad chocolate-brown eyes. The third was close to Erin's age and terrified; the fourth was a flaxen-haired Adonis. Her job was to stabilise them so they could travel as prisoners to a construction camp five miles away. Whenever Iris and Meg had a spare half-hour, they came to help. Despite her good intentions, Iris was soon banging her dressing tray down on the men's lockers, nearly frightening them out of their wits, while Meg's care extended to playing long drawn-out games of whist with the melancholic Captain Adonis.

'Dutton would make up to a shovel if it wore a pair of trousers,' grumbled Iris as she stacked basins on a trolley. 'It won't look good on her record.'

Addie followed her into the washroom. 'If the warmongers were as compassionate as Meg, the peace bells would ring.'

MEG CAME OFF night shift, ate a light breakfast and had a wash. It was an overcast day, although shortly after she left camp the sun came out. Wallace had organised a lorry on the pretext of picking up essential equipment for the lab and she was to wait for him at a farm gate a mile away, near a stand of larches. He'd told her earlier he regretted his glumness, which had nothing to do with her. He loved her.

Not far down the road, a blue tablecloth was flapping on a clothesline and as she drew closer, a child waved from the roof of a henhouse. She blew him a kiss, which he pretended to wipe off. Fifty yards further on an elderly man scratching about his yard with a rake gave her a toothless grin. She sent him a kiss too. There were plenty in reserve for Wallace. Beside a creek, she found two middle-aged women beating their laundry with sticks. The women greeted her as if she were an old friend. 'I'll come back after the war,' she called. Actually, she was thinking of staying on if Wallace would consider doing the same.

When he drove up behind her and stopped the lorry on the side of the road she climbed in without speaking. He eventually parked behind a dilapidated barn that couldn't be seen from the road. His hands rested on the steering wheel. Hers stayed in her lap. A large black spider spun an elaborate web on the windscreen in front of her.

'Do you think he knows what he's doing?' she finally asked, tapping the glass.

The spider scuttled to the centre of its lacy web. Beauty, she thought, shouldn't double as a trap.

Wallace took her hands, turned them over and kissed both palms.

He'd lost more hair but that didn't necessarily mean what she feared. War strain might be responsible. She waited for him to speak.

'You won't be pleased,' he said. 'I'm going on a top-secret assignment.'

234

She jerked away. 'What? Fritz is dropping gas and bombs all over the show. You're not indestructible.'

He gave a slight laugh.

She wanted to shake him. 'I mean it, Wallace. Please don't go.' Her voice was rising but she couldn't stop. She was almost out of control.

He gripped her shoulders. 'I leave tonight. It's for the best, darling girl.'

His voice faded to a whisper. She closed her eyes as he kissed her throat, neck, lips. The same electric feeling was there, but it was no good. She couldn't count on him, or trust him.

They travelled back in silence. If he wouldn't end it, she'd have to be the strong one.

He turned the engine off close to a bend in the road not far from the camp. Reaching across to open her door, he dropped his head unexpectedly into her lap. Instinctively she placed her hand on his cheek; his skin had always felt right against hers. Knowing she might weaken if she lingered, she slid from under him and climbed down from the lorry. He begged her to stay, to talk. They might never have another opportunity – she couldn't go, not like this.

Turning to face him, tenderness catching in her throat, she said, 'Goodbye, Wallace.'

'I'm going for the best of reasons.' His voice sounded far away and tears were welling in his eyes. 'Meg. Meg. Meg!'

MIDWAY THROUGH MARCH the army announced that it needed nursing sisters for eight weeks of anaesthesia training at British hospitals, to be followed by a month of practical experience at a clearing station. Addie was hoping to be among the chosen. Edward had shown her the basics but she was keen to master the intricacies.

When she saw her name on the list, a tremor of excitement ran through her. Iris had missed out and the only other familiar name was Jean Porteous, who was from Winton and had trained at Riverton. Addie hadn't seen her for years but remembered her as a woman always willing to help those in trouble. She hadn't known she was in France.

Instead of celebrating Addie's good news, Meg threatened to volunteer for another hospital train since everyone was leaving her. Addie said she'd better be here when she returned or she'd track her down and make her read a dictionary from cover to cover.

When it was time to say goodbye, Meg clung to her desperately, but Addie couldn't relinquish the chance to undergo extra training. 'Three months isn't long,' she said, hugging her tightly. 'If I hear news of Wallace, I'll let you know.'

'Don't bother,' Meg said, stepping aside. 'Watch yourself around those instructors. Never trust a stranger who can sprinkle ether on his handkerchief and render you helpless.'

Addie was chatting to Jean about the places they'd seen since leaving home when a short chap with thick wiry hair opened the door to the classroom.

'Listen and learn,' he said. 'I'll teach you to give ether and chloroform through a Shipway apparatus, which is simple to use and easier on patients. We'll cover open mask, drop method too, although it's fast going out of fashion. You'll also learn to administer nitrous oxide and oxygen. By the end of the course I expect you to think of the equipment as an extension of your own hand.'

He picked up a pair of forceps from a bench and held them up. 'Which hospital has a well-known association to these?'

'Guy's,' said Jean.

'Yes, well done.'

Next, he showed them a gag and asked for the name of the manufacturer. A North Islander correctly identified it.

Then he raised an ether inhaler. 'Who invented this?'

Addie raised her hand.

'Go ahead,' he said.

'Clover.'

'Good. Now we'll move on to an oxygen cylinder and fitting set.'

She wanted to remind him they were trained nursing sisters with extensive war experience but she held her tongue. If she made the most of this opportunity, it would give her more options when she returned home.

'Training and confidence, ladies,' he said, patting the cylinder.

She spent hours calculating body weights and charting appropriate doses, and almost as much time sheltering from bombs in a dugout. Initially she and her classmates donned tin hats and ran to the shelter immediately. After a week, however, they grew more blasé and paused to gather up cushions, rugs, thermos flasks and sandwiches, prepared in advance, although they did stop talking when they heard the telltale whine.

One night a Taube came over unusually low. She waited anxiously for the bombs to fall. The first dump landed some distance away, but the next was much closer. Three hours of terror wrecked her chance of a good night's sleep or studying for tomorrow's test on the uses of intravenous infusions, including blood.

Addie made the journey to a casualty clearing station south of Dunkirk in a lorry driven by a corporal who trained homing pigeons. When she arrived, the surgeon, a bear of a man with rather protuberant dark eyes under feathery brows, briefed her while she drank a cup of bitter tea. Although intermittent artillery fire drowned out portions of his talk, she caught something about a battle heating up nearby.

'We could face a tidal wave of injured men. I don't know how we'll care for them on top of those who are already coming in with raging temperatures and aching limbs.'

The following day she gave five anaesthetics, seven the next, using ether, nowhere near as many as Edward administered at No. 1. Mostly she cared for patients who were coughing up lumps of phlegm from congested lungs. The Bear was competent but she missed Wallace's astute observations. She was scrubbing mugs the morning the Bear came into the makeshift treatment room and said, 'Pack up, Sister. The Germans are retreating rapidly and we're moving further north.'

As Addie was preparing intestinal, spinal and head cases and the feverish chaps for the move, a chest patient opened a small volume of poetry and showed her a dog-eared page. She read the underlined stanza.

As the stars that shall be bright when we are dust
Moving in marches upon the heavenly plain
As the stars that are starry in the time of our darkness
To the end, to the end, they remain.

Recognising the lines from Laurence Binyon's 'For the Fallen', she asked the soldier if he considered them well written. He looked at her thoughtfully and said, 'They're memorable.' En route to her new posting, she described the conversation in a letter to Edward. He'd written first and she'd replied straight away.

Four days later the Bear joined her for a meal of bully beef. Between mouthfuls he said, 'I think you should rejoin your unit, Sister. Victory's in sight but there are reports of hand-to-hand fighting less than two miles away. Finish eating and grab your kit. I have a lorry waiting.'

Bouncing up and down in the front seat between the driver and a clerk, neither of them talkative, she surveyed the adjacent countryside for signs of enemy activity. In a field pockmarked with shell holes, something resembling a scarecrow caught her eye – no, not a scarecrow, a dead soldier with a bayonet through his belly pinning him to a tree stump. He wore a field-grey uniform, not khaki. The clerk opened the lorry door and vomited.

By the time she arrived back at Wisques, her entire body felt taut, as though a dressmaker had taken it in at the seams. She stood at the camp entrance, a battered kit at her feet, lorry dust disappearing down the gravel road.

There was no sign of life: everyone must be working or sleeping. In his last letter, Edward had mentioned that No. 1's influenza cases were growing. She hadn't heard from Meg for a fortnight, not that it meant anything. She mightn't have had time to write and mail often went astray. A letter from Addie's mother had taken six months to reach her, circumnavigating the globe twice. She checked the roster for Meg's name and found it in the day duty column.

A GERMAN PATIENT, shot by a sniper while he was on the frozen River Somme at night in makeshift skates, showed Meg a photograph of a young man receiving a trophy in Berlin.

'Dass bin ich. Ich war siebzehn.' He flicked his fingers open and closed until he reached seventeen. Placing his hands on the blanket where his legs should be, he said, 'Ich hatte zwei Beine.'

Meg patted his arm. At twenty, he had no legs and no dream. Thankful she'd managed to pick up a few words from the Germans she'd nursed, she nodded sympathetically. For two years, her dearest hope had been a future with Wallace. Now when she closed her eyes, she relived her nightmare of him in a watery coffin.

Another German patient was complaining of a severe headache and pain in his back and limbs. Half an hour earlier, his temperature had been 103; now it was 104. Meg rechecked his pulse – raised and thready. Any higher and he could convulse.

He lifted his head off the pillow. 'Wasser, bitte, Schwester.' The effort set him coughing violently enough to shoot clotted blood through his nostrils onto the sheet. It stank. He tried to apologise but she shook her head. 'Don't talk,' she said. 'Save your strength.' She cleaned up the mess, then fetched some broth. He gagged on the first mouthful, accidentally tipping over the bowl. More muck to clean up.

Leaving a VAD to strip and remake the German's bed, Meg moved to the next patient, an Australian, and placed a clean sputum mug in the hollow of his chest while she rearranged his pillows. 'That's better.'

His fingers plucked at the coverlet. 'I was fine yesterday.'

Scarlet froth dribbled from his mouth and she wiped his chin with a damp cloth. Wallace should be here taking samples, examining them in the lab, coming up with answers. 'So your symptoms came on quickly?'

His chest rattled like a bag of marbles as he tried to speak and more phlegm worked free. When she held the mug to his mouth, yellowish-brown mucus trickled over the rim. She took a cloth from a basin, squeezed out the excess water and gently washed his face.

He pressed his hands to his chest. 'One minute I was on my feet, the next on my knees. I feel real crook, Sister.'

'I'll put mustard leaves on your chest to ease the pain. You'll soon feel like a new man.' A dead one if she couldn't lower his temperature. 'I'll send an orderly to sponge you.'

He grabbed her arm. 'Sister, do you know what I've got?'

'Some badly behaved bug you need to biff on the chin.'

He made a fist. She smiled reassuringly, even though patients either side of him were drowning in fluids their exhausted lungs couldn't expel. She checked the time: five o'clock. Matron would be waiting on the list of new influenza cases. 'I'll see you after dinner,' she called to another patient who believed he would live as long as she was nearby. His eyes followed her to a cot near the door where she stopped to talk to Dora, who was supporting a fellow while he vomited into a basin. 'Can you hold the fort while I take over today's notes?' Dora waved her on.

Addie was waiting for her outside. Thinking she was seeing things, Meg seized her friend's arms so hard that she left imprints in the flesh. 'Oh Addie, I missed you so much.'

⁂

ON HER NEXT day off, Addie asked Edward if he could commandeer a vehicle with a full tank of petrol and drive her through the countryside from Ypres down to Lille, an area that was at last in the hands of the English. 'I'd also like to see Kemmel and Messines.'

Edward called in a favour and they were soon rumbling down dust-covered roads. A shaft of sunlight appeared between banks of dark clouds, making the fragments of ironwork partially buried in the shell-torn earth look like grotesque creatures that were about to rise up and devour her. She shuddered and looked ahead. On the other side of the road a boy on a bicycle, wearing an oversized jacket, swerved into a field and began to weave between a dozen graves. In a ruined village, returning residents hunted for remnants of earlier lives. Addie saw one woman about her mother's age triumphantly hold up a piece of a china tea set.

Two hours on, where the lie of the land reminded her of the rolling plains of Southland, she asked Edward to pull over. Navigating what was left of a charred stile, they made their way across a field, positioning their feet carefully, noting slight undulations, listening for the crunch of bones. When, eventually, they came to a ditch that heaved with sleek water rats, Edward took her hand and they jumped together. As she landed a twig snapped under her foot. It sounded like teeth breaking.

Below, in another destroyed hamlet, the ashen fingers of charred buildings stretched towards the pale horizon. An

241

abandoned rucksack lay beneath the blackened roots of an oak tree. She pulled back the rotting canvas flap, thinking there might be some form of identification inside, but only a broken compass remained. Nearby, though, she found a hand, its intricate network of weathered bones picked clean. She sank to her knees, a sob snagging in her throat. Whether these bones belonged to an Englishman, a German or a New Zealander, they deserved respect. She made a nest in the soil and buried the hand close to where a cluster of acorns had fallen. Thinking they would be a fitting reminder of this time, she dropped a handful into Edward's haversack, then stood shakily and recited the Lord's Prayer. When she opened her eyes, Edward passed her his canteen and she drank as if quenching a fire.

'I haven't been back to visit Hugh.' Her voice was heavy with sadness.

'No.'

'We're blighted, aren't we? Like this land.'

'We'll heal, Addie. So will the grass, and the trees, and the families who live here.'

'Farmers will be digging up human bones for years.' She squashed the tip of a grass blade between her fingers. 'You're from Dunedin, aren't you?'

'Canterbury originally, but I studied in Dunedin.' He gestured towards a pile of stones, once a low wall. 'Shall we sit for a while?'

'Could you please tell me about the city?'

He placed his haversack on the ground and sat beside her. 'Well, as I'm sure you know, it has an excellent medical school and a fine hospital. Dunedin's a progressive place, and it promotes the arts. There are bookshops on every corner.'

She smiled warmly at him. 'Is your father a medical man?'

'No, he's an archaeologist. He digs up the past. I'm the only one in my family who puts people to sleep.'

I want to take her in my arms. Instead, I remove my glasses and polish them with my handkerchief. She may not consider me a potential suitor, and for the life of me, I can't see why she would. I'm gangly, bespectacled, a bit of a brain, quiet rather than gregarious, not the type beautiful women go for. She seems to appreciate my humorous bent, though, and she enjoys discussing literature with me. She'd take pleasure in working her way through my parents' library. Goodness knows what she'd make of them, though. Both declared themselves against the war from the outset, a stance I've come to appreciate. I no longer believe I can control every aspect of my life. It's enough to have come through this horror in one piece and to realise there's still a place and a purpose for men like me. An unthinking brain is as quiescent as an anaesthetised one. The more contemplative I become, the more I realise how much of the mind remains uncharted, at least to me. Why, for instance, do some boys lose their minds at the front and not others? And why didn't I declare my intentions to Addie earlier? If only I could summon up the courage to kiss her. But not today. No man wants the dead witnessing his first embrace of the woman he loves.

Seventeen

MARLED GREY CLOUDS were sweeping across the late September sky. Back in Tuatapere, the first rays of light would be breaking over the Takatimus and Uncle Bert would have jammed on his size fourteen boots and set off to check which ewes were ready to drop spring lambs. When she'd first gone to live with him and Aunt Maude, the house had frightened her, with its unfamiliar creaks, and she'd often crept down the hall in the middle of the night and climbed into their bed. 'Houses need to stretch too,' Uncle Bert had told her. At daybreak, he'd made her a mug of milky cocoa and given her a plain biscuit to dunk in it. 'Don't leave crumbs on my side of the bed, Meg,' he would tease. 'Keep them for Maude. She likes surprises.' In the beginning, this routine had felt unnatural. You can't move from chaos to comfort and not feel uneasy.

If Uncle Bert and Aunt Maude had taken her at birth, she might have ended up more ladylike, though taking another path would have changed more than her manners. For starters, she mightn't have become a nurse. She could have had an easier life, but never met Wallace. So really, surviving her ghastly childhood, and later living comfortably with her aunt and uncle, had worked out just fine. In fact, it had given her a broader outlook.

She knocked on Matron's hut door, the latest influenza report in her hand. No response, so she rapped again. Matron must be inside: her ward shoes were on the steps. Gingerly she pushed the door open. Matron was slumped in an armchair in the far corner of the dimly lit room.

'Oh no, have you got it too?'

'Got it?' Matron said, lifting her head. 'What are you talking about, dear?'

Golly! Matron must have a raging fever. 'Shall I fetch a medical officer?'

Matron gripped the arms of her chair and stood up. 'I'm not ill, though I do have distressing news. But we must keep in mind that missing doesn't necessarily mean dead.'

Had she lost a relative? Meg had never heard her mention any family. 'The missing can turn up,' she said. 'Please, Matron, sit down. I'll make you a pot of tea.'

She took two mugs from a shelf and put them on the table. 'Are you sure you don't want me to notify someone?'

'Sister Dutton – Meg – I don't think you understand. One of ours is missing.'

Ours! Fear crawled up her spine. 'Not Addie . . . she can't . . .'

Matron flapped her hands. 'Harrington's fine.'

'Are you sure?'

'Yes, she's gone on a drive with Edward Ramsay.'

'Oh, yes, I remember.'

Matron patted the chair next to hers. 'Sit down.'

Then who is it? 'No, not . . .'

Matron's chin quivered as she nodded slowly.

An ice-cold void opened within Meg. She could no longer see Matron or the chair. Someone was screaming. She put her hand over her mouth: if she stopped saying his name, it wouldn't be true. 'No, no!'

'I'm sorry, Meg, dreadfully sorry.'

She tried to drive the words – 'lost in action', 'not accounted for' – from her mind. 'Missing can mean taken prisoner,' she said loudly. 'The Germans won't harm a surgeon. They need him. We need him. I need him!'

Matron took her by the shoulders. 'Listen to me. Our side suffered heavy losses. The authorities are sure he was among them. Someone saw him fall.'

Meg pushed the older woman away. The witness must have been wrong. He could have seen another captain, similar in height and build. There had to be a mistake. When she looked up, Matron's eyes were moist. 'No!' she screamed, running towards the door. 'I have to find him.'

Matron pulled her back but she twisted free. No one but Wallace could touch her. If he was gone, she wanted to die. Gripping her again by the shoulders, Matron urged her to be strong. Why should she? There was nothing to live for. 'Where is he?' she wailed. 'Where is he?'

Tightening her hold, Matron gave her a swift shake. 'Pull yourself together, Sister. We don't want a scandal.'

Meg shivered. 'What do you mean?' Her voice had dropped to a whisper.

Matron stiffened. 'His wife has been notified.' Her voice softened a little. 'Sister, this is a difficult situation.'

Meg slid further into the icy void. It couldn't be true. 'A wife – are you sure?'

Matron picked up a form from her desk and pointed to the words: 'Evelyn Madison, wife and next of kin.'

Meg closed her eyes, but her childhood game didn't work: she couldn't make Wallace's wife disappear. Deep down, she'd known he was married, but he could have filed for divorce. People did. Her parents should have. Now it was too late – for them, for Wallace, for her. She scraped her fingernails down her face, drawing blood.

'Sister Dutton! Meg! Stop that,' Matron said firmly. 'Take the next twelve hours off. Compose yourself. Report for duty tomorrow evening, mind on the job. We have an influenza disaster on our hands.' Meg tore off her apron and threw it to the floor, then kicked the leg of a chair. She couldn't stop clawing at her skin. 'Wait,' said Matron, 'while I fetch one of your friends.'

The door closing felt like her life shutting down. She thought of the last time she and Wallace had been together. He could have died thinking she no longer loved him. She fell to the floor and thumped it with her fists. He mustn't be dead. He could be married, but he mustn't be dead.

IRIS WAS PACING up and down outside the hut when Edward and Addie pulled up.

'Oh, thank goodness you're back, Addie. We don't know what to do.'

'What are you talking about? Where's Meg?'

Iris came to a standstill. 'She's with Netta in Matron's hut. Wallace has gone missing. And we were right – he's married.'

Addie's heart was pounding when she swung open Matron's door and found Meg crouched on the floor, uniform askew, lashing out at Netta, who was trying to wash her face.

Netta looked up. 'Addie, thank goodness.'

A desolate howl escaped from Meg as she caught sight of her friend.

Kneeling down, Addie gently pushed back the curls that had fallen over Meg's bloodied face. 'I'll take care of you.' She kept talking while she pressed Netta's damp cloth against the scratches on Meg's cheeks. 'You're safe now,' she said, 'you're safe,' and she held her until she stopped struggling.

When Iris arrived with a mug of tea, Meg pushed it away.

'Let's get you back to our hut,' said Addie. 'Come on. Up you come.'

Netta and Iris supported Meg as she staggered towards their

hut, head down, moaning pitifully. Addie ran ahead and opened the door. When they reached the doorway, Meg turned to Addie with a defeated expression on her face. 'He was married.'

'He loved you, Meg. He told me.'

'Words mean nothing.'

'I believed him.' Addie tried to make her voice as convincing as possible.

Meg shuddered. 'He never told me the truth.'

Addie was beginning to view truth as a shifting thing, like the mooring line of a boat, tied by time, place and circumstances. She had no idea whether Wallace would have fallen for Meg if they'd met in peacetime or what would have happened if he hadn't been married. What he wanted one day might have changed the next. It used to happen to her.

She settled Meg into an armchair and tucked a blanket over her while Netta went to the kitchen for soup. Iris poked the embers in the stove and put on a kettle. 'Hot-water bottle,' she mouthed to Addie.

Heat would ease the physical shock, but nothing could help Meg's despair. Addie thought back to the clearing station where Wallace had made a point of telling her that he loved Meg. Maybe he'd known he was going to die.

Iris handed her the hottie, which she put on Meg's knees, thinking she would perhaps pick it up, cuddle it, but she didn't move. Netta returned with a bowl of onion soup. 'Will you try a spoon or two, Meg?'

She shook her head. 'Did I hurt you before, Netta?'

'Don't give it a thought. I'm a toughie.'

'Not with Colin.'

'No, I'm a softie with him.' Her eyes filled with tears. 'Oh, Meg, I'm terribly sorry.'

At quarter to eleven that evening, Matron brought over a jug of cocoa. 'Drink up while it's hot, Sisters. Harrington, you're due on the ward at midnight. Have you slept at all?'

248

No, she hadn't left Meg's side. 'I'm fine, Matron,' she said, cupping both hands around her mug. 'Do we have more influenza patients?'

'Yes, beds are filling fast. Mild cases seem to progress well at first but in less than an hour they can deteriorate to a critical state.' She fixed her eyes on Meg. 'We need every pair of hands.'

Netta tried to get Meg to drink her cocoa but she clenched her teeth.

Matron carried on talking. 'We lost five boys this afternoon.' Her voice tailed off as she walked over to the table.

Addie followed. 'Have you noticed anything unusual about their condition?'

Matron scratched a rough patch of skin on her jaw. 'Coughing and expectoration cease towards the end. I can't tell if it's due to sheer weakness or a physical inability.'

Addie thought of the patients she and the Bear had treated. The pattern had been the same. She swallowed the last of her cocoa and put her mug back on the tray. 'It's destroying our boys.'

'The cook thinks it's a secret weapon of the Kaiser's disguised as poisonous gas,' Netta said.

Matron rapped her knuckles on the table. 'Tell him to concentrate on improving his beef tea. We could have an epidemic on our hands. Stay alert. Ventilate. Maintain rigorous cleaning standards.' She glanced at Meg. 'I need everyone on duty tomorrow.' She turned back to Addie. 'Understand me, Harrington?'

'Yes, Matron,' Addie said, but she doubted that she could get Meg to eat, let alone work.

❧

DURING THE NEXT fortnight, Meg swung from rage to grief and back again. She'd have thrown in the towel had fighting the influenza not given her something else to think about. The medics had different views on how to treat it. Wallace's replacement recommended hot packs on the thorax for pain relief. His sidekick favoured the cold variety. Blue nicknamed him the 'Piss Prophet' because he insisted on regular urine checks. Meg dished out oil of turpentine or cloves as a calmative for tympanites, a dangerous complication of pneumonia, and linseed and mustard poultices for those suffering chest pains. The relief was temporary. She had no time to reheat the poultices. It was hard enough keeping up with linen changes.

She fastened a gauze mask over her nose and mouth, pulled on a pair of rubber gloves and instructed her orderlies to collect and measure the prune-coloured sputum. Fearing a breakdown of lung tissue, she fetched a conical-shaped steam kettle from the storeroom and set about creating a warm vapour that would make breathing easier for the patients.

Germans were dying too, denting the theory of a secret weapon. The night before, an ambulance had dropped off a chap in a field-grey uniform. He had telltale dark-blue eyelids, and blood trickled from his nose and ears. If his papers were accurate, he died on his thirtieth birthday.

She ducked into the washroom to rinse basins and found Iris doing the same.

'Apparently, it's racing through Europe,' Iris said.

Meg dried a basin and put it on a trolley. The enamel gleamed like bones. 'What more can the top brass do to contain it?'

Iris shrugged as she hung her tea towel back on a hook. 'Visit hospitals, draw up plans, make speeches – it's our turn to listen to them this evening. If the influenza reaches New Zealand, there won't be sufficient nurses to care for the sick. We might be ordered home.'

Apart from Aunt Maude and Uncle Bert, who had money to pay for the best of care, there was no reason for her to return. 'I'm not leaving,' she said.

'Well, I suppose there's a higher chance of picking up a

military award from the French. They give out more than our lot.'

Meg glared at her and banged down the basin she was holding. 'I'm staying for other reasons.'

'Face facts. They may never find his body, and even if they do, it will go back to his wife. You should never have taken up with him. It nearly ruined you. Count yourself lucky that morals are more lax in France than at home. Not that I think that's anything to crow about.'

Meg gripped the bench to steady herself, but the room kept spinning. Iris must have realised that she'd overstepped the mark because she patted Meg awkwardly on the back as she left the room.

It didn't matter. Nothing did.

A CLERK at the door handed Addie two posters as she went into the mess to listen to the speeches. At first glance, they seemed more suited to the public than trained personnel. Perhaps there'd been a mix-up. The first was headed 'Advice to Sufferers – Official Instructions'. One phrase jumped out at her: 'Don't depress yourself by looking at the bad side.' What other side was there, when an illness could fell battle-hardened soldiers? The second poster, headed 'Influenza: Precautions and Warnings', advised citizens, among other things, to 'Avoid intimate contact, e.g., kissing and dancing'. Who on earth wrote these things?

A stiff-backed colonel cleared his throat before calling the gathering to order. 'I regret to inform you that a similar strain of influenza has hit New Zealand.'

Her parents! Erin! The world *was* slipping into darkness. She glanced at Edward, who smiled and tapped the underside of his chin with the back of his hand. She forced herself to pay attention to the talk.

'So far only North Islanders are affected,' the colonel continued. 'Health officials have begun spraying disinfectant in places of congregation. Don't worry, people are in good spirits. Apparently some wit has proposed large doses of beer as the sovereign remedy.'

There was a smattering of laughter, but she searched the faces around her for signs of worry. As usual, Meg was staring into space. Dora and Netta looked nervous and strained, but Iris raised her hand and asked which treatments would be of most use in France.

'Good question, Sister.'

His teeth caught the light when he spoke. They were yellow. He must be a smoker.

He issued a torrent of instructions, to which Matron added her contribution, interlacing her fingers and resting them on the buckle of her uniform belt. 'Watch for coated tongues, purple blisters, constipation or diarrhoea, icy sweating, nervous behaviours and, more worrisome, sudden and complete oedema of both lungs. Remember to place patients with pneumonia in a Fowler's or semi-Fowler's position.'

By now Addie's head was reeling.

'Put blocks under the cots of delirious patients to raise their heads,' Matron continued. 'Aim to rest bodies as well as minds.'

'But delirious cases disrupt the wards,' called an orderly who'd recently transferred from an Australian unit. 'Can we send them somewhere else?'

Matron sent him a withering look. 'Delirium is a serious and brutal complication caused by toxins that poison the brain cells. Never leave these patients alone. Their strength is phenomenal. If they have difficulty swallowing and can't take fluids, administer saline per rectum via a syringe to prevent severe dehydration. Does anyone have a sensible comment or question?'

The officials shifted their feet nervously.

Addie raised her hand.

'Sister Harrington?'

'Is alcohol of any use?'

'Yes, brandy will stimulate the circulatory system and it should help both delirious and convalescent patients.'

'Any rations for us?' the Australian shouted.

'Only if you become infected,' Matron said, 'which I would *not* recommend.'

'No more kisses for you, sweetheart,' he joked to a VAD standing beside him. The sensible girl backed away.

Addie suddenly saw her father pulling up carrots that he would take up to her mother in the kitchen. Please God, let this dreadful influenza spare them and Erin.

⁂

ALTHOUGH MEG wanted to collect her mail, she couldn't muster the strength to walk the extra thirty yards, so she stopped and leant against the laundry wall.

Wallace's death was official. As far as she knew, there was no grave for his wife to visit. A clerk had told her Mrs Madison held radical views – apparently she was a suffragette. Meg had heard about some of the militant women who'd been imprisoned and then gone on hunger strikes, so they had to be force-fed. She pictured Wallace's wife, a tube up her nostril, eardrums close to bursting, pain in her throat and chest, and felt a flicker of satisfaction, followed by a flash of despair. If she'd nothing better to do than wish misery on another woman, she might as well collect her mail.

Alone in the hut, huddled over the stove, she traced her uncle's big loopy handwriting on the envelope. He'd never written directly to her before; usually he just added a paragraph at the bottom of her aunt's letters. In her last reply, she'd thanked them both for all they'd done, for saving her when she was too young to save herself. Just in case she didn't make it home. Dora had already caught influenza and Iris was caring for her in the isolation hut. Every few hours a kitchen worker left them a glass bottle of soup on the doorstep. Twice a day Dora's sapper dropped off chocolate and encouraging notes. An hour ago, Netta had told them that Dora had developed pleurisy.

Slowly she opened the envelope and unfolded the single page.

'My dear Meg,' he wrote, 'I bring you sad news. Maude has succumbed to influenza. She went quickly. There was no time to hang a white tea towel on the gate.' No, please, not Aunt Maude. She put the letter on the table and backed away. A voice in her head blamed her for not being there, for thinking that money could buy health, for selfishly sinking head first into her own woes. Trembling, she picked the page up again and read on.

I'm sorry to tell you in a letter. I would prefer to tell you in person. But I'm feeling poorly myself. You mustn't fret if my number is up too. I had a good run with Maude, and you coming along made it a darn sight better. We love you, Meg. Remember us fondly. You'll know I'm gone if a letter arrives from our lawyer. Maude's last thoughts were of you. I can't tell you how proud she was. She kept your letters on her bedroom dresser. She wore them out just looking at them. She left you well-off. You won't have to scrimp.

Meg rubbed her eyes, looked again at the carefully written words. Then a black cloud pressed down on her and a queer sensation sent her reeling.

Sister Dutton's in a terrible state. I pray for the soul of her aunt and a miracle to save her uncle, and I comfort her until Blue fetches me to preside over the burial of nine soldiers. When I return to camp, she's nowhere to be seen. I can't find space in the hospital for my altar, so I set it up outside on the stump of a blackened elm. I say a prayer each time a stretcher goes into the moribund ward. Some die quickly, others with pitiful slowness. Many call for their mothers, and who can blame them? They're so young. I offer Holy Communion and Absolution, which most accept, including a few non-believers. One fellow counts up the number of Germans he thinks he's killed, then asks me to write and apologise to their mothers. All I can do is visit a group of German patients and ask if we can recite the Lord's Prayer together.

Vater unser im Himmel
geheiligt werde dein Name
Dein Reich komme
Dein Wille geschehe
wie im Himmel, so auf Erden.

Before I return to my own boys, I see a German lad arrive whose bowels spill onto the floor like a bundle of eels. He'll be gone before dawn.

Eighteen

WHEN ADDIE came off duty, Meg was outside their hut, scrabbling in the dirt with her bare hands, shouting that she had a tunnel to dig. Although Addie tried to reason with her, Meg continued to toss earth and gravel into the air. Fearful of what might happen next, Addie fetched Edward and the padre.

The men also pleaded with Meg, employing various tactics to distract her, but they couldn't get through to her either. She kept digging, faster and harder. Grime coated her hair, her face, her uniform. Her hands were bleeding.

'We have to help her,' Addie pleaded. 'Please Edward, try again.'

Crouching beside Meg, he talked to her calmly until finally her agitation tapered off and she began to shake, then he picked her up and carried her into the hut, where the padre helped to lay her on her cot.

'There are spiders everywhere,' Meg screamed, beating the blanket with closed fists.

'We should notify Matron,' said the padre thoughtfully. He ran a forefinger and a thumb down his chin and looked at them in turn. His eyes were misty. Recalling the reassurance Meg had sought after Lois lost her mind, Addie said, 'Meg's been through so much lately. If we get plenty of fluids into her and make her sleep, she might come right in a day or two. Can we at least try? Please.'

The padre looked at Edward. 'What do you think?'

'She won't sleep unless she's sedated.'

The padre brought his hands together and rested them against his chest as if he were about to pray. 'Yes, a good rest may be all she needs.'

'It would give us time to work out what to do,' Addie said. 'I'll watch her, Edward, while you fetch your medical bag.'

After he left, she asked the padre to stand on the other side of Meg's cot, ready to help pin her down should she try to flee. Jagged red streaks snaked from her elbows down to her wrists. Edward returned and filled a syringe with morphine. 'Pull back the blanket, Addie. Hold her leg steady.'

The gravity of what they were about to do made her hesitate, but there was no alternative. Meg was too busy unpicking the hem of her blanket to notice the prick. Soon her eyelids flickered and closed.

The padre watched over her while Addie and Edward drew up a revised roster. Quarter of an hour later, satisfied they'd organised sufficient cover, Addie said, 'I'd better show these changes to Netta and Iris, since we've got them down for extra shifts.'

'I'll come with you,' Edward said, 'in case you run into Matron, though I haven't a clue what I'll say if she asks awkward questions. If we look guilty, she's bound to know we're up to something.'

'Two first-class minds will surely outwit a matron distracted by an influenza outbreak,' said the padre. 'Off you go. I'll watch our patient.'

Addie walked the first few yards in silence. 'You know, poetry helped Tennyson through a terrible loss.'

257

Edward took off his glasses and wiped them on the cuff of his shirt. As he did so, his hand brushed against hers. 'I don't think it would comfort Meg.'

'Not even "In Memoriam"?' She stopped walking and quoted aloud:

Regret is dead, but love is more
Than in the summers that are flown
For I myself with these have grown
To something greater than before.

'Perfect,' he said.

She longed to ask if he meant the lines or the way she recited them, but this wasn't the time.

A car puttered through the gate and stopped directly in front of them. A black kid glove holding a small envelope came through an open window, followed by an olive-skinned face and a thatch of white hair partly obscured by a top hat. Addie recognised the mayor of Wisques. Unsure if local protocol required her to curtsey, she dipped a little and left it at that. He said, in heavily accented English, 'I cannot stop. I have a mass funeral to attend.' He gave Edward the envelope. 'Captain Madison treated many people in town, free of charge. To lose a mediocre man is a misfortune – to lose an exceptional one is a tragedy. Please give this letter of appreciation to his loved ones.'

Edward said, 'I'll make sure the right person receives it.'

After the car left, he handed it to Addie and said, 'You decide.'

She could feel the warmth of his hand on the envelope. 'Thank you.'

At the end of two back-to-back duties, Addie returned to the hut where Meg was sleeping under Netta's care. 'Edward called in earlier and gave her another injection,' Netta said. 'You're nearly asleep on your feet, Addie. I'll do the next double duty.

You rest.'

The stove threw out a cosy heat. Coffee was bubbling on the hob so she poured herself a cup, sank into a chair and removed the mayor's letter from her pocket. Her heart wanted to give it to Meg but her mind, especially her conscience, sided with Mrs Madison. She slipped the problem between the pages of her diary: it would be safe there until she reached a decision.

For the next five days she nursed influenza patients, covered for Meg, cared for her, ate when she could, ignored paperwork, snatched a couple of hours' sleep here and there.

As she set off for the mess one night before going on duty, hoping to pass Matron's hut unobserved, a familiar voice said, 'Harrington.' Addie's legs turned to jelly. 'While I'm sympathetic to Sister Dutton's plight, no one is to do more double duties without my permission. Mistakes will creep in. Get her back on her feet.'

So she knew. Addie took a deep breath. 'I don't think Meg's ready.'

Matron blew dust off the door handle. 'Loss is part of life. No one is spared.'

Although Addie wanted to say Meg had suffered more than most, all that came out of her mouth was 'Yes, Matron.'

She found Edward in the soup queue and filled him in.

He balanced a slice of bread on the side of his plate. 'Get her on her feet indeed. She's not a racehorse.'

The knife and fork she'd collected from the cutlery box on a side-table had seen better days. She polished them with a corner of her apron as she lined up for scrambled eggs on toast. A medic standing in front of her said, 'How's Dutton bearing up?'

'As well as we can expect under the circumstances. Thanks for asking.' Turning to Edward, she said, 'We don't have a choice. Matron needs her back on the ward.'

'All right, I'll lower the dose and we'll see how she responds.'

They headed for an empty table and Edward pulled a chair out for her. She draped her cape over the back and sat down, hoping he would realise she wanted company, not conversation. He passed with flying colours. Oh dear, she was behaving like a teacher marking a report card.

'Why do you think Wallace pushed his luck?' she said after she finished her toast. 'Meg's been terrified of losing him for a while.'

Edward picked up his cap. 'She might have anyway.'

There was no time to ask him what he meant. She was due in the ward and she dared not be late.

They were leaving the mess when Netta rushed in.

'Matron wants me in the medical storeroom to oversee an inventory. I sent a VAD to sit with Meg. Unfortunately she's a bit giddy.'

Edward put on his cap. 'You get off, Addie. I'll stay with Meg.'

'But you have loads to do,' she protested.

'I can write reports anywhere. Really, it's fine.'

'Well,' she said, 'if you're sure. I'll get back as soon as I can.' She wanted to reach out and tidy the piece of wavy hair sticking out above his right ear. 'Do you think Meg will pull through?'

'If she chooses to fight you'll get her back.'

'You've been a tremendous help.'

He smiled. 'Just making sure you can't do without me.'

A MAN'S SMELL stayed in his clothing. Meg remembered giving a dead Riverton man's belongings to his wife and watching her pull his jacket from the package, bury her face in the fabric and sniff hungrily. Wallace's clothes had had a fresh lemony tang. She must get his shirt and scarf before someone sent them to his wife. 'Now!'

Edward's fountain pen dropped to the floor. 'What did you say, Meg?'

She couldn't recall. Her eyes roamed the room searching for something familiar. They settled on her housecoat hanging on the back of the door beside Addie's cloak. Edward was walking towards her holding a pillow, to suffocate her, she hoped, but he placed it behind her head and handed her a mug of water. It was cold – like poor Wallace. She washed the stale taste from her mouth. If only she could remove sorrow as easily.

'Is there anything else I can get you?' Edward asked.

'Could you go to his quarters and bring me his clothes?'

'I will if you promise to go back to sleep. Can you do that for me, Meg?'

'Where's Addie? I want Addie.'

'She's working. I'm looking after you until she comes off duty.'

'Fetch his clothes. Please!'

'I will shortly, once you're asleep again.'

She sank back into the pillow and closed her eyes.

WHEN ADDIE returned, Meg was asleep among a pile of shirts, jackets and scarves. The probable nest-maker was dozing in an armchair, his spectacles pushed up over his unruly hair, both hands behind his head. A pot of coffee simmered on the stove, its bitter aroma offset by sprigs of rosemary arranged in an empty ether bottle on her bedside table.

Fighting back tears, she poured a little coffee into a tin mug. Half her duty had been spent pleading with fellows running raging temperatures not to jump out of their cots, and the rest applying linseed packs and taking pulses. Three chaps had convulsed. They would die before she got back to the ward. She dreaded writing to their mothers and telling them their sons survived the war, only to succumb to influenza.

Edward failed to wake when she untied her cape and hung it up. Walking past him to refill her coffee mug, she longed to stroke his forehead, but felt her own brow instead. No, she didn't have a temperature. All she needed was sleep.

Coffee finished, she wrapped a blanket around her shoulders and sank into a chair. The stubble on Edward's chin glinted in the candlelight. She wished she could lean over and kiss him. She must have been smiling because when Edward opened one eye he grinned back at her.

IT WAS DARK when Meg woke. Addie was breathing steadily beside her and Edward was no longer in the room. He'd done the right thing knocking her out. She'd have gone loony otherwise. Addie had been a brick – all the girls had. But judging by a conversation she'd overheard the previous evening, she needed to pull herself together and get back to work. Matron had picked herself up after losing her lover and she expected Meg to do the same. What's more, Edward had eased back on the dope. She was awake more often than not, although she didn't let on, because something delightful was taking place: Addie and Edward were falling in love. Not in the fiery explosive way that had engulfed her and Wallace; theirs was a slower burn.

Something else had happened too. Uncle Bert had said goodbye to her, maybe in a dream, but it felt real enough for her to believe it was true. If everyone she loved had gone, apart from Addie who now had Edward, she might as well act as if her grief was easing and offer to run an influenza ward where she could improve her chances of becoming ill and dying.

A false armistice on November the 8th sent hordes of coughing civilians into the streets, causing a rise in influenza cases. Even so, it didn't stop the stuffed shirts organising further celebrations for the real event on the 11th, starting with the ringing of bells at dawn. For the next hour, aeroplanes from a nearby hangar took to the skies and played merry hell. Inside the influenza ward, Meg removed her mask and hovered over the sputum mug of a young French girl with a bone-rattling cough, but she died without infecting her.

To keep up the pretence of a recovery, she went to No. 1's Armistice fancy-dress party, where Blue pranced about in a cook's uniform and Addie wore Edward's cap at a jaunty angle. When six clerks turned up as orderlies and four orderlies came as nurses, Iris took pictures for her photograph album. Earlier in the day, she'd removed a snap of Meg and Wallace coming off the dance floor last Christmas and given it to Meg to keep. Wallace's arm was around her waist and they were looking at each other.

At nine o'clock, four black-caped French musicians turned up to play show tunes for the patients. They wore the same haunted expression Meg saw on her own face when she looked in the mirror. After the concert, Edward drove the quartet back to town, returning to share a late supper with her and Addie.

'People were celebrating in the square,' he said. 'Two old chaps shinnied up a church steeple, quite successfully until they got vertigo inches from the bell. Fire brigade volunteers had to put up ladders and carry them down. And more trouble was waiting for them on the ground.'

Addie dished up three bowls of soup. 'What was that?'

Edward grinned. 'Wives brandishing rolled-up newspapers.'

As she listened to the rest of the story, Meg realised that if she were to die, she wouldn't be Addie's bridesmaid or godmother to Addie and Edward's children. She thought of the babies she and Wallace would never have. There was an ache in her breast where their small heads should have nestled.

The sound of the door opening broke into her thoughts. It was Iris. Tears were pouring down her cheeks and she was screwing her apron into a tight ball. Finally she got the words out: Dora had died in her arms. Meg wanted to go to her but her legs wouldn't move. Fortunately, Addie sat Iris down and comforted her while Netta filled the kettle. When Iris stopped weeping, she told them that two medical officers had refused to let her give Dora extra oxygen, as the Australian nurses were doing in their hospital, believing it improved the function of the lungs. They'd insisted that Iris wait for confirmation that the treatment actually worked. Now it was too late. Wallace would have bypassed the red tape. In a shaky voice Iris said, 'He was a marvellous surgeon, Meg. I'm sorry I judged the two of you so harshly.'

Anyone watching Meg sponge, incubate, inject and cajole would have believed she was putting the patients' needs before her own. In fact, she was doing everything possible to bring about her death, except climb into bed with a pneumonic and kiss him silly. Six weeks had passed – a hellish stretch of emptiness. More possibilities flitted through her mind. She could stash morphine under a loose floorboard. No, not if it meant depriving patients. She could loop a rope around her neck and swing from a beam in their hut. Only if she could be certain Addie wasn't first on the scene. She could make her way to the German line. If Edward and Blue weren't the kind of chaps who would put their own lives in danger searching for her.

※

IT WAS BUCKETING DOWN. The tin roof rattled as if a tribe of possums were scampering across it. Edward was in surgery. Addie thought of him often, in a way she never had with Hugh. Last month, she'd finally finished her apologetic letter and sent it off. She didn't expect a reply. Now it was time to decide what to do with the mayor's letter. She opened her diary and began to read what she'd written about Meg around the time Wallace had died. Slowly her reservations slipped away. She looked across to Meg's corner of the room. As usual, her bedclothes were in a jumble. Smiling, Addie walked over to straighten

264

them. Once she'd plumped up the pillow, she placed the letter in its centre.

✣

MEG WAS DOING back-to-back duties to cover for a staff nurse and a VAD desperately ill with influenza. Young women who wanted to live. None of them got what they deserved. Her sleep remained erratic. She dropped off easily but generally woke a couple of hours later, thinking of Wallace.

No one was born damaged. Things happened along the way. A chip here, a dent there, until you were committing unwise acts because you no longer cared what happened to you. She'd unlocked Wallace's pain, and he, hers. Yet he was fighting something else before he died, something he'd felt unable to tell her, not realising she would have loved him regardless. She was almost certain, as she'd been for some time if she were honest, that he'd picked up syphilis in Egypt before he met her. Weight loss and stiffness were common symptoms.

✣

'YOU TOLD ME months back that Meg might have lost Wallace,' Addie said. She and Edward were walking near the camp. 'Did you mean to his wife?'

'Not exactly,' he said, 'although it was a possibility. Actually I was referring to something else.' He lowered his voice. 'I think he was unwell.'

She stopped. 'Are you sure? What do you think he had?'

He rested a hand on her arm. 'He never said anything to me so I could have been mistaken. All I have to go on was a lesion I glimpsed in the bath hut one night and the fact that he was losing hair. I never saw him with Salvarsan or injecting mercury. Though I noticed when he turned moody that he never went anywhere without his kitbag.'

265

He could have visited back-door beauties in Port Said, Addie thought, before he fell for Meg. Men from every class frequented these establishments, some regularly. Then a terrifying thought occurred to her: months ago, Meg had been unusually tired and she'd mentioned a sore throat. 'Do you think he infected her?'

'He'd have ceased intimate contact as soon as he knew. Actually that could have contributed to his moodiness.'

'No wonder Meg was confused. Oh Edward, this is terrible. What are we going to do? Should we tell her?'

'It might make things worse.'

'But we talk about everything.'

'What if she knows and doesn't want to discuss it?'

'I need to at least give her the choice.'

She thought of asking Edward whether he'd visited the same places as Wallace but before she could formulate the question, he reached over and took her hand.

'Not my cup of tea.'

On Christmas Day 1918, their last together as a unit, fresh snow fell and gleamed under clear skies. Matron had told them they were leaving camp on Boxing Day and France at the end of January. Each ward had its own little decorated tree and the dinner table groaned with Red Cross parcels and festive treats. There was much knowing laughter when Addie pulled a cracker with Edward and a cheap ring fell out.

On their way to the unit's final fancy-dress party that night, dressed, at Meg's suggestion, as Antony and Cleopatra, Edward had surprised her by taking a longer route, down a dark alleyway that ran between the mess and the officers' headquarters. In the shadows, he drew her to him and kissed her. She liked the feel of his lips on hers and the way his hands stroked the back of her head. He was tender and gentle as he caressed her face, then kissed her a second time. A new and pleasant sensation rippled through her. It left her wanting more.

'Don't make it a late night,' a senior officer told them as they entered the mess. 'You have to be up at five-thirty tomorrow morning, luggage packed and ready to leave.'

'Everyone please raise your glasses.' The CO, dressed as the King of Spades, stood to demonstrate. 'Many soldiers benefited from our nurses' care and compassion. Thank you, ladies.'

'We're not ladies, we're sisters!' Iris shouted.

'And officers,' said Matron. 'Please accord my girls the long overdue military salute.'

'Hear, hear,' called Edward, executing a perfect example.

Blue sounded a hooter to get the party underway and dished out another dozen to the clerks. The room soon rang with toots and laughter. The padre and the CO blew up balloons, in between drinking to a better future. Addie stayed close to Edward but every now and then, when they were dancing, she looked over his shoulder to see what Meg was doing. At one stage she was teaching Iris a few dance steps, and later Addie overheard her cajoling Kemp to ask Iris to join him for the supper waltz. After sending Meg an appreciative smile, Addie led Edward back to the dance floor. Goodness knows what Father would think if he could see her now.

I can tell from her letters that my Adelina has come out of her shell. She says what she thinks and she gives advice. I suppose a nursing sister knows a thing or two about influenza. Thelma thinks she's become far too uppity but I'm relieved. I turned sixty last November and if Adelina remains a spinster I need to know she can look after herself. Not all is lost on the marriage front, though. Last night we re-read her last three letters. There were five mentions of a chap called Edward. Erin warned us not to make a song and dance of it: 'Don't stick your nose in or she'll stop referring to the Great Male Hope.' Then she told her mother to stop rifling through wedding cake recipes. The fellow who gets my Erin will have a bumpy ride. Even so, every Sunday, I thank the Lord for giving Thelma and me two daughters. This senseless war has taken far too many sons.

Nineteen

MEG WAS SITTING in front of a vanity table in her hotel room in Wisques combing her hair when there was a knock on the door. A youth in a postal uniform waited in the hallway. Before he could speak, she snatched the telegram from his hand. He backed away as if stung by a wasp. She'd almost not had her mail forwarded from the camp, wanting to avoid this moment, but it would have been futile. Trouble always caught up with you. 'Sorry,' she called to the boy, who was already nipping down the stairs, desperate, she supposed, to deliver the rest of the grim news in his postbag so he could cycle home and forget the people who'd turned white at the sight of him.

For an instant the frightened child she used to be wanted to scrunch the telegram into a ball and throw it into the smouldering embers in the fireplace, but she made herself walk over to the chaise longue and sit down. The sender was Mr Maurice Sutherford, a solicitor from Invercargill. 'Condolences. STOP. Maude and Bert Eastwood buried Tuatapere Cemetery. STOP. You sole beneficiary. STOP. Letter & personal note follows. STOP.'

Addie and Edward had gone to the dining room. She hadn't told them about Uncle Bert, preferring to keep the news to herself tonight. Yesterday Addie had quizzed her about Wallace's state of health before he died and asked if she was feeling the slightest bit unwell. She'd reassured her as best she could. Addie deserved a nice evening with Edward, not listening to more of her woes. To avoid awkward questions, she had a tray sent to her room.

She told her friend at breakfast. 'Don't worry. I'm not going to fall to pieces.' Meg liked the certainty she could hear in her own voice. Something had shifted in her now that she knew the answers to her questions were on their way.

The winter sun threw lean shadows across the dirt track that wound up a gentle knoll. A sparrow flitted from the stump of a tree to a scraggly thorn bush where icicles were melting on the brown tips. Meg wandered through the graveyard that surrounded the little chapel, reading the names on the stones. She thought of what happened between birth and death. How you believed something one day and the next discovered it was a lie. How you could nurse close to a front line for years then wake up one morning and find that part of your life was over. How you thought you would die of grief when you lost your dearest love, only to discover, gradually, that you could go on living.

After brushing a scattering of leaves from a chipped stone step, she sat down, adjusting her skirt so that it didn't bunch up. She eased a finger along the flap of the envelope that had arrived from New Zealand earlier in the day. It opened easily. Inside was a sheet of plain paper filled with crabbed script: it was from the solicitor. There was also a smaller sealed envelope, addressed in Aunt Maude's handwriting. She tackled the solicitor's letter first. Did she appreciate the magnitude of her bequest? Fifteen thousand pounds was a great deal of money. Did she know how much interest it would accrue if she invested it wisely? Did she want him to arrange her passage home? Then, further on:

> Your uncle and aunt instructed me not to impose impediments or make judgements regarding your financial decisions. You are free to handle your affairs as you see fit. However, it would be remiss of me not to strongly urge you to return to Southland and take up activities befitting a woman of your means. My wife and I can guide you in these matters. It would be our duty and privilege to help you establish a respected position in society.

As if she could go back and twiddle her thumbs when there was so much to do in France. With this amount of money, together with Wallace's, she could set up something worthwhile. She picked up the second envelope and warily removed the contents.

> Dearest Meg,
>
> This is not an easy letter for me to write and it will be even harder for you to read. Please remember that nothing of what happened was your fault. I will try to answer your questions. Your mother, my sister, was always delicate of mind, a little fey some said; others used stronger words – depraved, unnatural. Our parents considered her wilful because she wouldn't obey them. She was always wandering off, often returning with stray animals. At eighteen, she progressed to men. The horse-trainer asked for her hand on her twenty-first birthday. Our father agreed, thinking it might settle her, but she became more restless. Two years later, she suffered her first mental collapse. Using her husband's razor, she made crosses and other religious symbols on her skin. He thought it best to commit her to a mental asylum. When she came home eight months later she was in the family way. She

couldn't or wouldn't explain. They fought night and day. He started drinking. She got the blues. After you arrived, she had a second collapse. He insisted on caring for her at home, which meant she didn't get the medical care she needed. Bert and I tried to help. We should have taken you earlier. It was my fault – I thought she might get better. You do the daftest things in the name of hope. Forgive me, Meg. We loved you from the start and we love you still. Hold your head high. Believe anything is possible and you will have a bright future.

Heartfelt blessings always,

Aunt Maude

On her way back to the hotel, Meg passed an abandoned stable. Peering inside, she could see that the layout was similar to the one owned by Ma's husband – she could no longer refer to him as Pa. The smell was familiar: man, horse, manure. Reins hung over the door of a stall.

He used to hide his whisky under the straw. From the loft, she'd watched him search for a bottle. Sometimes when he went off with the horses, she poured the leftovers down a drain. He'd caught her once and walloped her, calling her 'daughter of the devil'. Later, ashamed she supposed, he promised to quit drinking. But he never did.

More childhood memories came back, scene by scene, as if a film were playing inside her head. Without warning, a wall of grief gave way and she sank to her knees, weeping for what she'd lost and for what she'd never known.

Afterwards, she felt cleansed, almost reborn. She scooped a handful of water from a rain barrel outside the stable and splashed it over her face. The coldness made her gasp. She dried herself with the sleeve of her coat and tidied her hair with her fingers.

A DRIVER TOOK Addie and Edward to Boulogne via St Omer, along roads littered with machinery, discarded boots, sandbags, rubble. In the fields, slimy green water overflowed from huge pits into depressions that contained graves. Crucifixes, grouped and solitary, dotted the landscape, sleet nestling like gulls along their beams. Wreaths hung on semi-intact dwellings. Beside a barn, printed in large letters in English, was a sign that read 'Horse Buried Here'.

At a crossroads, the driver stopped so she and Edward could check a blanketed form abandoned on a stretcher. They were two or three months late.

As they drove on, a gull swooped in front of the windscreen, its pinkish legs a splash of colour against the snow-white torso. Addie could smell the sea. The driver dropped a gear as they came over the brow of the hill and there, in front of her, were Boulogne's steep-roofed houses and irregular-shaped hotels, and the arc of the English Channel, like an elegant swathe of black tulle. Smoke gusted from the funnels of ships in the harbour. Edward stretched his arms, twisted his neck from side to side and arched his back. 'Motorcars aren't designed for tall fellows.' He peered through the side window. 'We're almost there.'

They parked near the entrance to the wharf. Across the road, a throng of ship workers spilled from a scruffy eatery, cigarettes clamped between their lips.

There was no sign of her nursing unit.

While the driver and Edward unloaded their luggage, two Frenchmen set down baskets of fish on the quayside, some species still flapping, clear-eyed and translucent. In no time, black-skirted housewives were stampeding through the gate, intent on procuring a portion of the day's catch, and laughter filled the space between Addie and the sea.

Author's Note

APART FROM well-known historical figures, and nurses who appear under their own names, the characters depicted in *Lives We Leave Behind* are entirely fictional. However, in the interests of historical authenticity, I drew on primary sources such as diaries, autobiographies, memoirs and first-hand accounts published in *Kai Tiaki*, the New Zealand nursing journal of the time. I have also set the novel in locations that loosely followed the route of New Zealand's No. 1 Stationary Hospital from 1915 to 1918.

During the course of researching and writing the novel, I viewed film footage, attended symposiums and read historical, academic and literary texts. These secondary sources also informed my thinking and therefore this novel.

Of the thirteen nurses portrayed in *Lives We Leave Behind*, five served in the war.

Fictional	Actual
Meg Dutton	Marion Brown*
Addie Harrington	Isabel Clarke*
Iris Hutchison	Helena Isdell*
Dora Kennard	Jean Porteous
Lois Moore	Margaret Rogers*
Netta Smith	
Joan Watson	
Nancy Wilson	

*Died as a result of the torpedoing of the *Marquette*

Despite suffering 'war strain' themselves, New Zealand nurses worked their passages home, caring for convalescents and war-weakened influenza patients on ships such as the *Tainui* and the *Marama*. Not surprisingly, many arrived back exhausted and in a poor state of health. They then had to face both employment challenges and a society that did not understand what they had been through and expected them to return to their old lives.

After years of excitement and heightened emotions, some of these nurses struggled to adjust to mundane routines and family duties such as caring for ailing parents. Returning to their former jobs in peacetime hospitals also proved difficult, as various positions were no longer available. A number of nurses found employment in military hospitals such as Hanmer, Rotorua and Trentham, where they cared for soldiers with disabilities, including shellshock; others clubbed together and set up private nursing homes.

In a few instances, family and friends supported those unfit to work until the New Zealand Trained Nurses' Association established a memorial fund for members in straitened circumstances. Even so, there were army nurses who experienced on-going financial hardship, a situation exacerbated by male military discrimination at the onset of war when officials denied them the title of 'officer' and the higher pay rate.

Military records show that many First World War nurses died prematurely.

Acknowledgements

I AM ESPECIALLY indebted to Bill Manhire, who read and commented on numerous drafts of this novel and engaged me in stimulating conversations about craft and content. Thanks also to Pamela Wood for her advice on nursing practices of the era and her astute comments on historical details. Bill and Pamela's support and enthusiasm nourished more than this novel.

Sincere thanks to Pip Adam, Angela Andrews, Michalia Arathimos, Stephanie de Montalk, Laurence Fearnley, David Fleming, Lynn Jenner, Marian Evans, Kerry Hines, Christine Leunens, Tina Makereti, Gavin McGibbon, Hannah McKie, Lawrence Patchett and Steve Toussaint from the PhD in Creative Writing programme at the International Institute of Modern Letters, Victoria University of Wellington, for their helpful feedback and stimulating company during the writing of this novel. Thanks also to Katie Hardwick-Smith and Clare Moleta for helping me keep on top of the paperwork and for checking in from time to time.

I am also grateful to friends Jackie Ballantyne, Elizabeth Brooke-Carr, Martha Morseth and Miranda Spary, who read the manuscript in embryonic form and offered suggestions that invariably made their way into the work.

Key aspects of this novel benefited from the generous input and expertise of Pieter van Ammers, Claire Beynon, Bill Gillespie, Konstanze Ehlebrecht, Gundula Güldner, Alison Holst, Peter Holst, Helen Leach and Axel de Maupeou d'Ableiges.

As always, members of my writing group contributed in useful ways and celebrated significant milestones as the novel took shape. The women in my book club also showed a keen interest in its creation, as did friends and colleagues at Otago Polytechnic.

Others helped through conversations and acts of kindness. Annie Price sent me her mother's Queen Alexandra Imperial Military Nursing Service cape and medal from which I drew inspiration. Prue Donald talked to me about her role as interpreter at Te Papa for part of the Great War section of the 'Slice of Life' exhibition. Frances Steel and Tom Bond shared their knowledge of steamships, while Glenda Hall told me about her great-aunt, Jean Porteous, who trained and worked as a nurse anaesthetist in the Great War. Detta Russell accompanied me on a trip to Riverton and Tuatapere, the hometowns of my fictional nurses, Addie and Meg.

Staff at the Hocken Collections and the Alexander Turnbull Library assisted me with essential reading material, and Rachael Manson at Wellington City Archives and Dean Miller at Museums Wellington sent me detailed plans of the steamship *Maheno*, which I drew on to authenticate the nurses' initial sea voyage.

Verona Cournane, Elaine and Carl Fisk, Alison Gerry and Alistair Nicholson, Paula Haines-Bellamy and Phillip Bellamy, and Sonia Jones and Mark Richter provided me with inspiring spaces to write in beautiful locations in New Zealand and Australia. I am extremely grateful for their generosity.

Once again, the love and support of my family: Noel, Kate, Jo, Nic, Damara and Kiwa, my parents, John and Lorna Ferns, and members of our extended family, sustained me as I worked on this novel.

Geoff Walker commented on early draft chapters and later read the entire manuscript. His steadfast faith in *Lives We Leave Behind*, a title he and Laurence Fearnley helped to choose, kept me writing in my den under the stairs on evenings and weekends when other pleasures beckoned.

Thank you, too, to the entire team at Penguin, who turned my manuscript into a book and showed unwavering commitment to design, production, marketing and sales. Special thanks to Katie Haworth, a perceptive reader, for her thoughtful comments and contributions, to Leanne McGregor, who ably oversaw the final editing stages, and to Debra Millar for her enthusiastic support.

I am also indebted to my editor, Anna Rogers, for her forensic attention to detail, sensitive suggestions and skilful editing. Her in-depth knowledge of military nursing proved invaluable.

Finally, I want to thank all the nurses I have worked with or come to know in other contexts for their friendship, and for their stories.

Bibliography

THE FOLLOWING BOOKS, diaries, memoirs and other material proved immensely helpful to me during the writing of this novel. I am extremely grateful to these sources and to their authors.

Historians, other scholars and writers provided significant background information: Margaret Darrow, *French Women and the First World War* (Oxford: Berg, 2000); Santanu Das, *Touch and Intimacy in First World War Literature* (Cambridge: Cambridge University Press, 2005); Paul Fussell, *The Great War and Modern Memory* (Oxford: Oxford University Press, 1975); Margaret R. Higonnet (ed.), *Nurses at the Front: Writing the Wounds of the Great War* (Harmondsworth: Penguin Books, 1999); Richard Holmes, *Tommy: The British Soldier on the Western Front 1914–1918* (London: Harper Perennial, 2005); David Mitchell, *Women on the Warpath: The Story of the Women of the First World War* (London: Jonathan Cape, 1966); Jane Potter, *Boys in Khaki, Girls in Print* (Oxford: Oxford University Press, 2008); Peter Rees, *The Other Anzacs* (Sydney: Allen & Unwin, 2008); and Michael Roper, *The Secret Battle* (Manchester: Manchester University Press, 2009).

Two works of Charles Brasch — *In Egypt* (Wellington: Steele Roberts, 2007) and *Indirections: A Memoir 1909–1947* (Wellington: Oxford University Press, 1980) — provided atmospheric prompts, as did John Miller and Kristen Miller (eds), *Cairo: Tales of the City* (Vancouver: Chronicle Books, 1994). To familiarise myself with poetry and other relevant literature I studied: Harry Ricketts, *Strange Meetings: The Poets of the Great War* (London: Chatto & Windus, 2010); Angela Smith (ed.), *Women's Writing of the First World War: An*

Anthology (Manchester: Manchester University Press, 2000); and George Walter (ed.), *The Penguin Book of First World War Poetry* (London: Penguin Books, 2006). I also acknowledge the importance of reading some time ago the powerful novels of Pat Barker and Sebastian Faulks and, more recently, those of Deborah Moggach, Bruce Scates, Shirley Walker and Louisa Young.

To better understand the New Zealand context I read: Michael King, *The History of New Zealand* (Auckland: Penguin Books, 2003); Nicholas Boyack and Jane Tolerton, *In the Shadow of War* (Auckland: Penguin Books, 1990); H. T. B. Drew (ed.), *The War Effort of New Zealand* (Christchurch: Whitcombe & Tombs Ltd, 1923); Richard Rawstron, *A Unique Nursing Group: New Zealand Army Nurse Anaesthetists of WW1* (Christchurch: Rawstron Publishing Company, 2005); and Jane Tolerton, *A Life of Ettie Rout* (Auckland: Penguin Books, 1992). John Meredith Smith's *Cloud Over the Marquette* (Christchurch: Caxton Press, 1990) informed the chapter that re-imagines the torpedoing of the *Marquette*.

I gleaned medical and surgical facts from Ian Hay, *One Hundred Years of Army Nursing* (London: Cassell, 1975) and Cuthbert Wallace and John Fraser, *Surgery at a Clearing Station* (London: A. & C. Black, 1918). Judith Roddick's 2005 MA thesis, 'When the Flag Flew at Half Mast: Nursing and the 1918 Influenza Epidemic in New Zealand' (Otago Polytechnic), informed my chapters on the Spanish influenza pandemic.

Other crucial nursing information and insights came from: Marianne Barker, *Nightingales in the Mud: The Digger Sisters of the Great War 1914 – 1918* (Sydney: Allen & Unwin, 1989); Jan Bassett, *Guns and Brooches: Australian Army Nursing From the Boer War to the Gulf War* (Melbourne: Oxford University Press, 1997); Christine Hallett, *Containing Trauma: Nursing in the First World War* (Manchester: Manchester University Press, 2009); Kirsty Harris, *More than Bombs and Bandages: Australian Army Nurses at War in World War 1* (Newport: Big

Sky Publishing Ltd, 2011); Lyn Macdonald, *The Roses of No Man's Land* (London: Penguin Books, 1993); Yvonne McEwen, *It's a Long Way to Tipperary: British and Irish Nurses in the Great War* (Dunfermline: Cualann Press, 2000); Melanie Oppenheimer, *Oceans of Love: Narelle – An Australian Nurse in World War One* (Sydney: ABC Books, 2005); and Anna Rogers, *While You're Away: New Zealand Nurses at War 1899–1948* (Auckland: Auckland University Press, 2003).

I also drew on: Enid Bagnold, *A Diary Without Dates* (London: Virago, 1979); Kate John Finzi, *Eighteen Months in the War Zone: The Record of A Woman's Work on the Western Front* (Breinigsville: Kessinger Publishing, 2010); June Richardson Lucas, *The Children of France and the Red Cross* (Liskeard: Diggory Press, 2005); Susan Mann (ed.), *The War Diary of Clare Gass 1915–1918* (Montreal: McGill-Queen's University Press, 2004); and Agnes Warner, *Nurse at the Trenches* (Liskeard: Diggory Press, 2006). The nursing journal *Kai Tiaki*, now available on the National Library website Papers Past, also contained valuable first-hand accounts of nurses' experiences.

Integral to the entire novel were experiences depicted in the memoirs of First World War nurses and VADs, most notably: Catherine Black, *King's Nurse – Beggar's Nurse* (London: Hurst & Blackett, 1939); Mabel Clint, *Our Bit* (Montreal: Nurses' Edition, Royal Victoria Hospital, 1934); Rosa Kirkcaldie, *In Gray and Scarlet* (Melbourne: Alexander McGubbin, 1922); Shirley Millard, *I Saw Them Die* (New York: Harcourt Brace, 1936); Edna Pengelly, *Nursing in War and Peace* (Wellington: Wingfield Press, 1956); May Tilton, *The Grey Battalion* (Sydney: Angus & Robertson, 1934); and Kate Wilson-Simmie, *Lights Out* (Ottawa: CEF Books, 2004). Mary Roberts Rinehart, a former nurse, war correspondent and author of *Kings, Queens and Pawns: An American Woman at the Front* (New York: George H. Doran Company, 1915), yielded another worthwhile perspective.

Maxine Alterio

Ribbons
of Grace

Ribbons of Grace

Maxine Alterio

Arrowtown, a goldfield settlement with an explosive mix of inhabitants, is the scene of an unlikely love story.

Ming Yuet, a young Chinese woman seeking riches, disguises herself as a male miner and comes to the goldfields, where she meets Conran, an Orcadian stonemason escaping a family tragedy. A secret love affair develops amidst suspicion, fear and hostility, culminating in an act of violence that irrevocably shatters the lives of those involved.

Maxine Alterio's beautiful novel about love, forgiveness, alienation and friendship moves between past and present, homeland and adopted country, and from the living to the deceased.